# Spur of the Moment

# SPUR OF THE MOMENT

# MOMENT

A Renata Radleigh Opera Mystery

# DAVID LINZEE

coffeetownpress
Seattle, WA

coffeetownpress

Coffeetown Press
PO Box 70515
Seattle, WA 98127

For more information go to: www.coffeetownpress.com
www.davidlinzee.com

Cover design by Sabrina Sun

Spur of the Moment
Copyright © 2016 by David Linzee

ISBN: 978-1-60381-341-9 (Trade Paper)
ISBN: 978-1-60381-342-6 (eBook)

Library of Congress Control Number: 2015957346

Printed in the United States of America

A12006 820685

To Claire

*il "mio dolce tesoro"*

# PART I

—

## SATURDAY, MAY 22

# 1

HEFTING HER HEAVY BAG OF musical scores and water bottles, Renata Radleigh pushed through the stage door into the heat and humidity and the glare of the sun. She shut her eyes and gripped the handrail. In St. Louis, May could be like August. She'd been here a month and still hadn't got used to it.

She opened her eyes to see Hannah, the receptionist from the admin building, waiting at the bottom of the steps.

"Oh, Renata, there you are. Your brother wants to see you in his office."

"I'll see him later."

But as she descended the steps, Hannah did not step aside.

"It's all right. I'll see him later. I'm staying at his house, you know."

"He said he wanted to see you now."

Renata sighed. A bad day of rehearsal had left her exhausted, but it was a point of honor with her not to snap at assistants or secretaries who were only doing what they'd been told to do. She mustered a smile, nodded, and headed for the admin building.

Don was on the phone when she entered his office. He grinned and waved her to a chair, but Renata remained standing in hopes of shortening the meeting. As he leisurely wound up his conversation, she wondered, not for the first time, how it was that though he had been in America for a decade while she still lived in England, his accent was stronger. Posher too, though they'd shared the same middle-class upbringing.

"Renata darling." He replaced the receiver, put his feet on the edge of the desk, and pushed back into the depths of his comfortable chair, interlacing his fingers behind his head. He was always striking the sort of poses television actors did. Not the best actors, either. "How would you like to be my guest at Carmen's Cornucopia tonight?"

"At what?"

Irritation rippled across his face. "The season kick-off donor appreciation party. Only our biggest do of the year."

"Oh, Don. You know I'm no good at those things."

"You needn't scintillate. The donors will be thrilled just to meet the singer they'll see playing Mercédès."

"No. They'd be thrilled to meet the singer they'll see playing Carmen."

"Yes, well, Carmen's busy."

"Oh. And Micaëla and Escamillo? Am I the best you could do?"

Don swung his feet to the floor and sat up, glowering. "A lot of the *artists* round here lack a sense of their larger responsibilities."

"Don, please, I'm knackered. There are serious problems with Act Three—technical problems. I've been sitting in the theater all day listening to the director shouting at the boffins. I've had hardly a chance to sing."

"Then how can you be tired? This is what I mean about a sense of larger responsibilities. You're upset about a technical problem in Act Three. Until last week, we weren't sure we'd be able to put on *Carmen* at all. It was a co-production with Opera Oklahoma and they had a funding crisis of their own and dropped out, leaving us with a stack of unpaid bills. Do you remember any of this?"

When her brother fished for compliments, he didn't use a hook and line. He used dynamite. "Yes. And I remember you went out and got the big donation. You're the man of the hour. Your name is on everyone's lips. It ought to be a thrill for me to be at your side tonight."

Don nodded contentedly. Over the years in America, his irony detector had become rusty. "My feelings aren't important," he said unconvincingly. "What matters is that the Stromberg-Brands have a lovely evening. This will be the first public announcement of their gift. Considering that without them you wouldn't have a job, it doesn't seem too much to ask that you say a civil word to them."

The strap of her shoulder-bag was wearing a groove in her clavicle. There was no point standing here arguing any longer. "Oh, very well. But you ought to know by now, Don, how easy it is to make me feel guilty. You needn't be so heavy-handed about it."

But he had lost interest as soon as she capitulated. His smartphone was in his hand and he was bowing over the little screen. "See you under the tent in half an hour, then."

"Half an hour? Is it all right if I come as I am?"

He looked her up and down and returned his gaze to the screen. "Renata. Of course not."

# 2

---

E MERGING FROM THE SHOWER, SHE found that eighteen of her thirty minutes had passed. It would serve Don right if she were late for the party, but she didn't think she would be able to manage it. Years of showing up on time for auditions, rehearsals, and performances had made unpunctuality difficult for her.

She was in the tiny dressing room she shared with two other soloists. Luckily, she'd found the best of her recital dresses—a dark-blue silk gown only three years old—hanging in the closet. Before putting it on, she sat at the dressing table and gave her face a moment of hard appraisal in the well-lighted mirror. Was there time to make herself beautiful?

It took longer and longer. She had one of those fair English complexions that picked up wrinkles as readily as fine linen did. Without a foundation layer, she looked five years older than her real age, which was thirty-six. The gray hairs that kept sprouting at her temples were certainly no help.

A touch of lipstick and eye shadow and she'd look good enough for the donors. For performing, luckily, a few wrinkles didn't matter. Looking good under stage lights required chiefly a prominent chin and high cheekbones. Those she still had. No, it wasn't the fault of her face that she wasn't a star.

Her body, on the other hand …. She wasn't fat, by the standards of any sensible era. But she was a tall, broad-shouldered, large-breasted, full-hipped woman, and these days opera managements wanted sylphs. Sylphs with big voices, and the two rarely came in one package.

"No whingeing," Renata said aloud to her image, before getting up. For a struggling singer, self-pity was a more dangerous habit than drugs or booze. She constantly patrolled her mind, casting out excuses. There were women built like storage units still getting star parts—if they had the talent. And she did.

She put on the blue-silk dress and twirled, eying the hemline. Too much leg showing. She wouldn't be able to get away without tights, or pantyhose as Americans called them, which was an appropriately ugly name. Unceremoniously hoisting her dress, she sat and struggled into the wretched things. Then she was ready, and right on time.

# 3

—

S HE CLIMBED THE STAIRS AND pushed through the door to
the Charles MacNamara III Auditorium, then went up the
aisle and through the door to the Emmanuel Gerwitz Lobby.
As she left the Jane B. Pritchard Theatre she repeated the
names to herself, since she might be meeting some of these
people tonight.

The sun had set and the heat was letting up a little. The St.
Louis Opera was located in the leafy suburb of Webster Groves.
Don and his colleagues in fundraising called it "the American
Glyndebourne" and made much of its park-like grounds, with
tall oaks, broad lawns, and beds of pansies and petunias. The
interior of the white-and-green striped pavilion where the
party was being held glowed invitingly in the dusk. It was
already about half-full, and more guests were filing down the
path from the parking lot.

As she stepped into the tent, a man with a drinks tray
approached. It was someone she knew. "Well, hello, Ray."

He grinned, showing a fine set of dentures, white against his
ruddy skin. A lock of his still abundant gray hair had fallen
over his right eyebrow. Since his hands were full, she thought
of brushing it back for him, but he was not the sort of man to
welcome feminine fussing.

"What are you doing here?" she asked. "I would have thought you'd done enough for the opera today."

"They nailed me on the way to the parking lot. Said they needed more waiters."

Ray was a supernumerary—a volunteer extra—in *Carmen*. The St. Louis Opera, being located in a city with a small supply of out-of-work actors, had to fill out its crowd scenes with retired men like Ray. He'd volunteered simply because he lived nearby and had time on his hands. Being an engineer who had spent his working years in a factory, he had little fellow-feeling with theater people. During the long technical delays in Act III he tended to grow irascible. Renata, doing her bit for the show, took it upon herself to jolly him along.

"How come you're not home with your feet up?" he asked.

"Oh, they thought it would be nice to have someone here from the cast of *Carmen*."

"And The Slope couldn't be bothered?"

Amy Song, the fast-rising mezzo-soprano playing Carmen, was Korean-American. Ray, like so many white American men of his age, took delight in these slips of the tongue that weren't slips but taunts. He was trying to get a rise out of her. She said mildly, "Ray, please don't call Amy that."

"Okay. But I'm right, I'll bet. She couldn't be bothered."

Renata conceded with a shrug.

"Be sure and tell the donors you might be singing Carmen some night," Ray went on. "If she gets sick or something."

"Only happens in films. I've covered a dozen parts in the last year and haven't sung a single note."

In these cost-cutting days, opera managements didn't just let understudies sit around. Renata was contracted to sing Mercédès unless Amy Song became indisposed. Then Renata would sing Carmen and a chorister would take over Mercédès. In reality, Amy Song would be fine and Renata would just sing Mercédès. Such arrangements did at least bring in some extra income that Renata had come to count on. She belonged to that class of singers—experienced, reliable, and cheap—whose fate was to spend a lot of time preparing roles they would never get a chance to sing.

*No whingeing*, she told herself again, silently this time. She took a glass of white wine from Ray's tray. "Time for me to start chatting. Cheers."

She put a smile on her face and went looking for someone to talk to. It ought to be easy enough. Fundraisers in New York or Los Angeles could be intimidating. You might find yourself chatting with an international arms trafficker, or a super-model so coked up she was practically shooting sparks. But these were the solid folk of the Midwest, CEOs, senior partners, and surgeons—men with gray hair or bald spotted pates. Most seemed to have kept their original wives. All she had to do was catch someone's eye, make a rueful comment about the hot weather, and ask about their grandchildren.

Renata wasn't a shy person. After all, her job was to step into a spotlight, open her mouth, and sing to thousands of people. Although being comfortable on stage didn't necessarily preclude shyness. But tonight she could not get going. She was preoccupied with the suspicion that her brother wasn't just being typically self-absorbed in browbeating her into attending the party—that he had also been motivated by a touch of malice.

The St. Louis Opera offered her a part almost every year, which meant that she spent May and June in St. Louis. This had begun when their parents were still alive, and she stayed with Don because it was impossible to explain to them why she didn't want to. The habit survived their parents' deaths. Her quarters grew more luxurious as Don moved from apartment to condo to house, but relations between the siblings were as strained as ever.

When Renata's latest therapist had suggested that Don was secretly in awe of her, she'd sacked him. *Awe indeed*. There was a theory to make a cat laugh. Oh, perhaps he'd been a bit envious when they were children. He was the younger by three years. She'd shown talent early on, and their parents, both maths teachers at a grubby suburban comprehensive, had made a fuss over her, buying her recital gowns and driving her to faraway competitions where she usually won prizes. By their teens, though, Don had discovered and was capitalizing on his own talent, which was for sucking up to toffs. As he went out to ride horses with Saskia or sail a boat with Rupert, leaving her at the piano, symptoms of awe weren't manifest.

Anyway she had become less and less awe-inspiring. The high point of her career had probably been here, eight years ago. SLO was considered one of the best regional opera companies in America, a proving ground for talent bound for the Met and Covent Garden, and Renata had sung a widely praised Dorabella in *Così*. Invitations had come in, to sing big roles at little companies, and little roles at big companies. Reviews were generally good and important people said encouraging things to her. But the flurry died down, for reasons she had not been able to figure out in a thousand sleepless nights. Things just hadn't worked out.

Not for her, anyway. Don, who like most English snobs couldn't wait to leave his damp homeland for the States, had just collected an American MBA. Trading on her name and contacts, he had wangled a job as a fundraiser at SLO. It had all been uphill from there. His title was Director of Development now, and he was one of the youngest in the country to hold such a post.

As for Renata, she lived in a cramped flat In London W. 11 that she shared with four other singers. Not that she saw much of it. Most of the year, she wound her way around Europe and America, taking pretty much any part she could get. It was all a bit hard on the ego. Wandering through this jolly crowd with glass in hand, she hesitated to talk to people because she knew what they would say. In an effort to be polite and interested, these affable Midwesterners would twist the knife:

"And will this be your debut at SLO?"

"Erm … no, I've been coming here for ten years."

"Oh … what might I have seen you in?"

"Last year I was Flora in *La Traviata*."

"Oh … I saw that. Who was Flora?"

Renata played a lot of roles like that.

*No whingeing.* It was all part of the job, and if she was tired of the job, she should go back to England and give piano lessons. But it bothered her to think that Don knew what he was asking of her and relished causing her embarrassment. No, better to think he was just being his usual thoughtless self.

Above intervening heads and shoulders, she saw Don enter the tent, wearing a beautiful cream-linen suit and striking another of his studied attitudes, the one she called the JFK— left elbow crooked and hand in pocket, right hand brushing back his blond forelock. His handsome face was full of pleasure and excitement. Carmen's Cornucopia was the high point of his year.

She turned away, put her empty glass of Chardonnay on a waiter's tray—and took a full one. This was inadvisable. Renata hardly drank at all, because alcohol redoubled the effect of her antidepressants and was dehydrating—bad for the vocal cords. But now she felt the need to soften life's sharp edges.

She had reached the edge of the tent and remained there, her back to the crowd, sipping Chardonnay. Well, gulping it, actually. It was completely dark now. A single light, a few feet above ground level, very bright and wavering occasionally, caught her eye. It was moving slowly toward her. This was like something in a science fiction movie, Renata thought. She gazed at it for some time before figuring out that it was the headlight of a bicycle, coming up the path from the street. The bike stopped a few yards away and a man swung gracefully off of it.

# 4

—

H E WAS TALL AND SLENDER, dressed in a blue blazer much
the worse for wear, white shirt and jeans. When he took
off his helmet and turned, she saw that he had an intelligent
face, which to her meant a high forehead, spectacles, a neatly
trimmed beard, and an aloof, critical expression. In brief: her
type. She walked toward him.

He had a U-lock in his hands and was looking around.

"The nearest bike rack is miles away. I think you can just
leave it."

He looked at her and smiled. "True. It'll be safe. They're all
millionaires here."

"Well, except for me."

"And what are you?"

"A mezzo-soprano."

He hung the lock on a handlebar and stepped up to her. He
had a pleasant smell, a salty tang of good, clean sweat from
having got here on his own muscle-power. "Oh, you're actually
in an opera. You outrank the rest of us, then. Nice to meet you.
I'm Bert."

"Renata. You know, you don't look like a Bert."

"Short for Bertrand, after Lord Russell. My parents actually
wanted me to be a philosopher."

"Mine actually wanted me to be an opera singer. Tell me, how did you get to be a millionaire in philosophy?"

"I didn't. I'm just a professor. In fact this is my first donor party. Perhaps you could explain a few things to me?"

"I'll do my best."

"Why is this event called Carmen's Cornucopia?"

"Well, aside from the allure of alliteration, you and the other guests are going to receive a bag of presents."

"Presents?"

"Oh, T-shirts, discount coupons, that sort of thing."

"And why are you giving us these presents?"

"So you'll feel you're getting something back for your donation, I suppose."

"But if it's a donation, why would we expect anything back?" Without waiting for an answer, which was lucky, because she didn't have one, he pointed between his feet. "I can't make out the writing on these bricks."

She glanced down. They were standing on the Donor's Walk. "It's people's names. Each paid one hundred dollars."

"Ah. And as they were coming in this evening, were they side-stepping to avoid treading on their own names?"

"They're not here tonight. This party's for people who give buildings, not bricks."

"Which reminds me." He pulled a rumpled copy of the evening's program from his side pocket. "Our names are grouped under cryptic headings. Divas, impresarios, maestros—"

"Divas gave the most. They get a private cocktail party with the stars of this year's productions. Impresarios gave the second most. They get their own parking spaces right next to the theater. I forget what maestros get, but it's all in the back of the book. It's not meant to be cryptic. Everyone's supposed to know."

"And why is that?"

"SLO wants maestros to aspire to become impresarios, obviously."

"Oh. So the donors ... are competing with each other for status? They're not opera lovers, giving as much as each can afford to?"

"No."

"That's illuminating. Thank you. Because I was wondering, why hold this event at all? I thought the donors were giving because they loved to see good operas. So why not cancel the party, put the savings into the operas, and the donors could come see them, and that would be their reward?"

"You're having me on, aren't you?"

"It depends on what that means."

"People as naive as you're pretending to be aren't allowed to wander around loose."

He shrugged and smiled, charmingly. "Sorry, I was employing the Socratic method, which I shouldn't really do outside the classroom. But this evening is confusing to me. I'd expect modern charitable giving to be constructed upon Western religious paradigms. Jesus said, when you give, never let your left hand know what your right hand is doing. And Judaism teaches that the intention is inseparable from the gift. If your intention is impure—if you're giving just to be recognized—God will know and give you no credit."

Bert was her type, all right. Thoughtful, slightly askew. And the third finger of his left hand bore no ring. This evening had taken a turn for the better. She said, "Let's get you a drink." And herself another one. "Perhaps you'll get up on a chair later and explain your thoughts to the party."

"Perhaps."

They stepped into the tent. She spotted Ray with his drinks tray and headed for him. He was talking to a guest, a large man in a loud madras jacket with brown hair spilling over the back of his collar. The man turned as they approached, revealing a bearded face. He gave a formal nod to her companion and said, "Mr. Stromberg-Brand."

Renata did not catch Bert's reply. She was thinking that while in Britain a hyphenated name usually meant upper-class twit, in America it could mean only one thing: married. Her plan for a jolly evening with Bert collapsed.

The bearded man was walking away and Bert was taking a glass from Ray's tray. Renata restrained herself, because another unwelcome thought had just struck her. She had heard the name Stromberg-Brand before. Quite recently. But she couldn't remember why it was important. Better not have that third glass of Chardonnay.

When Bert turned back to her, she said, "Sorry, I didn't introduce myself properly. I'm Renata Radleigh. May I ask—"

Bert's eyes widened. "Sister of Don Radleigh? I wouldn't have guessed. You're not at all like him."

"We look quite different, true."

"Different in other ways, too, I would say." He took her arm. "People seem to be sitting down. My wife's over here, I see. Come along. Don will be joining us shortly."

By now she had remembered. The Stromberg-Brands were the stars of the evening. Saviors of *Carmen*. Don would expect her to sit with them, so this was all right. But somehow it did not feel all right. The playfulness had dropped from Bert's voice, and he had a tight grip on her biceps. Feeling a cool ripple of unease in her belly, she allowed herself to be towed across the pavilion.

They approached a table where a woman in white was sitting. Standing and talking to her was SLO's General Director, Philip Congreve. He departed with a charming smile and a little wave to Renata. She was glad that he did not greet her by name, because he could never remember it. "Rebecca" was as close as he got.

Bert said, "Dear, this is Renata Radleigh."

The woman smiled but did not rise or offer her hand. She

said, "Helen Stromberg-Brand." She would be the Stromberg part, Renata thought. Her hair was blond going gray and her eyes were a wintry-fjord blue. They exchanged how-are-yous, and then she asked, "What do you do?"

Renata answered and reversed the question. She welcomed this forthright American conversation opener, because she was very curious about what Helen did. She had to be the moneybags of the family; philosophy professors did not get invited to fundraisers.

"I'm a doctor. I do research at Adams University."

"I see. What do you research?"

"UTIs."

"Urinary tract infections," Bert supplied.

"Oh," said Renata with feeling. A few years ago she'd suffered through one, and vividly remembered the itch and burning, the constant need to go to the loo. Worst of all, every time she thought she'd got rid of it, the wretched thing flared up again. "Well, I hope you eradicate them."

"I will."

Renata stared at her. Americans did say the most extraordinary things. She was trying to come up with a response when Bert said, "I've asked Renata to join us."

Helen gave a curt shake of her head. "Don's bringing someone."

"My wife never listens when people are introduced to her," Bert said to Renata. Turning to Helen, he went on, "This is Renata *Radleigh*. Don's *sister*. She's who he was bringing."

Helen shrugged and said, "She doesn't look at all like him."

Again Renata did not know what to say. There was no hint of apology in the woman's firm tone. It sounded as if she suspected that Renata was an impostor. Ought she to produce some ID?

Bert pulled out a chair for her, and reluctantly she sat down. She hoped that the Stromberg-Brands weren't going to turn out to be one of those couples for whom arguing in private had lost its savor, so strangers had to be brought in and urged to take sides. She glanced sideways at Bert, who was taking a long swallow of his wine, glaring over the brim at Helen.

She was talking to another table-hopper, an old man in a yellowing, puckered seersucker suit whom Renata recognized as the chairman of SLO's board. Even sitting down, Helen Stromberg-Brand looked tall. She had a rather narrow and long-jawed but handsome face. Her hair was in one of those short, bouncy cuts that look as if you never have to comb it; you just have to visit the salon every other day. Her fingernails were manicured but unpainted. Her wrinkles were becoming lines of authority at the corners of her eyes and mouth. She was wearing a simple white dress that bared firm upper arms and looked comfortable in the heat. She gave off glints whenever she moved: her jewelry was plain and expensive, gold disks in her earlobes, a tennis bracelet on one wrist, a Rolex on the other.

Renata attempted to chat with Bert, but he did not respond. Had he practically dragged her to this table just to ignore her? He sat very still, shoulders hunched, absently twirling his wineglass. It was empty, but when a waiter offered him a full one, he shook his head. He reminded her of a singer waiting for a big audition—his mood a mix of dread and determination.

Renata felt a stab of alarm. Perhaps she ought to get word to Don that one of his donors needed tending. He was nearby, standing at the center of a knot of guests, relating an anecdote. They were all laughing, but not as hard as he was.

As far as Helen was concerned, her morose husband might have been in Patagonia. She was fully occupied with a series of table-hoppers. From what Renata could hear over the background roar of conversation, each offered the same sort of compliments—pleasure to meet you at last, what a wonderful gift you're making. One woman said something about UTIs, and it must have been a repeat of Renata's remark, because Helen again replied, "I will." She was one of those people,

Renata thought, who did not agree with Emily Dickinson. They *liked* being public like frogs. Telling their name the livelong June to an admiring bog was just fine with them.

Finally Don arrived. Dropping into his chair, he gave a smile around the table and said, "Ah, splendid. You've found each other."

Bert straightened up and locked eyes with Don. He was not smiling. Renata realized, with a tightening of her innards, that it was Don he had been waiting for.

"So, Don. What's next on the schedule?"

"The general director's welcome to Carmen's Cornucopia. And thanks. Prepare to take a bow."

"Are we first on the list?"

"That I don't know."

"But surely ours is the biggest gift."

Helen had seen off the last of the table-hoppers. People were taking their seats. She caught her husband's words as she turned back to the table. "That's enough, Bert; it doesn't matter."

"Where we are on the list is germane. It will determine how long Don has to find his boss and tell him to remove us from the list."

Don frowned. "Remove you from the list? You mean, you want your gift to be anonymous?"

"No. We want our money back."

"Ignore him, Don," Helen said. Turning to her husband, she went on without dropping her voice, "We've already discussed this, too many times."

"This time will be different." He leaned toward Don. "I've reconsidered the figure. Instead of three hundred and thirty thousand dollars , we are going to give you … nothing."

Don was visibly trembling. He said, "Bert, please. Let's not spoil the evening. I'll come over tomorrow morning and we'll address your concerns, whatever they—"

"My concerns? I'd tell you about them right now, but you don't have time to waste. You need to find your boss. Because if he starts to thank us for our gift, you will leave me no choice but to stand up and tell him he's in error."

"Stop this now, Bert. You're embarrassing no one but yourself."

Ignoring his wife, he continued to gaze at Don. Now that the die was cast, he was enjoying himself. "Still sitting there? Then I *will* tell you about my concerns. I'd prefer to give the money to fight homelessness in St. Louis. Starvation in Haiti. In fact I can think of a hundred better uses for three hundred thirty thousand dollars than an opera." Now he turned to Helen. "Can't you?"

Don was on the verge of panic. The whites were showing all around his irises and his mouth was hanging open, disclosing a thread of saliva connecting his upper and lower teeth. He started to rise. "Look, I'll just tell Phil not to mention—"

"Don, sit down," Helen said. "I've made my decision. That's that."

"But it's such a puzzling decision, dear. Three hundred thousand dollars for an opera, when you've never so much as bought a ticket to one. In fact you've never been able to stay awake for a piece of music that lasted longer than five minutes."

Helen still seemed to be the calmest person at the table. In a quiet, even tone, she said, "Shut up, Bert. I'll do what I want with my money."

He gave the gratified smile of a chess player whose opponent has made the move that created the opening he was waiting for. "'I'm just asking you to explain. Why does a person who doesn't give a shit about opera *want* to donate three hundred grand to an opera company?"

Helen did not reply.

Don gave a jerky glance over his shoulder. Following it, Renata saw Phil Congreve rising from his chair. He was still talking to the woman seated beside him, but in a moment he would begin to make his way to the lectern.

Bert had noticed too. He said, "Better go to your boss now, Don."

"Stay where you are, Don." Helen said. She sounded a little less calm now.

His gaze sweeping from one to the other, Bert said, "The Five Gables Inn. Last Tuesday afternoon. I know, and I'll tell."

Helen stood. She picked up her handbag, which was slung over the back of her chair. Looking down at her husband, she said loudly, "I'm going home now. You are not. I want *my* house to *my*self tonight. Get on your fucking bike and pedal off somewhere."

She turned and walked away. The last Renata saw of her was her formidable profile. Her jaw looked as if it could cleave the Arctic Sea.

Bert was staring at her back. The scene had been playing out according to his expectations, until this last move stunned him. After a moment of paralysis he jumped to his feet, so abruptly that his chair tipped over backward. Then he too left the tent, in the opposite direction from his wife.

Renata looked around the nearby tables A couple of people dropped their gazes in an embarrassed reflex, but most seemed not to have heard. They were chatting, laughing, drinking. The hush had been only in her mind; conversation roared on. Across the tent, Phil Congreve was now standing at the podium. Smiling, he mimed tapping a glass.

Her friend Ray, who was standing a couple of paces away, picked up an empty glass and a knife and started tapping. Clinking noises were arising from all over the tent, and conversation faded.

She turned to Don, "Hadn't you better tell Phil?"

"What?"

"Not to mention the Stromberg-Brands."

Don got unsteadily to his feet. But he didn't head for the podium. He too left the tent.

# 5

—

RENATA WAS NOW ALONE AT the table. An odd thought crossed her mind: how flat and disappointing real life was, compared to opera. If Verdi had written music for Carmen's Cornucopia, this scene would have been an act finale quartet, with the four of them pouring out their opposed emotions, weaving a rich braid of sound. In opera, time when weighted with feelings and consequences slowed down. In real life, dramatic moments were wasted. They went by too fast, like car crashes. You sat there dazed, trying to figure out what had happened, but already knowing that it was going to cost a lot to mend.

*Come on, Renata.* So much to think about, so much to do, and here she sat musing about her art. She rose and strode out of the tent as Phil Congreve's amplified voice wished everyone a good evening.

Out on the lawn it seemed very dark compared to in the tent. She blinked about her, half expecting to see Don and Bert rolling around on the ground, fists flailing. But there was no one. She headed for the parking lot. Now she could see the pale smudge of Don's cream-linen jacket, far ahead. She quickened her pace and caught up with him just as he reached his car.

"Don! Where are you going?"

Surprised, he turned to look at her. "Helen's. We have to talk."

"Oh, Don, no. Leave it till morning. What if he's there?"

"He won't be. You heard what she said. She'll be alone."

"All the more reason not to go there."

He was swaying with nervous energy. He pulled out his smartphone and began to finger it. This was a tic she knew well. When her brother didn't know what to do, he would scroll through his contacts, desperately looking for the person who could tell him.

"Don, let's go home."

Without raising his eyes from the tiny screen, he shook his head.

"Well, take me home at least." If she could get him into the house, she could keep him there till morning, which would surely be for the best.

He swore under his breath. Then he put the phone away and took out his car keys. The horn beeped, the lights flashed, and they got in. He pulled out of the parking space with a screech of tires; he always drove too fast when he was upset. Fortunately the streets of Webster Groves were quiet at this hour, and the house was just minutes away.

"You can do without their gift if need be, can't you?"

He gave a humorless laugh. "Renata Radleigh, past mistress of the worst-case scenario. We are not going to lose the gift. You heard what she said. Anyway we *can't* lose the gift. I've told you all this. Did it go in one ear and out the other?"

"Someone will give you the money. SLO is a well-established company."

"Well-established opera companies go broke all the time. That's what happened to Opera Oklahoma. They said, we can't be your partners with *Carmen* after all. Goodbye, and here are the bills. No gift from the Stromberg-Brands, no *Carmen*. And you're back in London, trying to get a job singing at a wedding or a funeral. Now do you understand?"

"Yes, I understand. But her husband seems determined to make trouble. What was he on about with the Five Gables Inn?"

"No clue. Never heard of it."

"It's that pretty little hotel in Clayton, remember? We've had drinks there."

"Yes, yes, but I have no idea what Bert was talking about."

"Well, he seems to suspect that you're having an affair with his wife."

"That's absurd. Bert's problem is envy. His wife is so much more successful than he is, and he can't stand it. You've no idea what it means to be a top medical researcher. She's not some frump holding a test tube over a Bunsen burner. She's an executive, running a lab with a dozen employees and a seven-figure budget. And this vaccine she's working on may well win her the Nobel."

"Right. Um … Don? When you're trying to persuade her husband that you two are not having an affair, I would try to speak a little less warmly of her."

He gave her a sideways glare and flung the car into a squealing left hand turn. When they had swayed back upright, he said, "I am *not* having an affair with her. I'm trying to make the point that someone like her is not going to be scared by Bert's threats."

"Yes, but shouldn't you be just a bit scared by them? Stay away from his wife until—"

Don slammed on the brakes. The car nosedived and Renata, who hadn't fastened her seatbelt, plunged forward. She caught herself on the dashboard and looked up. They had arrived home. He did not switch off the engine.

"Don, come in. We'll have hot tea with milk and sugar, like at home, and we'll talk this over."

"I don't need any advice from you. You don't understand the situation. Bert doesn't matter. His wild accusations don't matter. All that matters is that Helen does not ask for her money back."

"Right. I do understand."

"I don't think so. Money's not *your* problem. You think you're above people like me, because you have *talent*."

"Yes, Don. Come on in and tell me all about it." If he wanted to row with her, fine. Once the two of them got to fighting, it could go on for hours. It would keep him in the house.

"Don't patronize me. The only thing makes you special is your capacity for guilt. If you don't practice for three hours every day, you feel guilty. You've been that way since you were five. And the result is, you can hit the right notes."

"Well, thanks for that."

"Only people aren't willing to pay to hear you hit the right notes. There aren't enough opera fans in the world to support all the aging journeyman mezzo-sopranos like you—"

Renata gasped. It didn't stop him.

"So people like me have to go out and get money. From people who have some. Whether they love opera or not. Understand?"

"Perfectly." She had the door open and was sliding out. "Go make a bloody fool of yourself for all I care."

She slammed the door and the car roared away.

# 6

—

BERT STROMBERG-BRAND WAS SITTING IN a sports bar on Big Bend Boulevard. His bicycle helmet rested on the table in front of him, next to a half-empty beer stein. He was gazing at a baseball game on the big-screen TV. Brilliant greens, reds and whites were reflected in his eyeglasses. His high forehead was deeply furrowed, as if he was having trouble following the game.

A short, broad-shouldered man with tousled black hair approached the table. He looked very tired; his eyes were hooded and his arms hung straight down. His T-shirt was on backward. He said, "Mr. Stromberg-Brand?"

"Oh hello, Luis. Sit down. It's Bert, especially after I wake you up from a sound sleep."

"It's okay. I wasn't asleep," said Luis, rather unconvincingly, as he sat in the chair next to Bert.

"I want you to know, I didn't call you because you're our gardener. I mean, it's not your job to come pick me up at eleven p.m. I called you because you're the only person I know with a pickup truck. For my bike. I have a flat."

Bert drained his beer. Luis folded his arms on the table and leaned heavily on them. He watched Bert. Bert watched the baseball game. After a few minutes he said, "About ready to go?"

"I'd like to see how this inning … no, sorry, let's go."

Bert put his hands on the table and pushed himself upright. Picking up the helmet, Luis followed. They stepped out into the humid darkness of the parking lot. Bert waved at his bicycle, which was lying on the asphalt, and walked to the cab of the truck. Luis swung the bike into the bed and got in.

Once they were out on Big Bend, Bert wound down the window and hung his head out in the wind, as if he were a dog. After a few moments he slumped back in his seat. "Uh … Luis? How about we go back to your place?"

Luis gave him an alarmed sideways look. "What's wrong with yours?"

Bert was silent for a minute. Then he said, "Nothing. Not a damned thing. And it is my house. Mine and hers. Ours. Community property, under the laws of the State of Missouri. She can't say, it's my house and you can't come home, not even if you have a flat tire."

Luis kept quiet and drove. A few minutes later, they turned into the Stromberg-Brand's street, which was quiet. There was only a man walking along the sidewalk, who averted his face from their headlights. Luis pulled into the driveway. He left the engine running.

There were lights in the front windows of the house. Bert gazed at them a moment, then opened his door. "I was actually hoping she'd gone to bed. So I could tiptoe in and sleep on the couch. Isn't that pathetic?"

"Good night, Mr. Stromberg-Brand."

Getting out of the truck, Bert noticed his bicycle in the bed. "Oh, uh, Luis, could you help me with the bike?"

"Sure. You want me to put it in the garage?"

"It'll be locked. Just put it inside the front door, please."

Luis hefted the bicycle and followed Bert up the front steps. Only the screen door barred their way; the front door was open. "She's letting the cool air out," Bert said. "You ought to hear her complain when I leave a door open."

He opened the screen door and paused. Tiny rainbows were scattered over the white walls of the hall. Bert looked down at the blond-wood floor. There were nuggets of crystal lying all over it, creating the prism effect. And there were small red stains. Bert ran to the doorway of the living room, looked in, and screamed.

Luis let the bicycle fall as he rushed over. Helen Stromberg-Brand lay motionless on the floor, face down. Her blond hair, white dress, and the Kashmiri rug under her were soaked with blood. Red flecks of it marked the wall behind her. Her head looked as if it were resting in a depression in the carpet, but that was an illusion. Her skull was caved in. Scattered all over the floor were fragments of the crystal bowl that had been broken over her head.

Bert was backing away, still screaming. Luis took his cell phone out of his pocket and tapped in 911.

# 7

—

RENATA WOKE ABRUPTLY FROM A deep sleep. It took a moment to figure out where she was—her brother's house. After their argument, she had considered going to a hotel, but it was late and she had no car. The next moment she realized what had awakened her. Male voices were talking loudly and excitedly, directly below, which meant they were in the front hall. A lot of them, all talking at the same time. Even so it was easy to pick out Don's voice. He sounded frightened.

She swung her feet to the floor and staggered through a wave of dizziness to the window. It was still dark outside. The street was full of police cars. She would not have thought the peaceful suburb of Webster Groves had so many police cars. Some cops were standing in a group, shoulders hunched against the chill, with the unashamed indolence of a road-repair crew. Ted's next-door neighbors, an elderly couple, were standing at the foot of their drive in their bathrobes, watching.

Renata made for the stairs, pausing only to see that she had something on. It turned out to be last night's blue dress. She threw open the door and hurtled down the stairs in her bare feet.

Don, in his striped pajamas, was backing away from a group of bulky, grim-faced men. The one in the lead had a black mustache, no hair on his head, and a badge dangling from a lanyard round his neck. He stepped forward, grasped Don by the wrist and biceps, and spun him halfway around. A few more vigorous movements and Don was leaning both hands on the mantle of his fireplace. She saw, without registering it, that his right hand was wrapped in a blood-stained bandage. The lead cop kicked Don's bare ankle with his heavy black shoe, moving his feet farther apart.

In Renata's mind, thirty years fell away: this was her little brother, set upon by bullies.

"Stop that!" she roared. "Leave him alone!"

The cops froze and stared at her. No wonder: her voice could fill a three-thousand-seat opera house. She ran straight at the cop who was kicking Don. Flinging out both hands, she struck him in the chest. She was a large, strong woman and he staggered back. That gave her room to swing at the cop beside him. Her open hand smacked him in the side of the face and sent his glasses flying.

Renata often played characters transported by emotion. It had never happened to her in real life until now. It was strange to have no control of her words or actions, no thought for the consequences. It was rather restful.

Strange as her behavior was to herself, it was no novelty to the police. Many hands grasped her limbs. In no time at all they had her lying on the floor, on her belly. Trying to kick, she found that her ankles were immobilized. Trying to get her palms to the floor to push herself upright, she realized that her hands were behind her back. Something hard-edged bit into the flesh of her wrists. A great deal of grunting and shouting was going on, some of it produced by herself, but even so, she distinctly heard the click as the handcuffs locked.

# PART II

—

## SUNDAY, MAY 23

# 8

---

THE DOOR OPENED AND A man walked in. He had a pistol on his hip and ID clipped to his shirt pocket: another detective, one Renata had not seen before. He was young and heavy-set, and his light-brown hair was cut short on the sides, with a spiky forelock projecting over his smooth brow. His madras shirt was redolent of smoke from the Sunday barbecue from which he must have been summoned. Without looking at her he sat down across the table and opened a laptop computer.

Not a pad of paper but a computer. From what little she had seen of Clayton Police Headquarters, it was brand-new and lavishly equipped, as she would expect of this small, posh suburb. The interrogation room in which she had been sitting, or pacing, for hours and hours had the same fixtures—table, chairs, mirror, presumably one-way glass—as the ones on television cop shows, but it was as bright and clean as an expensive hotel bathroom, with a lot of beige tile and stainless steel. Surely no criminal more down-market than an embezzler had ever been questioned here. A murder investigation must be a rare event for the Clayton Police, and to judge from the footfalls and voices she had been hearing from the corridor, they were rather excited about it.

"I'm Detective McCutcheon."

"Can I speak to my brother?"

"Not at this time."

"Where is he?"

"I'm just here to take your statement, ma'am." He spread his fingers over the keys of the laptop. "Name and address?"

"Look, I know that Dr. Stromberg-Brand is dead—"

"What makes you say that?"

"Because somebody who's less bloody-minded than you told me." This was the sort of riposte Renata thought of saying and usually managed to suppress. Her nerves were badly frayed. "It's the only question I've got an answer to. I've been here since dawn, and all you lot can do is offer me coffee. You seem to think a person is some kind of plant that needs coffee instead of water. As long as you give it coffee every few hours you can leave it sitting in a corner forever."

"Sorry you had to wait so long. Name and address?"

"You've arrested Don for murder, haven't you?"

"What makes you think so?"

"Because it would be a stupid thing to do and you strike me as stupid people. Why haven't you arrested the husband?"

"What makes you think we should do that?" he asked in the same neutral tone. Her insults were bouncing off him; she might as well throw rocks at the tile walls.

"Surely Don told you what happened last night. It's all true. The Stromberg-Brands had a flaming public row and she stormed off, telling him not to come home. But he did, didn't he? They must've quarreled again. He killed her."

"We'll get to what happened last night, ma'am. Name and address?"

"No. I won't answer your questions until you answer mine."

"I'm afraid it doesn't work that way, ma'am. Name and address?"

"I refuse to answer. A sister can't be forced to testify against her brother."

Until now McCutcheon's face had seemed as incapable of

forming an expression as, well, his elbow. But now the corners of his mouth turned up slightly in amusement. "What?"

"It's in the Constitution, isn't it?"

"It may be in Magna Carta, Ms. Radleigh, but not the Constitution. You must be thinking of spouses."

"Well, if a spouse can't be forced to, how can a sister?"

McCutcheon sighed and looked at his watch.

"What time is it?" Renata asked.

"Twelve fifteen."

"Finally, a question you'll answer. Wasn't so hard, was it? Now when can I see my brother?"

McCutcheon's face turned to stone. "Let me explain your position, Ms Radleigh. You interfered with the police arresting your brother. You assaulted two officers."

"Oh come on. I didn't do them any harm."

"You can be charged. I can put the cuffs on you right now and take you to jail. And since this is Sunday, you can't go before the judge until tomorrow. So here's your choice: you want to spend the night in jail, or answer my questions and go home?"

Renata was silent. Strange. She'd had plenty of time to think about the questioning to come, and it had occurred to her that the police might threaten to lock her up. She had planned on being brave. But somehow it was a lot scarier when he said it than when she'd imagined it.

"Renata Alice Radleigh," she heard herself say. "Thirty-seven Crosswell Road, London W. 11."

# 9
—

A N HOUR LATER, SHE STEPPED into the corridor, where she
planted her shoulders against the wall, shut her eyes, and
breathed deeply. She felt dazed. It was partly standing up after
sitting for so long, but mostly the after-effect of the interrogation.
It hadn't been at all like a cop show on telly. McCutcheon had
skipped around, varying innocuous questions with ones she
didn't want to answer, seeming to accept what she said and
move on only to repeat a question. She would have to review it
all to figure out how much she had let slip.

*Stop kidding yourself,* she thought. McCutcheon had
emptied her out. Everything that could incriminate her
brother, like the time he had left her and where he'd said he was
going. It embarrassed her to remember her attempts to insult
McCutcheon. The worst thing about anger was that it made
one cocky. She would not underestimate the police again.

As her brother had reminded her last night, Renata had
a brooding, perfectionist side. Just as she went over her
performances feeling a stab of chagrin for each recollected
false note, she reviewed her actions in real life, pouncing on
things to feel guilty about. The disgraceful way she had caved
as soon as McCutcheon mentioned jail was something for
which she reproached herself bitterly.

"Renata? They told me they were finished with you."

She opened her eyes to find a man standing in front of her. It was someone she knew. Thinning gray hair, hooded eyes behind horn-rimmed glasses, sardonic smile: Dick Samuelson, SLO's general counsel.

"Want a ride back to Webster?"

She supposed that she did. Nodding, she fell in beside Samuelson as he walked down the corridor. He was in fully lawyerly rig, suit, tie, and briefcase.

"Are you handling this ... I mean, representing Don?"

"For the moment. I was a public defender for as long as my idealistic youth lasted."

That was the first bit of good news, she thought. Samuelson was one of those lawyers who made her feel glad that their relations were social and not professional—that she'd never tried to wriggle out of a SLO contract. He was affable and glib, but in even the most casual discussion, he would never let you get the better of him. He thought that he was a very clever fellow, and as far as Renata could tell, he was right. "Where is Don now?"

Samuelson stopped walking. Raising the hand that held the briefcase, he pointed his index finger out the window. "There."

They were looking at the skyline of Clayton, a satellite business center with a cluster of skyscrapers that were not very tall. Samuelson was pointing at one green-glass-and-tan brick tower that looked much like the others.

"What is it?"

"County Justice Center. The jail."

Renata thought of the London equivalent: the grim, sooty Victorian pile of Wormwood Scrubs, not far from her flat. One glance and you knew what it was. How many times had she driven by the County Justice Center, assuming it was just another insurance company headquarters? It seemed sinister to her, as if it had been waiting in camouflage for the moment when it would play its role in her life and her brother's.

"He's being processed now, probably," Samuelson said.

That meant fingerprints, delousing powder, body cavity searches. Renata shivered as she was hit by a wave of simple fellow-feeling such as she was not used to experiencing for her brother. She wondered if he had his watch on—that fancy diver's watch he'd bought after seeing it in a James Bond movie. None of Renata's gibes about successful product placement had dented his pride of ownership. They'd take it away and put in an envelope, which would go on a shelf. He might never see it again. Suddenly her eyes were hot and itchy, her throat was blocked, and tears coursed down her cheeks.

Samuelson looked at her, appalled. He reached into his breast pocket and handed her his handkerchief. It was fine white cotton, so heavily starched it resisted her attempts to unfold it. "That's all right," she said, "I don't want to get mascara on it."

He readily took it back as she mopped her cheeks with her sleeve. She could wait no longer to confess. Leaning closer to Samuelson, she whispered, "I told them when Don left me. About ten thirty. And that he said he was going to the Stromberg-Brand's house." She thought a moment. "It must be here, right? That's why we're in Clayton. Because she lived here."

"To be exact, because she died here. In her house on Linden Avenue, a few blocks away. Anyway, you don't have to feel bad. Don told them all that himself and more. Before I got here and told him to shut up."

"Oh!" said Renata. Seldom, in a lifetime of feeling guilty, had she received such prompt and total absolution. But there was no time to luxuriate in it. "Did he tell them things that incriminated him?"

She was leaning in and whispering. But Samuelson seemed to see no need for discretion. He resumed walking and spoke in a normal voice, heedless of the police passing by.

"I'm hoping I can get some of that stuff suppressed. Problem is, Don didn't think it was incriminating at all. He didn't see any harm in telling the cops. He found Dr. Stromberg-Brand composed and calm. She assured him that her husband's efforts to get the donation back would come to nothing. In fact she suggested old Bertrand was not going to be her husband much longer. Don was only in the house about fifteen minutes, he said. He left her alive and well."

"And she was alone? Her husband wasn't there, I mean?"

"She was alone."

"What I can't understand is, why isn't the husband in jail? Don't the cops always suspect the husband? I told them all about what he said at the party last night."

"I'm afraid you were wasting your time. Bertrand is in the clear."

They had reached the elevator lobby. Renata turned to face him in surprise.

"He has an alibi witness. One Luis Reyes. The Stromberg-Brand gardener. Bertrand had a flat tire, stopped at a bar, and called this Reyes guy for a ride. Reyes drove him home and was with him when he discovered the body."

As Samuelson pressed the call button, Renata folded her arms across her middle and walked in a distracted circle. This was bad news. In the interrogation room she had told McCutcheon all about last night's party and the argument. It had seemed so inescapable to her that Bert was guilty. McCutcheon had listened impassively. Now she knew he had been dismissing everything she said. She felt foolish.

The doors opened and they stepped into the elevator. No one else was in it. Renata said, "The main thing now is to bail Don out."

"He'll be arraigned tomorrow. I'll make the argument for bail."

"Yes, of course. He can put up his house, can't he? You'll need the deed. I'll look for it."

Samuelson pressed the button for the ground floor, then put his hand in his pocket. He looked at the floor. "The thing is, Renata, I'm not confident the judge will grant bail. It's far from automatic, in a high-profile homicide. And, well, the prosecution case is firming up."

The words chilled Renata. She looked hard at his averted face. "Dick, my brother is innocent."

"Well, of course he is. Don couldn't kill anybody. But there are problems. The cops can place him in the house that night. He admitted it himself. Of course I haven't seen the M.E.'s report yet. I don't know what it'll say about time of death. But they've got him in the house. And it looks like they've got his blood in the house, though again we have to wait for the lab work."

"His blood?" Renata remembered a detail of the arrest that had gone out of her head until now—the bandage on Don's hand, which she hadn't seen before.

"The murder weapon was a large crystal bowl that sat on a hall table in the house. The murderer broke it over Dr. Stromberg-Brand's head. Fractured her skull. Apparently the bowl shattered in a hundred pieces. Don had a cut on his right hand—"

"What does Don say?"

"That she gave him a glass of Scotch while they talked. He dropped it, and then picking up the pieces he cut himself. Dr. Stromberg-Brand bandaged it for him."

"But that must be true! That's just like Don. He's so clumsy. He's always breaking glasses and cutting himself picking up the pieces."

"Yes, but if they do have his bloodstains in the house ... well, the prosecutor could do a lot with that. We just have to wait for the report."

"But why would Don kill Helen Stromberg-Brand? There is absolutely no reason."

She had made this point numerous times to the stolid McCutcheon. It didn't impress Samuelson either. "At this stage—I mean the initial bail hearing—they don't get into motive or lack thereof so much as physical and circumstantial evidence."

The doors opened and they stepped out. The small lobby was empty, apart from one uniformed man at the security desk. The glossy tile floor reflected the colors of the flags lined up around the walls. Samuelson started to speak, glanced at the desk man, and took her elbow to guide her out onto the sunny pavement. There was no one around.

She wondered why he'd suddenly become concerned about being overheard. "Renata, what did you tell them about Don's relations with Dr. Stromberg-Brand?"

"Relations?"

"Sexual relations."

"Well … nothing. Don said those accusations Bert made were completely groundless. That's what I told the detective."

"Did the detective ask if you believed that?"

"I told him I had no reason to disbelieve my brother."

Samuelson's eyebrows rose, clearing the tops of his horn rims. "Nicely put. As it turns out, Bert's accusations were not groundless."

She said nothing.

"Don and Helen spent last Tuesday afternoon and evening together at the Five Gables Inn. The cops didn't go into detail, but apparently Bert was able to document it to their satisfaction."

"Oh, he's a DIY matrimonial investigator as well as a philosopher?" asked Renata bitterly. She was trying to remember last Tuesday: rehearsals had run late; she'd been at SLO until 10 in the evening. She did not recall that she had spoken to Don at all that day. "Did Don admit the affair to the cops, too?"

"By that point in the interrogation, I was at Don's side, so he admitted nothing."

"I suppose I ought to ask what Don told you."

"I'm afraid that's covered by attorney-client privilege."

"Good. I can't face anymore today."

Samuelson walked to the curb and looked down the street. Following his gaze, she saw a big, expensive-looking sedan slowly approaching. Renata had never owned a car and couldn't tell one make from another, but she recognized this one from the SLO parking lot. It occupied the space closest to the entrance, the one reserved for the general director.

The car stopped beside them and the tinted window glided down. Congreve looked up at her in silence. A thoughtful, appraising gaze? Or had he forgotten her name as usual?

Samuelson obviously thought it was the latter. "Phil, I've offered *Renata* a ride back to Webster, if that's okay."

Congreve shook his head. "We're not going to Webster. Renata can get a cab at the Ritz-Carlton."

"I, uh, don't have any money." She had not been able to grab her purse as she left Don's house last night, being handcuffed at the time.

Congreve opened the door and got out of the car to face her. This time it was definitely the thoughtful, appraising gaze. He was wondering how she was going to respond in this crisis. She was asking herself the same question about him, and her thoughts were not reassuring.

Philip Congreve was not tall, but he had wide shoulders—or at least his expensive suits had a lot of padding—and he seemed to loom over her. Twenty years ago, when he was making his name as head of operations at the Metropolitan Opera, he had had a magnificent head, and it was still imposing, with a wave of silver hair topping a high forehead and chiseled cheekbones. Now, though, his jowls sagging over his collar rather muddled the effect.

SLO was a young company, and when its dynamic founding director moved onward and upward, the board thought an experienced hand on the tiller would be a good idea. It might have been, but Congreve arrived with a secret plan, which was to rest on his laurels. SLO's abbreviated season made it possible for him to spend most of the year at home on Central Park West. His management style stressed delegation. When a crisis arose—and there had been a few lesser ones before this—he roused himself and acted decisively, which generally meant firing the people he had delegated to. You never knew how you stood with Congreve, but you could be certain that he cared more about what people in New York might be saying about him than the future of the company or the well-being of its employees.

"Renata, reporters will be trying to contact you," he said as he took out his wallet and extracted a bill. "Don't talk to them."

"Oh. I suppose the media interest has been rather intense?"

"Not one word," said Congreve, and handed her a $50 bill. He glanced at Samuelson and got back in the car.

The glance had been peremptory, but the lawyer lingered to say one more thing to her. "Um … Renata? By tomorrow afternoon, Don ought to be cleared to receive visitors. I'll make sure you're on the list. Go see him if you can."

"How is he?" Renata's stomach dropped sickeningly as she asked the question that she should have asked hours ago.

Samuelson opened his mouth, but for once words failed him. He sighed and shrugged, and walked around the car to get in on the passenger side.

# 10

—

Fifteen minutes later, Samuelson and Congreve were sitting at a long table surrounded by high-backed chairs. They were alone and not speaking to each other, being fully occupied with their text messages. Tall windows behind them overlooked the collegiate gothic spires and verdant quadrangle of the main campus of Adams University.

Adams had been founded by an eminent Unitarian clergyman. But since he thought the slaves should be freed—a controversial position in St. Louis before the Civil War—the benefactors had decided to name the fledgling university for the second President of the United States instead of him. It turned out to be an appropriate choice. John Adams was called the under-appreciated Founding Father, and Adams U would come to feel that it was under-appreciated, too. By the early 2000s, it was consistently ranked in the top fifteen universities in the country by *U.S. News & World Report*, but something, perhaps its location in a fly-over town, denied it the name recognition of Harvard or Stanford.

The upshot was that Adams spent a lot of money improving its image. This conference room in the public relations department was paneled in dark, lustrous wood and richly carpeted. The table at which the men from SLO sat was polished to a high gloss, reflecting their images as they plied their cellphones. The door opened and Roger Merck entered, apologizing for his tardiness.

"Hello, Roger," said Congreve. "This is our counsel, Dick Samuelson."

The men shook hands. Roger, the Associate Deputy Vice Chancellor for Public Relations, was an African American of around sixty, with a head of pure white hair and glinting gold spectacles. He had a round face and a benign smile.

He turned grave as they sat down. "I'm sorry you folks are in such a tough position. I've fielded some calls from the local media already, and some of the questions were very unpleasant."

"It'll be the national media soon," said Congreve. "To be frank, we're hoping for a little help from you."

Roger folded his hands and deliberated silently for half a minute. "In a case like this, with a high-profile faculty member who can no longer defend herself, we're prepared to go proactive."

Congreve looked relieved. He brushed back a lock of silver hair and glanced at Samuelson. The lawyer said, "Those unpleasant questions, I assume they concerned a possible affair between the defendant and Dr. Stromberg-Brand?"

Roger nodded and sighed. "They were just fishing. They didn't know anything. They had a murder and were hoping to turn it into a romantic triangle."

"I'm afraid that's going to happen on this evening's newscasts."

Roger frowned. "Your guy, Radleigh—do you mean he said something to—"

Samuelson and Congreve shook their heads vigorously. Congreve said, "He won't be our guy much longer. I'm just waiting for the next news cycle to suspend him. In the cycle after that, he'll be terminated."

Samuelson said, "He's not a problem anyway. He's in jail. Tomorrow he'll go before the judge, say 'not guilty' and then go back to jail. Our problem is the husband."

"Bert?"

"I got a call from Justine at Channel 5 News not an hour ago," said Congreve. "She claimed Bert had just given them an interview, in which he said he had proof of a … I suppose you'd have to say an assignation between his wife and Don, at a Clayton hotel last Tuesday."

"And you said—"

"No comment."

"But we're going to have to give ground," said Samuelson. "Don admitted to me that he and Dr. Stromberg-Brand were having an affair."

Roger emitted a grunt of surprise and pain, as if someone had punched him in the stomach.

"He said that in finalizing her gift to SLO, they were thrown together a lot, and in the atmosphere of excitement surrounding a new production of an opera … well, they lost their sober judgment. Don said he was sorry for her. She told him she was very unhappy at home."

Roger continued to look as if he was in pain. He kept silent.

The men from the opera company exchanged glances. Congreve leaned forward. "The damage is done. We'll cope. But we don't want to be hit with something else in the next news cycle. Bert works for the university. Do you know him—I mean, personally?"

"Yes."

"Well, can you talk to him? Make him see that blackening his dead wife's name this way is … well, indecent?"

"I'm afraid I've never had much luck talking to him about anything. Bert's the head of a committee of humanities professors who've made it their business to complain about Public Relations. They say we don't devote enough space in our publications and press releases to their departments. All I can say is that seventy-five percent of the university's income is research grants to the medical school, so it's not surprising that the medical school gets most of the attention. Bert has not been receptive."

"In other words, he's mad that medical professors, like his wife, get so much attention," said Samuelson. "How far back does this resentment of his wife go?"

"I suppose there's no point trying to be discreet about this anymore. Fifteen years ago the head of our molecular microbiology department spotted Helen Stromberg-Brand's potential and set out to hire her away from Indiana University. She asked if Adams had a spot for her husband, who was also on the Indiana faculty. Of course we do our best to accommodate a hire we want as badly as Helen, but budget realities being what they are, the only possible position was NTT."

Puzzled, Congreve looked to Samuelson, who said, "Non Tenure Track. Had he been tenure track at Indiana?"

Roger nodded.

"Fifteen years ago, and he still holds a grudge?" asked Congreve.

"You don't know academics, Phil," said Samuelson, smiling. "Just because they dress like slobs and don't make real money, we think they're not competitive."

"They're the most competitive people in the world," said Roger. "Their first-grade teacher gave them an A, and it changed their whole lives."

"And when you're Non Tenure Track, the best you can ever hope for is C-plus."

Congreve massaged his jowls thoughtfully. "So Bert's bitter towards Adams, and bitter toward his wife for not making them improve their offer?"

Roger nodded. "And bitter toward a society that would rather be well than wise. It never ends. He's not the most mature person, I'm afraid."

"But there must be someone who can talk to him," said Congreve. "Surely he has friends."

"Of course. But they're resentful humanists like himself,

who would not be receptive to a call from me, asking them to do something for the public image of Adams U."

"How about the public image of Helen herself?" asked Samuelson. "Do you know some friend of hers who has leverage with Bert?"

Roger looked at him. Then he took off his glasses, breathed on the lenses, and pulled out a handkerchief to polish them. All this took several moments. The men from SLO waited patiently.

"I've thought of someone," he said finally. "But I can't call him myself. I'll have to talk to his doorkeeper, who guards the door rather zealously, I'm afraid." He rose to his feet. "I'll be in touch, but probably not as soon as you'd like me to be. This person is very busy."

"Who is it?"

"I'd rather not say until I talk to him."

Samuelson was smiling. "I think I can guess."

"Please don't."

"Do you really think *he* would help? That would be great."

Roger did not reply. He put out his hand to Congreve, ending the meeting.

# 11

—

CLAYTON'S BUSINESS DISTRICT WAS ALL but deserted on a hot Sunday afternoon. The clean and pretty mini-city would have to wait until Monday morning to be repopulated. Here and there a car parked at the curb indicated that somebody was in one of the glittering office towers, but sidewalk cafés had no diners, shop windows no browsers, shaded benches no loungers. Flowerbeds bloomed only for the bees, and small fountains roared like Niagara in the silence.

On the wide, sun-blasted sidewalk of Bonhomme Avenue there was only one pedestrian, a tall woman with tousled black hair, wearing a badly wrinkled blue party dress. She walked slowly, with a long, hip-swinging stride, her arms folded and her head down. She had a beautiful face full of woe. Had her hair been red, she would have looked like an Old Master's Magdalene.

Renata was completely absorbed in going over her conversation with Dick Samuelson, so brief but so over-charged with bad news. What was vexing her at the moment was the end of it. Samuelson and Congreve had driven off in the direction of the Ritz-Carlton. They could have given her a lift to the hotel and its cabstand. But they needed to talk, and she was not to hear. She wasn't sure what that meant, but it did not bode well for her brother.

She stopped and looked up. In her preoccupation she had given no thought to which way she was walking, and she found herself not at the Ritz-Carlton, but the County Justice Center. The name was etched over the locked front doors. There was a window display touting the attractions of St. Louis County's parks. She ran her eye up the ten-story building. Behind these tan-orange bricks and opaque green windows was her brother. She could hear men shouting. A riot? No, there was also the regular, hollow beat of a basketball being dribbled. So that was one way the prisoners passed time. It wouldn't do Don any good; basketball was one American enthusiasm he'd never managed to embrace.

Tomorrow afternoon she would be able to visit him, Samuelson had said. He seemed to have little hope that Don would qualify for release on bail, so she would have to come back here and enter this building tomorrow. She had never visited anyone in jail, and her memory could produce only movie scenes: actors sitting on either side of a thick pane of glass, talking to each other on telephones. She shuddered. In real life it couldn't be that bad, could it?

Even if there were no pane of glass or phones it would be hard. Her brother's life had been smashed to bits. He wasn't just in jail but in disgrace, and he was the sort of person to feel disgrace keenly. How was she to console him? If only they loved each other. Even liked each other a bit. If only he hadn't been so beastly to her the last time they had talked. She knew why, of course: she had been questioning him about his affair with Helen, and Don often got angry when forced to lie. Still she couldn't forget that last shaft of his, "aging journeyman mezzo-soprano." It hit too close to home. No, it hit home squarely.

She touched the $50 bill Congreve had given her for cab fare. It was tucked into her bra, because the blue silk dress had no pockets. Tomorrow would come soon enough. Now it was time to head for the Ritz-Carlton and home.

Home? No doubt the police had turned the whole house over by now. They might still be there. Even if they weren't, the phone would be ringing. Reporters. A few might even come to the door. Congreve had made it crystal-clear she wasn't to talk to them.

Renata started walking. But not toward the Ritz. Samuelson had mentioned that Helen Stromberg-Brand had been killed in her house on Linden Avenue. That was only a few streets away, an easy walk even in her pinching party shoes. She wanted to take a look at the scene of the crime.

# 12

—

Roger Merck, Associate Deputy Vice Chancellor for Public Relations, went directly from his meeting with the men from SLO to the near empty parking lot where his Volvo was parked. He got in and drove east on the Forest Park Expressway, into the eponymous park. Above the trees rose the apartment towers of the Central West End, St. Louis's most fashionable neighborhood, and in amongst them, the tall, blocky silhouette of Granger Hospital, Adams University Medical School's teaching hospital, and other buildings housing the school's classrooms and laboratories. Adams University's sense of being underappreciated was not shared by its medical school. Many believed that it was the best medical school in America. What wasn't a matter of opinion was that it regularly ranked first among institutions receiving federal research grants.

Roger continued eastward on Forest Park Avenue, to a stretch where medical school buildings alternated with old row houses, factories converted into loft condominiums, a microbrewery, and the headquarters of the Salvation Army. He parked in front of a new building, lustrous in white and pale green, that took up an entire block. Amygdala, said the stainless steel letters on the facade.

It was familiar territory for Roger. He and his minions devoted much of their time to singing the praises of Amygdala, the university's "incubator," where the discoveries of faculty members and the investments of venture capitalists were combined to hatch a company that would preserve health or banish sickness, and produce a lot of money for scientists, investors, and Adams University.

Roger swiped his key card at the door, showed his ID at the security desk, and headed down a quiet corridor to a door marked *Ezylon*. His brow was furrowed and his lips turned down at the corners, as if he was not anticipating this meeting with pleasure. He paused with his hand on the doorknob and took a deep breath. His face blandly genial again, he went in.

There was no one in the outer office but a young man sitting at a desk, talking on the phone. Roger, always tactful, did not hover over him, but stood between the rows of chairs in the waiting area. Ezylon's busy partners were rarely on hand to greet visitors, and to make up for that, their pictures were here to be gazed upon. They were good pictures, produced by Roger's department. Helen Stromberg-Brand in her white lab coat stood beside the celebrated venture capitalist Keith Bryson, who wore the sort of clothes he was almost always photographed in—blue jeans and checked sport shirt. His famous features, framed by longish silver-blond hair and Elizabethan beard, wore the usual calm and intelligent half-smile. She was showing him a chart in her lab. People, including Roger himself, were standing around in the background grinning.

The man at the desk hung up the phone and looked at Roger, who approached with hand extended. "Hello, Jayson. How are you?"

"Hey, Rog, what's so important that you're here on a Sunday?" said Jayson Mentis, who shook hands briefly without rising.

"It's this terrible business with Dr. Stromberg-Brand, of course. Have you spoken to Keith yet?"

"He's aware of the situation."

"How quickly can you put me in touch with him?"

"Just as soon as you convince me that it's necessary."

"Well, let me endeavor to do so," said Roger with a smile that looked only a little forced. Deciding that Jayson was not going to invite him to sit down, he took the chair in front of the desk. Then he explained that the news media were trying to turn Helen's murder into a scandal, and receiving help from her husband.

"Isn't this the opera company's problem? They're the ones who have a murderer working for them."

"Dr. Stromberg-Brand is one of the most high-profile faculty members Adams University has."

"So? Put out a press release saying the private lives of faculty members are no concern of the university and you're done."

"It's not that simple."

"Oh. You mean, 'cause your medical school's senior faculty is eighty percent men and you catch a lot of heat for that, you've given Helen big play as a role model Woman in Medicine, and now she turns out to be a slut. Is that the complication?"

Jayson's face was beaming, and Roger evidently decided that the sight of it was not helping him keep his temper. He gazed at the floor for a while, and when he spoke it was in an even tone.

"I think that if Mr. Bryson talks to Bert," Roger said, "he can convince him to stop behaving in this destructive way."

"Keith doesn't even know this Bert guy."

"No, they've met several times. At the cocktail party the med school hosted to launch Ezylon, at the tour of the lab for the media—"

"Keith has forgotten all those people," Jayson said. "I have to brief him every time he comes back to St. Louis. Anyway, the main point is, this is a mess. It's ugly. It's smelly. It's the kind of thing Keith can't afford to get within a mile of. Just because he drops by for some grip-and-grin every few months, don't get the idea Ezylon is important to him."

"But at the media picnic he said—"

"No, don't quote him back to me. I probably wrote the speech."

The furrows on Roger's brow had returned. "He's spoken to me privately about his warm personal regard for Helen. I thought he meant it."

Jayson shrugged and tapped keys on his laptop. "Okay. Let's bring up the sked and see if it's feasible. At the moment, Keith is in San Diego, where his contender yacht in the America's Cup trials is being fitted out. Then he's off to Death Valley, where he's founder and grand marshal of the triathlon. They're expecting him to compete, too, but they may be disappointed. Then he's off to Tokyo, where he's hosting the Third Wave Conference on Sustainable Hi-Tech. On the way back he stops off in Los Angeles, where he has no public appearances scheduled, but rumor has it he's getting together with his great and good friend Angelina Jolie to discuss her UN ambassadorial duties. So, help me out here. Which of these events shall we ask him to cancel so he can come to St. Louis and try to persuade an angry husband not to talk trash about his dead wife?"

"I'm only asking for a phone call."

Jayson leaned sideways and dug his cellphone out of his pants pocket. "I'm sending a text to his personal cell. That's the best I can do for you." He tapped keys, then put the phone away and looked at Roger. "It'll be a few hours. No use hanging around."

As Roger got to his feet, Jayson's phone played its incoming-call tune. He pulled it out and looked at the screen in surprise. Pressing the talk button he said, "Hello, Keith." He listened for half a minute, said, "Will do, 'bye," and hung up.

A good deal of the bounce seemed to have gone out of Jayson. He spoke to Roger without meeting his eye. "Uh, turns out he's *here*. He told me to ask you to go straight to his condo. Four-nine-oh-nine Laclede."

"Thanks, Jayson," Roger said, and there was no trace of

sarcasm detectable in his tone, no gleam of triumph in his eye. At times, the Associate Deputy Vice Chancellor's politeness rose to the level of heroic.

# 13

—

In Clayton, Maryland Avenue was the boundary between the commercial and residential districts. Renata crossed it and stepped gratefully under the shade of the tall oak trees that lined Linden Avenue. The houses were a mix of agreeable old Victorian, Queen Anne, and Craftsman buildings of wood and brick with wide porches, set far back from the street, and pretentious new mansions of stone and marble that practically bulged from their lots.

It was one of these new mansions whose door was barred by yellow crime-scene tape. Parallel tracks flattened the grass where something wheeled and heavy had run over it, probably the gurney bearing the body. Otherwise the lawn was smooth and green as a pool table, and not much bigger. Boxwood hedges lined the drive and there were flowerbeds on either side of the steps leading to the front door. The rest of the lot was taken up by the house. That must simplify the job of the Stromberg-Brand gardener. What had Samuelson said his name was? Luis … something.

In fact he must have been here recently, for the grass was glinting in the slanting sunlight and the earth in the flowerbeds was dark with moisture. There was not a withered bloom among the flowers and the hedge tops were even to a fraction of an inch. A constant gardener, she thought, not neglecting his duties even on Sunday.

Didn't the police find it a bit suspicious that Bert's alibi was being provided by his employee? Renata certainly did. It would be interesting to have a chat with this man. It would be wonderful to find out he was lying. She looked up and down the street. There was no man at work in any of the yards; in fact, there was no one in sight at all. She could hear children's laughter and splashing from a pool behind one of the houses, and the wind in the leaves, and the thrum of central air conditioning units, but otherwise Linden Avenue was quiet.

Abruptly Renata was deafened by a howl. The racket would make you expect to see a fighter jet taxi down a driveway—if you weren't as familiar with American suburbs as Renata, who knew it was a leaf-blower. Possibly a gardener at work. Maybe even Luis, who had other customers in the neighborhood. Most likely not, but she walked toward the noise anyway.

She descended the street to the corner and turned left, where she found a pickup truck parked in a driveway. "Reyes Gardening" was painted on the door. That was the name Samuelson had said, Luis Reyes. The noise ceased. A man came around the corner of the house—a short, broad-shouldered man with thick black hair escaping in all directions from under a baseball cap. He swung the leaf blower into the bed of the truck.

Here was luck, throwing open a door to her. Or possibly it was the tug of a really bad idea. Either way, Renata could not resist. She walked up the drive.

"Mister Reyes?"

He regarded her warily as she drew near. "Are you from the newspaper? Because I already talked to somebody from the paper." His accent was faint. Lighter than hers, in fact.

"No." She realized belatedly that she should have dreamed up a pretext. "I, uh, my name is Renata Radleigh."

He looked at her blankly.

"It's my brother they've arrested."

"Oh. I'm sorry. That must be tough." He waited for her to say something, but nothing came to her. "Uh, what can I do for you, miss?"

*Retract your story so Bert becomes prime suspect.* She decided to say something equally true, but a bit less pointed. "I'm sorry. I've just gotten out of the police station after spending the whole day there. I don't know what I'm doing, really. Just wandering around. I suppose the cops kept you waiting around a long time, too?"

Reyes shrugged. "A person like me, he always has to be ready when the cops call." Reaching into his breast pocket he lifted out a blue U.S. passport. "But they didn't give me a hard time. Just asked a lot of questions about last night." Without prompting, he told her the story. Grudgingly Renata found that it all sounded plausible. She asked, "Does Bert do this sort of thing to you often?"

"Oh, he's all right. I see him a lot because he's home most of the day. His wife, she was practically never home. He just has one or two courses to teach at the university. That's not enough teaching for Bert. He comes out to help me build my vocabulary."

Renata smiled. "I expect you'd much rather get the job done and move on to the next yard."

Reyes smiled back.

*Well, this is a disaster*, she thought. She ought to be subjecting the gardener to a withering cross-examination that would make him break down and admit he'd lied. And here they were having a friendly conversation. This wasn't doing Don any good at all.

She heard herself blurt out, "My brother didn't do it. He could never kill anyone."

"Of course you think that, miss. He's your brother and you love him."

She did not reply.

"Look, I … maybe it'll help …." He shook his head. "No, never mind. Sorry."

"Go on."

"Well, Doctor Stromberg-Brand—she was a brilliant scientist they say, doing a lot of good in the world, but she could really make a person angry."

"Did she make you angry?"

"Well … yes. She had this bed near the front door? Last spring, she says, I want azaleas there. I told her, they won't get enough sun. Let me plant hostas. But she wanted azaleas, so I planted them, and they died.

"Early one morning the phone rings and it's her. She's in an airport in Tokyo. Or Oslo, or someplace. She's just opened my bill, and she says, I'm not paying for those azaleas."

"Did you remind her they were her idea?"

He nodded grimly. "Big mistake. Did that ever make her mad. I'll never forget that phone call. Somebody on the other side of the world shouting at you. People in Oslo or wherever would interrupt her—she was real busy, always—and she'd tell me to wait, and I'd think, when she comes back, she'll be calmer. But no, she took up yelling at me right where she left off. I ended up eating the loss."

"She pretended to forget and you had to go along."

"She wasn't pretending. The azaleas hadn't worked out. So they couldn't have been her idea. It was impossible for her to be wrong. Sorry, I'm not explaining this real well."

"I understand," said Renata. She had encountered many singers, directors, and conductors like that. Encountered wasn't the word. They had run over her and never felt the bump. Just bringing the incidents to mind caused her fists to clench and her heartbeat to quicken. Then her feelings took an abrupt, sickening swerve. "You're trying to convince me Don's guilty, aren't you?"

"I just mean, you could be a really good person, and Dr. Stromberg-Brand could make you mad enough to—" He broke off. "Forget what I said. The police told me practically nothing about the case. I'm sorry."

"You didn't see him, did you?"

"What?"

"I mean, you didn't tell the police my brother's car was driving away when you arrived or anything like that?"

"Didn't see any cars, I told them. Or anybody. Oh ... I forgot to tell them about the guy walking his dog."

Turning, he looked toward the Stromberg-Brand house. "Now that I think about it, I didn't see a dog."

"What?"

"The only reason people walk around this neighborhood at night is they're walking a dog. But I didn't actually see a dog with this guy."

"What did he look like?"

Reyes thought for a long while before he could come up with anything. "I didn't see his face. He was wearing a long coat. Like a raincoat. White or tan. I remember 'cause it was a clear night. Otherwise he was just average."

Renata was relieved: Don hadn't been wearing a raincoat when he left his house. In fact, he didn't even own a coat that matched this description. "He was coming toward you? How come you couldn't see his face?"

"He turned away." Reyes mimed the movement, burying his chin in the hollow of his shoulder.

"He was hiding his face."

"Or he didn't like the headlights shining in his eyes."

"Did you tell the police about this?"

"Didn't think to."

"Would you call them?"

Reyes hesitated. "You know how stupid they make you feel. Did you see him coming out of the Stromberg-Brand house? No. Did you see him get in a car? No. Oh, so I suppose you can't tell us the license plate number either."

"Please call them. It could be very important."

"Okay. Look, I got to be going." Reyes opened the door of the truck and climbed in.

She was almost dizzy with the rush of hope. She wanted to grab him by the collar and make him swear to call the cops. But she managed to thank him and step back as the truck reversed out of the drive.

# PART III

—

## MONDAY, MAY 24

# 14

—

ON MONDAY MORNING, PETER LOMBARDO entered the office of Medical Public Relations by the back door, which meant that he did not pass the reception desk, and had no warning. He just walked into his office and found the Associate Deputy Vice Chancellor for Public Relations sitting in his visitor's chair.

Peter had not seen Roger Merck since his job interview eight weeks before. He'd learned enough of the office routines to know that when Roger wanted to see one of his medical writers, he summoned him to the main campus of Adams University, to his office just down the hall from the chancellor's. Roger liked being close to the chancellor.

In fact, that was how the conversation began. After rising to give Peter a smile and handshake, Roger said, "I was up early to have breakfast with the chancellor. At his house." Roger turned around and spread his coattails. Long white hairs made a spiral pattern on the seat of his black trousers. "They're from Mavis, the chancellor's Persian cat. I shouldn't have sat on the sofa." He chuckled.

Peter did too. "So … uh, you want me to take a lint roller to your butt or what, boss?"

Roger swung around quickly, to show an embarrassed face.

Peter winced inwardly. He was still struggling to find the right tone for this place. People were nice, they liked a joke, but the crudeness and raucousness of his previous workplace, the newsroom of the Springfield *Journal-Register*, wouldn't fly here. Trying to recover, he politely invited Roger to resume his seat, and went around the desk to drop into his own chair.

Roger slowly, mournfully shook his head. "This is a hell of a thing, isn't it?"

Peter nodded back. He had no idea what his boss was talking about. Obviously some bad news had broken over the weekend. As a PR man, he was supposed to know about it. Unfortunately, he had spent the weekend trying to forget all about his job.

"Have you gotten a lot of calls?"

Peter covertly glanced at his phone. The light was blinking, meaning he had messages, but he didn't know how many. What to say? "Um … yes."

"Have you returned any yet?"

Each answer was a step into the fog, possibly toward a cliff edge. "No."

"Good. Forward them all to me. I'll handle all Stromberg-Brand media queries personally."

So whatever had happened was connected to Sturm und Drang. No surprise there, she was the newsiest doc on his beat. He hoped he wouldn't have to talk to her.

"What I'd like you to do, Pete, is get to work right away on the obit. I don't suppose you have a draft on file?"

The obit. *Holy mackerel.* Sturm und Drang was *dead.* He strove to feel a pang but couldn't. He had never met her or even talked to her on the phone, but she sent him stinging emails whenever she was unhappy with her media coverage. He pulled himself together to reply to the question. "No, we don't prepare obits on people until they turn fifty."

"And she was only forty-eight," said Roger, nodding sadly. "Who'd expect her to die? Let alone be murdered."

Murdered.

Nothing since he had left the *Journal-Register* newsroom had thrilled Peter as much as that word. Questions filled his mind—none of which he could ask Roger. He couldn't wait to get on the phone to reporters. Adjusting his glasses on his nose, he said, "Uh, Roger, I wouldn't mind returning those calls myself."

"Thanks, Pete. I'm not looking forward to it. But the chancellor was firm on that point. As you can imagine, it's very delicate, now that the local media have chosen to focus on the scandalous aspects."

Scandalous aspects.

Peter could hardly sit still. He said, "Any tips on how I should deal with the scandalous aspects in the obit?"

"Ignore them," said Roger, getting to his feet. "Do our standard obit. Call around for some quotes, play up her scientific and teaching accomplishments, get a draft to me by noon if possible. I'll leave you to it."

Before the door even closed behind him, Peter had swung to his computer and flicked the power switch. The prospect of another boring Monday, which had weighed upon him since he woke up, was forgotten.

# 15

---

In THEIR LAST CONVERSATION BEFORE his arrest, Don had ridiculed Renata for feeling guilty if she did not practice her singing for three hours a day. Because of his troubles, yesterday had been one of the few days in her life when she had not sung for even three minutes. And this morning she was missing the vocal warm-ups before rehearsal to catch Dick Samuelson before he went to court. She felt guilty for neglecting her profession. Considering the crisis Don was in, she also felt guilty about being so selfish as to feel guilty for neglecting her profession.

She entered the Peter J. Calvocoressi Administration Building and climbed the steps to the corporate counsel's office. Dick Samuelson looked up from his computer screen and frowned in a puzzled way at the suit on a hanger she was carrying.

"For Don to wear in court," she said. "Is that all right? I didn't want him appearing in an orange jumpsuit or whatever."

"People are arraigned in all manner of get-ups, but I suppose it can't hurt. Just drape it over the chair back."

The charcoal pinstripe was his favorite suit. Last night she had spent a long time weighing the pros and cons: it would give him confidence today, but would he ever want to wear it again in his life? Either way, he wouldn't want it draped over a chair. She hung it from the door handle.

"You'll need the deed to the house for bail. Is this it?" Never having owned real estate, she wasn't sure she had found the right paper.

"Renata, I'll do my best, but don't get your hopes up. Judges are reluctant to grant bail in a case like this, especially if they think the defendant is a flight risk. Don being a foreigner—"

"He's an American citizen. Do you want me to get his passport?"

"No, that's okay." He glanced at his watch. "I better head for the courthouse. I'll call you."

"When?"

"Depends on the docket."

She left him shoving papers into his briefcase. She wondered where his normal smugness was when she really needed it. Checking her watch, she crossed the Emerson Electric Picnic Lawn, still glittering with dew, and entered the Jane B. Pritchard Theatre by the stage door. The corridors were empty, because rehearsal was scheduled to begin in five minutes and everyone else was on stage. Ordinarily Renata would have been too, but she was trying to avoid being consoled and asked a lot of questions about Don. So she leaned against the corridor wall and waited. Precisely on time, she pushed through the heavy door to the dimness of the Charles MacNamara III Auditorium.

The plan didn't work. She was halfway up the aisle when she heard an urgent whisper of "There's Renata!" By the time she climbed up to the Ruth Baxter Irwin Mainstage, the whole cast was gathered round, taking her hands, hugging her, saying how terrible it was, asking how she was bearing up, offering to lend her a car or take her to lunch. Looking over shoulders, Renata uneasily watched Bernhard von Schussnigg, the director, a paunchy, gray-headed figure in black, pacing the aisle. He had a filthy temper at the best of times. If they didn't get on with rehearsal soon, he would make everyone pay for it the rest of the day.

She tried to get across the stage to take her position, but here were more people coming up to manhandle her. In the lead was Amy Song, the Endeavor-Rent-a-Car Endowed Artist and star of the show. She had actually bestirred herself to come up early from her dressing room and assume the expression she had worn as Suzuki, when she condoled with Madama Butterfly at the San Francisco Opera last fall.

Renata hurried through the brave smiles and hand-clasping and shoulder-petting. As she finally made her way downstage to stand on the piece of tape that marked her position, she thought, *This is all awfully wet. How opera singers do love an emotional binge, especially when it breaks the tedium of rehearsal.* But the asperity of her thoughts was only to help keep her equilibrium, for there was an undeniable lump in her throat. Mustn't burst into tears. That would bring everyone round for more shoulder-pats and the director would get very cross indeed.

The way Renata saw it, she was a gloomy, irritable person who pretty much deserved the lonely life she led. It escaped her notice that in a theater, gloom and irritability were not her leading characteristics. She had a love for music that she didn't have for anything or anybody else, and it transformed her into an enthusiastic, patient, tolerant person. A trouper. Whatever it would take to make an opera score live, she would do. In fact, the middle rungs of the opera world rang with praise of Renata Radleigh's dedication and generosity, though it never reached her ears. Perhaps that was just as well, because the conversations generally ended with some variant of, *Poor Renata, she's a better musician than X, and so much nicer, but she never got the breaks, and now it's too late.*

The stage managers were rushing around, urging the others to their places. Ray the super loped to his place next to her.

"I'm not much for hugs, Renata, but I'm sorry for your trouble, too."

"That's all right, Ray. Seems a bit much, doesn't it? I'm not the one in jail."

"It's harder to feel sorry for your brother."

She turned to him, but he avoided her eye. She said, "He's innocent, you know."

"Of course you say that. You're his sister. But I saw the husband on TV."

"Bert Stromberg-Brand gave an interview?" This was the first she had heard of it. Last evening she had obeyed Congreve's orders and ignored the telephone. In the interests of a night's sleep, she had avoided the television and computer, too.

"The poor guy laid out the whole story. What your brother did was sleazy."

"Sleazy isn't the same as guilty."

Not the most ringing defense, but it was the best she could do. She wondered if most of the St. Louis television audience sympathized with Bert and agreed with Ray.

"He should never have gotten mixed up with that Stromberg-Brand woman," Ray said.

"What do you know about her?"

"Nothing, except she had way too much money."

She shook her head; Ray had some very reactionary ideas. "For a woman?"

"For a doctor."

"Quiet everyone!" bellowed the stage manager, as Bernhard von Schussnigg walked down the aisle.

# 16

―

IT WAS MID-MORNING AT THE Office of Medical Public
Relations, and Peter Lombardo was gazing out the window.
He had nothing else to do.

His day had gotten off to such a fast start. He had written
up a list of people who he knew would feel that they ought
to be quoted in the Stromberg-Brand obit and put in calls or
dispatched emails to all of them. Then he had written up the
rest of the obit, which had taken about fifteen minutes, because
it was mostly a matter of cutting and pasting paragraphs from
the many press releases he had churned out about Sturm und
Drang's triumphs. Now he could only sit and wait for return
calls. It could be a long wait. Docs were busy people.

Meanwhile, the view: the roof of the Amygdala building,
the helipad atop Granger Hospital, and the glass and concrete
towers of various medical school buildings and luxury condos.
In the gaps between he could see the green of Forest Park.

In his early days here it had excited him to have an office of
his own with a window. At the Springfield *Journal-Register*, he
had sat at one desk in a long row. He had to hear his neighbors'
phone conversations. People walking by would snatch bits of
his lunch. Others would interrupt his writing to tell a joke
or let slip a bit of salacious gossip from the State Capitol.

Periodically somebody watching the TV in one corner, always tuned to CNN, would shout that something big was happening and they would all rush over to watch and kibitz.

God, the paper had been wonderful.

Peter swung his chair around, breathed on his glasses and wiped them off with the broad end of his tie, and faced the computer screen. Reading what he had written was like chewing Styrofoam pellets. At the paper he had written stories that were like Reuben sandwiches.

His phone rang.

"Mr. Lombardo, this is Dr. Patel returning your call."

Anisha Patel MD, assistant professor of molecular microbiology. She was very junior in the department, and he hadn't spoken to her before. Her name had made him expect an accent, but she sounded as middle American as he did.

"Thanks for calling back, doctor. It's about the obit for Dr. Stromberg-Brand, of course."

"Yes. I should let you know that I'm going to record this conversation."

"Um ... why?"

"In case you misquote me."

"That's not necessary, Dr. Patel."

"Reporters have told me that in the past, and then they've misquoted me."

"I'm not a reporter. When the article is finished, I'll send your part to you for your okay. Public Relations never sends out a piece until all quotes are approved."

"Oh. You mean I can make sure it's what I said."

"Or you can change it. Whatever you want is what I'll run."

"Oh. That's good. What about the rest?"

"Sorry?"

"Do I get to approve the whole article?"

"You mean, change other people's quotes?"

"Well, or recommend they be dropped, if in my opinion they're inappropriate?"

"I think you would have to take up that with Roger."

"Who?"

Medical profs were notoriously unimpressed with the satraps and pooh-bahs of the main campus. "Roger Merck, Associate Deputy Vice Chancellor for Public Relations. I'm working directly for him on this."

"Who else are you asking for quotes about Helen?"

The list was lying on his desk, and there was no reason not to read it to Dr. Patel. But this conversation had been hard on his self-esteem. He dug in his heels.

"I'm afraid not, Doctor. That's something else you would have to clear with the vice chancellor."

He heard a sigh of impatience that ought to have intimidated him, but alas, only gratified him. "Mr. Lombardo, all I'm asking is that you tell me one thing. Have you called Dr. Chase?"

Peter hadn't. In fact, he couldn't place the name. "No."

"All right then."

The rest of the conversation went well. Dr. Patel became quite affable and gave him a nice, sincere-sounding quote about what an inspiring mentor Sturm und Drang had been.

After hanging up, Peter pushed off with his feet and spun around in his chair a few times, cackling to himself. Nothing he had done in the past month had exhilarated him like that phone call. It had been like being back at the paper, fencing with a source at City Hall. If he really was back at the paper, his next act would be to contact the person he had been told not to talk to.

Peter could not resist.

He consulted his directory: Ransome P. Chase MD, associate professor of molecular microbiology. Now that was interesting. Chase was on his beat, but no one had ever mentioned his name. Turning to the computer, he rattled off his standard query, asking Dr. Chase for a quote about his late colleague Dr. Stromberg-Brand, and sent it off.

Only as he turned back to his desk did he notice that he

hadn't hesitated before clicking "send." The cover-your-ass instincts of an Adams University underling, which should have warned him that he was about to create a permanent record of his insubordination toward a faculty member, had failed to kick in. *Oh well, too late now.*

The computer gave its incoming-mail beep. Dr. Chase must have been at his computer, too, because his reply popped up on the screen:

> Yes, I have a quote for you:
> "Ding Dong! The Witch is dead. Which old Witch? The Wicked Witch!
> Ding Dong! The Wicked Witch is dead."

Peter stared at the screen for a long time. Then he pressed "print" and ran down the hall to the office printer, to grab the message before anyone else saw it.

# 17

---

IF AN OPERA FAN WHO couldn't wait for opening night
had happened to wander into the Charles MacNamara III
Auditorium this morning, he would have been puzzled by
what he saw on the Ruth Baxter Mainstage. He would have
been able to figure out that the twenty-odd people standing
around in their street clothes, mostly T-shirts and jeans, were
opera singers. Their tendency to barrel-chestedness would
give them away. The puzzling part was the set.

Act III of *Carmen* takes place on the border between Spain
and France in the Pyrenees Mountains in the mid-nineteenth
century. There was nothing to suggest that here, except
perhaps, for a jagged line of orange neon across the back of the
stage that could have been a mountain range, and an electric
simulation of a campfire burning stage right. Most of the
stage was taken up by vertical rows of oversize video screens,
showing recent news footage of illegal immigrants rushing
the Texas and Arizona borders and being apprehended by
helicopters and SUVs of the U.S. Border Patrol. Upstage left
was a red-velvet banquette and more neon squiggles, this time
suggesting a Las Vegas casino. The dominant fixture was an
oversize slot machine.

The curious opera fan would have gazed upon all this

in bewilderment, until, with a smile of comprehension, he exclaimed, *Of course. It's a Eurotrash production!*

When SLO's two productions for the season were announced, the *New York Times* had commented that Philip Congreve was making bold, risky choices. Congreve had ordered this quote placed on the cover of the season brochure—and had chosen the music director as scapegoat if the season turned out to be a disaster. Such was the rumor around SLO, anyway. The world premiere of *Catch-22* would bring prestige to the company. But like most new operas, it was glum and tuneless and would play to half-empty houses. Congreve had paired it with the world's most popular opera to put bottoms on seats. So far so good, but then he got to thinking about the critics who flew in from New York to review the season, and how they wouldn't even bother to write about *Carmen*, which they had seen countless times. So he had hired Bernhard von Schussnigg to jolt the old warhorse back to life. Von Schussnigg was internationally notorious for his radical productions. He was able to discover an anti-American message latent in practically any opera. His *Rigoletto* set in the locker room of the Pittsburg Steelers had electrified the Aix en Provence festival. His *Pelléas et Mélisande* set aboard a Polaris submarine had incited a riot at Innsbruck. With his *Carmen* set in present-day Mexico, he was going to tell Americans what he thought of their immigration policy.

The problem was that the stage machinery at SLO was not up to the spectacular effects for which von Schussnigg was famous. One *coup de théâtre* in Act III was still going wrong, and opening night was tomorrow. So the cast, who would ordinarily have been enjoying a day of rest, were going over it again and again.

The only cast member who didn't mind was Renata. She never got enough rehearsal, and the moments leading up to the tricky bit happened to be her character Mercédès's best number in the whole show. Like everyone else she was "marking," singing at half-volume to save her voice for tomorrow, but otherwise she was working hard, trying to imagine herself into Mercédès's head. There were gestures and expressions she wanted to refine, for one of the few moments when the audience would be looking at her.

She and Carmen's other sidekick, Frasquita, were standing at the giant slot machine, pulling its lever and telling their fortunes. In the original, ordinary playing cards were used, but Bernhard von Schussnigg wanted the slot machine to symbolize the mechanistic workings of Fate as Carmen perceived them.

Renata pulled the lever and peered at its screen. Nothing actually happened, of course, as the screen was too small for the audience to see, but she imagined four ripe red cherries rolling up. Renata liked cherries. Her face beaming with delight, she sang of the very rich, very old man she was destined to marry, and of her enviable future as a rich widow.

Then Amy Song, who had been feuding with von Schussnigg for weeks and was in a very bad mood this morning, trudged over to the slot machine, muttering Carmen's lines about trying her luck. She pulled the lever.

A trapdoor in the stage swung open. Swiftly and smoothly a wooden frame bearing a giant canvas ace of diamonds arose. Just as it reached its twelve-foot height, another ace of diamonds dropped like a guillotine blade from the ceiling.

"*Carreau!*" Carmen sang, back to the audience, staring up at the cards.

As the second ace of diamonds settled into its slot, an ace of spades shot up from the stage floor, followed by another ace of spades dropping in to complete the row.

"*Pique!*" Carmen sang, putting her hands to her head in terror as she read her fate.

Next she was supposed to sing "*La mort! J'ai bien lu*" but Amy Song clapped her hands and threw back her head, laughing delightedly, because this was the first time in a dozen run-throughs that one of the cards hadn't moved too slowly, or too quickly, or simply gotten stuck halfway. The other cast members were applauding or hugging one another. Hearty cheers resounded from the back of the theatre, where the technical crew were gathered around their control board. Even Bernhard von Schussnigg, seated in the auditorium, smiled. As the ruckus died down, the stage managers could be heard calling the end of rehearsal.

Walking offstage, Renata switched on her cellphone. No call from Dick Samuelson. She decided to go to his office and see if his secretary had heard anything. She stepped outside. It was noon, blazing hot, and she was sweating by the time she reached the Peter J. Calvocoressi Administration Building.

Samuelson's office door was open. He was standing behind his desk, talking on the phone. Don was not there. His suit, back on its hanger, was lying on the sofa. As she entered, Samuelson hung up the phone with one hand and lifted his coat off the chair back with the other. "Renata, I'm sorry, I have to go. That was Phil Congreve."

An experienced unimportant person, Renata knew a few tricks for delaying important persons long enough to get her questions answered. "That's okay, Dick. Where's Don's suit?"

He had to detour round the other side of the desk to pick up the suit and hand it to her. "You might as well take it home. He won't need it until the preliminary hearing, which is two weeks off. Oh … the judge denied bail. I'm sorry, I should have texted you."

He was out the door by now. She chased him down the corridor. "How do I get to see him?"

"Just go on over. Anytime this afternoon. You're on the list."

"I will. Dick, how is he? How did he take it when he realized he'd have to go back to jail?"

But they were descending the stairs, and she had lost Dick's attention. He was staring straight ahead. Renata followed his gaze. Standing before a window overlooking the parking lot, between a potted ficus tree and the front doors, were Congreve, whose high forehead was corrugated with anxiety, and another man whose back was to her.

As they drew near she saw that it was Bert Stromberg-Brand. He was wearing a black suit and white shirt with open collar. Above his graying beard, his features were locked in a stern but serene expression. He looked like a mullah.

"Come on up to my office, Bert, we'll talk," Congreve was pleading. No wonder he wanted to get Bert out of here, Renata thought. The lobby resounded with a clamor of footfalls and voices. People were streaming through the doors, heading for the parking lot and lunch. They looked curiously at Bert as they passed. He paid no attention to them. His feet were planted on the glossy tile floor. He was gazing over Congreve's shoulder into the lot, as if he was expecting someone.

"I'm not here to talk. Just give me a check for three hundred thirty thousand dollars." He glanced at Samuelson and Renata. "She can tell you. That was my demand on Saturday night. Between then and now, your employee murdered my wife. I don't see that as any reason why I should alter my demand. You might see it as a reason to comply. Don't you think?"

"Your wife gave us the gift that's made it possible for us to mount a wonderful production of *Carmen*. The work is done. It's ready. Tomorrow night the audience will see it, and they'll say—"

"Is this your way of telling me the money's spent? In that case I won't take a check. It'll have to be cash." He nodded his head toward Samuelson. "Send this guy to the bank."

Congreve repeated desperately, "Let's go up to my office. Please, Bert."

Bert was gazing into the lot, and now he said, "Ah."

Renata turned. In the lot, a white van was pulling up. Channel 5 News was painted on the side.

Congreve frowned, causing his jowls to droop further than usual. "What are they doing here?" he whispered.

"I called them. Also Channel 4 and Channel 2 and Channel 30."

Samuelson said, "Mr. Stromberg-Brand, please, let me go out there and tell them it's some mistake."

"Nope. Once they get their cameras set up, I will repeat my demand. And I will tell the whole story of Radleigh's strategy for getting the gift from Helen. The *whole* story."

"I don't know what you're talking about," said Congreve.

"That's going to be your line, is it? That you didn't know what Don was up to that weekend in Chicago? I guess we'll just have to see how that goes down with the media."

Renata wondered what Chicago had to do with anything. She glanced at Congreve and Samuelson, but they seemed as baffled as she was.

Samuelson said, "Please, sir. Think this over. We understand your feelings toward Don. But it will not do anybody any good to bring the media in."

Bert paid no attention. Outside the truck was raising its high, stout antenna. Men in T-shirts and shorts were taking equipment out of the back. Another man, who must have been the on-camera correspondent because he was wearing a dress shirt and tie and had an expensive haircut, was walking up the path to the building.

As he opened the door, Bert stepped forward. "Hello, I'm Stromberg-Brand. You want to set up right here?"

The correspondent looked at him blankly, then turned to the other three, "Anybody know where Bryson is?"

They stared back at him. It was Samuelson who recovered first. "Keith Bryson?"

The correspondent nodded. "We got word he was on his way here."

"I'm Stromberg-Brand," Bert repeated. "I called you. You're here for me."

But the correspondent was turning away and the door was closing.

Samuelson pulled Congreve a couple of steps away, whispering urgently to him. The lawyer seemed to have some idea what was going on, but Renata was clueless. What would America's most media-friendly billionaire be doing here? Waiting in airports in Europe or America, she often saw Keith Bryson's handsome head on magazine covers and television screens. He'd started out as one of those Silicon Valley boy wonders. Dropping out of Stanford, he had invented some bit of software—she forgot what it was, but everybody in the world had used it every day for a few years, until it became obsolete. By that time Bryson had cashed in and moved on. He started up quirky little enterprises: a company that made umbrellas that wouldn't turn inside-out in the wind, a chain of undertakers specializing in low-cost ecological funerals, a string of vegan, gluten-free sandwich shops. People were surprised that they made money, until they decided that everything Bryson did would make money. Once they made up their minds, it became true. He was a billionaire several times over. Now he spent his life traveling the world, being photographed and admired. He ran triathlons and sponsored racing yachts, gave TED talks about emerging technologies, wrote bestsellers about management technique, did stunts for charity that showed he didn't take himself too seriously, and dated film stars. He was the sort of person who never showed up in places like St. Louis.

She noticed that other SLO employees were coming up to the window while talking into their cellphones or thumbing text messages. True or not, the rumor of Bryson's imminent appearance was spreading fast. Everyone was staring at the unremarkable parking lot as if a crack had appeared in the earth, or a tsunami on the horizon. Another news truck, this one from Channel 4, pulled up behind the first. Then a huge black SUV lumbered into view. A trio of broad-shouldered, short-haired young men with Bluetooth devices on their ears climbed down from it. Politely but firmly, they began to clear the path from the parking lot to the building. A helicopter passed noisily overhead and everybody looked up, expecting Bryson to descend like the president, but it continued on its way.

A nondescript sedan pulled up and the passenger door opened. An *oooooh* rose up from the crowd that Renata could hear even through the glass wall. Many people had their phones over their heads, taking pictures. A slender man in worn blue jeans and a check shirt stood up from the car. The famous face bore an expression blending affability and alertness. The outfit and the expression were familiar from a thousand photographs.

One of the security men came up beside Bryson and pointed toward the Calvocoressi building. The other two fell in behind him. Behind them came the media people, some with video cameras perched on shoulders, others shouting questions.

Bryson spotted Bert through the glass and nodded and smiled to him. They knew each other? Renata's bafflement deepened. The security man opened the door and Bryson came through. He was as oblivious to Congreve and Samuelson as he was to the crowd behind him. He was interested only in Bert. He put out his hand, and Bert, who seemed to be in a trance, slowly reached for it.

"Bert, I'm so sorry for your loss. Helen was a wonderful woman."

*So he knew her too*, Renata thought. Probably like everybody else, she was adjusting to the jolt of seeing a celebrity in real life. She'd experienced it a couple of months before, bumping into Renée Fleming in a corridor of the Metropolitan Opera House. It wasn't the face and voice that threw you—they were familiar—it was the contrast with the everyday environment that was so jarring. You had never believed until now that the celebrity occupied the same world you did.

Bryson was a man of average size, but he seemed somehow more solid, denser than an ordinary person. After all those

triathlons, his BMI must be an astounding number. His jeans
were not some designer brand but ordinary Levi's. She could
see the leather patch between the belt loops: his waist was 30
and his inseam was 32. His graying light brown hair was long
enough to curl slightly over his collar and the tops of his ears.
His thick, short beard framed a wide mouth and brilliant white
teeth. Opera singers showed their teeth a lot and were vain
about them, but she had never seen a set of choppers this even
and effulgent.

Keeping hold of Bert's hand, he turned to Congreve. "Is
there somewhere we can talk?"

Congreve gave a huge smile of relief. "My office is right
upstairs."

Bert freed his hand. "No. I'm not going anywhere. I have
something to say. I've thought it through and I know what I'm
doing." But his voice sounded hollow.

Bryson clapped a hand on his shoulder. "Fine. Just tell me
first. We're partners now, you know."

She did not know what that meant, but Bert seemed to alter
before her eyes. Videographers and still photographers were
filling the doorway, and maybe it was all the lenses pointed
at Bert that made her imagine that a caption was appearing
under his face, spelling out "Partner of Keith Bryson."

Congreve started up the stairs, followed by Bert and Bryson.
More news people were pushing through the doors. Some
were still calling out questions. But the three security men
stationed themselves at the foot of the stairs, and no one even
tried to push past them. Renata turned to Samuelson, but he
was wandering away, talking on his cellphone.

Renata felt like a coat rack, and not just because she was still
carrying Don's suit. Apart from Bert, no one had noticed her
in the last five minutes. Now that only she and the news people
remained, they were eying her.

One stepped forward. "Do you work here?"

"Yes."

"Have any idea what they're going to talk about up there?"

"No. I'm just a mezzo-soprano."

One of the men carrying a video camera on his shoulder said, "Hey, she's the guy's sister."

"What guy?' a woman with a notebook asked.

"The killer."

"My brother did not kill anyone," Renata blurted.

The media people exchanged looks. They were stuck here until Bryson came back down the stairs anyway. Might as well. Tripod legs splayed and cameras locked in place atop them. Lights glared in her eyes. A microphone was pinned to her blouse.

# 18

—

PETER STOOD OUTSIDE THE DOORWAY of his supervisor's office and waited to be noticed. At Medical PR, you didn't barge in the way people did at the newspaper.

"Pete! Come in. How's it going? Want to go downstairs for lunch?"

"Thanks. Sorry, I'm on deadline. The Stromberg-Brand obit for Roger."

"Need more time? Want me to talk to him?"

"No, I'm fine." Diane the chief medical writer always had time for him and kept looking for ways to make his job easier. You never had a boss like that at a paper.

"I just had a question," Peter went on. "Who's Ransome Chase?"

"Oh, is he bothering you? Ignore him. Just forward the email to me."

"No, I, uh, someone mentioned the name to me, and he's on my beat, so—"

"You don't have to worry about him. We don't do press releases or articles about him. We steer reporter queries away from him. That's straight from Roger."

"Isn't that unusual?"

"Unusual but not unique." Diane used words with precision.

He liked that in a woman. If she wasn't his boss and married with two kids he would definitely put the moves on her. "What did Chase do?"

"I'll give you Roger's exact words: 'The purpose of your department is to make good news about Adams U. Medical School. Chase is of no use to you.' "

"Oh. He must've done something really bad."

"Before my time. All I know is, he's one doc I don't have to worry about."

Peter's next questions were: *Aren't you curious? How can you stand not to know?* He did not ask them. He thanked Diane and headed back down the corridor to his office. Along the way, he passed four colleagues. Three paused to ask him how things were going. The other invited him to lunch. They were always going out to lunch together in Medical PR. Or meeting for a drink after work. Or having coffee and cake to celebrate somebody's birthday. Everybody got along. Feuds and grudges were rare. It wasn't like a paper at all.

He sat down in front of the screen and started making final revisions to the obit. The fly in the ointment was that your own writing bored you. That didn't seem to bother anyone else. Why not? Most of them were ex-reporters. He pondered the mystery as he automatically trimmed words and corrected punctuation. He'd asked a few of them if they missed journalism, and they said no, they liked going home at five o'clock. They were all married, and most of them had children. They weren't counting on the job to make life worth living. It was only Peter who at five o'clock went home to an empty apartment. He was thirty-four, but he'd never been married. Except to the paper.

Which made him a widower. The Springfield *Journal-Register* had died the slow, ignominious death that was the common fate of newspapers these days. He had foolishly stayed on until the end. Then he had no choice but to go back home to Edwardsville, to the room he'd last lived in as a teenager.

He was the first in his family to make it all the way through college. How proud and hopeful his parents had been … even if he had majored in journalism. Now he was back. There had followed eight months, two weeks, and four days of delivering pizzas and applying for jobs.

The offer from Adams U Med School had been a godsend. He would have jumped at much worse jobs. His parents saw it as a move up from the paper. No more consorting with cops, crooks, and politicians. Now he would be the colleague of doctors and professors.

He hit a snag in the press release that interrupted his reverie. Two quotes in a row called Sturm und Drang a "dedicated" researcher. Could he change one of them to "deeply committed?" No, then he'd have to get the quote re-approved and there wasn't time. He would have to move the second quote to another paragraph.

"Pete?"

Diane was in the doorway. "Annie and I are going to lunch. Sure you can't join us?"

"Sorry."

She hesitated. "I remembered something. I mean, if you're really curious about Chase, you could ask Marian in fundraising."

"Marian?"

"Yes, she handled the Blixes. You know, when they endowed the chair."

Sturm und Drang had been the Chaim and Hadassah Blix Professor of Molecular Microbiology. He thanked her and she went away. Peter reached for his directory to look up Marian's extension. Then he thought he'd just go to her office. Then he thought not.

Why should he bother to find out why Chase was glad Sturm und Drang was dead? There could be many reasons. Peter was glad she was dead himself. Writing the obit, he'd been delighted he would never have to submit anything else for her approval. His press releases had usually "missed an opportunity" to fully sing her praises, as she used to say in complaining emails to Roger and Diane, with copies to him. Then there was the time he had set her up with the medical reporter of the *New Yorker*. She had given him a full hour of her valuable time and he had only included two brief quotes in his story. Peter's fault, obviously. Or the time an envious colleague had criticized her in a letter to *Science* and Peter had failed to find out about it before publication and notify her so she could threaten to sue. It was actually a good thing that her complaints were so unreasonable; Roger and Diane had always told him not to worry, while they sent groveling responses to Sturm und Drang. No doubt she could be just as disagreeable with the other professors. It didn't matter why Chase had disliked her.

Unless he had killed her.

He hadn't, though. It was the sleazy fundraiser. From the media accounts, the cops seemed to be building a solid case against him.

Anyway, doctors didn't kill people. Not on purpose, anyway. But if he fed his curiosity by going to see Marian, it might grow. Then he'd keep digging, and sooner or later it would come to the attention of his superiors. Diane had just quoted Roger to him: "Our job is to make good news about the med school." It would not be good news if one professor had murdered another.

Like most reporters—former reporters—Peter was quick to imagine disaster. If Roger found out what he was doing, he'd order Diane to fire him. Poor Diane would be in tears. And then what? The long drive back to Edwardsville. Correction, the long train ride, because his car would be repossessed.

He shook his head to dispel catastrophe. *Come on, focus!* All he had to do was solve the problem of the repetitious "dedicateds" and he could send the obit to Roger and never have to read it again. But first he took Ransome Chase's message, the "wicked witch" one, crumpled it up tight, and threw it in the trash can.

# 19

—

THE GENERAL DIRECTOR'S OFFICE TOOK up one corner of the Calvocoressi building. Sun poured into the broad windows, illuminating the fronds of plants and the intricate hues of the Persian carpet, but at midday did not reach far into the air-conditioned depths of the vast room. Bert was perching on the edge of a sofa, hands clasped between his thighs. Bryson sat in an armchair, turned at an angle, giving Bert the choice of whether to look him in the eye or not. Congreve was standing, leaning his back against the door as if he was afraid the reporters might break through the roadblock of Bryson's security detail on the stairs.

"I am going down to talk to them," Bert was saying. "The truth has to come out."

"Why?" asked Bryson, in a neutral tone.

"Because it's the truth."

"Then tell me."

"Don Radleigh had been sniffing around Helen for months. 'Cultivating a donor,' I guess they call it. Calls. Emails. Half the parties we went to, we'd bump into this gigolo for the arts with his Masterpiece Theatre accent, wanting to kiss my wife on both cheeks.

"And then early this month came the big push. He asks for a

meeting. He says now is our chance to contribute, as if it's what we've been waiting for." He looked at Congreve. "You were desperate, weren't you?"

Congreve avoided his eye and spoke to Bryson. "Our music director has made some mistakes. The other production this season is a world premiere, *Catch-22*. It has been more expensive than he anticipated. Then our production partner on *Carmen* dropped out. I won't deny that we were facing a cash-flow problem."

"Go on, Bert," said Bryson.

"Don found out we'd never seen *Carmen*. That should've discouraged him, but no. He's delighted to tell us that by sheer luck, the Lyric Opera is putting on *Carmen* this weekend. Won't we allow him to take us to see it?"

"Where is the Lyric Opera?"

"Chicago."

There was no change in Bryson's expression. But his left leg was crossed over his right knee, and the foot was rotating slowly. It stopped. He said, "When was this? The date you went to Chicago?"

"May fifteenth. But *we* didn't go. Helen and I spent several days discussing the question of why we should travel three-hundred miles to spend a boring evening, when we were not going to give a third of a million dollars to an opera company anyway. The discussion did not end until Helen said she was leaving for the airport and I said I was not."

Congreve straightened up. "Don and Helen went to Chicago alone?"

Bert smiled humorlessly at Bryson. "The first he's heard of it. Right. He's planning to tell the media it was all Don's idea."

"What was Don's idea?"

"Seducing my wife to get three hundred thirty thousand dollars from her."

"No," said Congreve "I don't know what he's talking about, Mr. Bryson. Don said the first time they, uh, had relations was at the Five Gables Inn on May eighteenth. *After* Helen made her gift. There was no connection between the affair and the gift."

Bert looked at him. "You admit to that because you have no choice. I can prove they were at the Five Gables Inn on May eighteenth."

"What about Chicago?" asked Bryson, in the same neutral tone. "Can you prove that?"

"I can't prove that they had sex, no. But from the way she acted when she got back .... I'm her husband. I'm not wrong about this."

"I'm not questioning you, Bert," said Bryson. "Okay. You're going down to tell the reporters all this. What do you think is going to happen next?"

"You actually want me to suppress what happened in Chicago."

"I do. Absolutely. What's to be gained? Radleigh has been arrested and charged. The St. Louis Opera had no idea what he was up to in Chicago. Why punish them?"

"This is a murder investigation. The truth has to come out."

"I'm not asking you to suppress evidence. You have none. Just a suspicion. Which you are under no obligation to share with the police, let alone the media."

"The cops or the media will find the evidence if I steer them toward Chicago."

"Oh, Bert. Do you really want to turn on the TV and see some reporter interrogating some maid about the state of the bed sheets in Helen's hotel room?"

"There's nothing you can tell me about the media. I'm already getting worked over. They were waiting for me outside the police station yesterday morning. It's only hours since I found my wife's body. I've had no sleep. And here's this guy saying I've got to get my version of events out. Because in the court of public opinion—he actually said that, 'the court of public opinion'—I'm the prime suspect. Because I'm the poor husband of a rich wife."

"The reporter said *that*?" Bryson shook his head with disgust and sympathy.

"All he had to do was look at the Adams U website. There she is, the Chaim and Hadassah Blix Professor. And there I am, instructor of philosophy. Everybody knows that means they pay me shit and I'll never get promoted."

"Helen felt very badly about that."

Bert's brow furrowed with surprise. "What?"

"About how you had to give up a tenure track position at Indiana when she moved to Adams. She told me she should have pushed Adams harder to give you a job equal to the one you were giving up. But she was inexperienced and over-eager. I hope you don't mind her confiding in me, Bert, but we were friends, and she felt terribly guilty about that. I remember she said, when you're on the way up you do things you're not proud of. You're only thinking about making it to the top. You think once you get there, then you'll be able to make everything right. But you find out you can't turn back the clock."

Bert was gazing intently at Bryson. He waited after Bryson stopped speaking, as if hoping he would say more. Finally he murmured, "She never said that to me."

"You were angry and she couldn't handle it."

"She couldn't be bothered talking to me when there were plenty of people waiting to kiss her ass."

"You're right. I'd just add that they all wanted something from her in return for the ass-kissing. When you're responsible for something that's terribly important to millions of people, like Helen's vaccine, it's overwhelming. There isn't enough room in your mind for everything you have to think about. You'll find out."

"What?"

Bryson smiled. "It hasn't had time to sink in, has it? You have inherited responsibility for the vaccine. Along with me, of course. That's what I meant downstairs when I said we were partners."

From Bert's expression, this was a new thought to him, and a mindboggling one. "I know shit about biomedical science."

"Shit is exactly what I know about it. Don't worry, we'll have expert advice. But the big decisions will be ours. You are now an important man. My condolences."

"Condolences?"

"People treat us like gods. Meaning they don't permit us any mistakes. I hope you'll someday find it possible to forgive the mistake Helen made back at Indiana."

Bert was silent. He was visibly thinking hard. Bryson left him to it for a full minute. Then he resumed, in a different tone. "All right. We have a pack of reporters down there. There are several subjects we can talk about to them that will be useful to us in what we have to do. Chicago is not one of them. Are we agreed?"

Bert nodded slowly.

Bryson turned and beckoned Congreve to join them. "We need a reason for us to be here. Any ideas?"

# 20

—

In the lobby of the Calvocoressi Building, Congreve, Bert, and Bryson were standing halfway down the steps, so that they could address the crowd of journalists, which had swelled while they were upstairs and now filled the room. Congreve had the floor. He was announcing that Keith Bryson would match the Helen and Bertrand Stromberg-Brand gift to SLO. He said that he was proud and happy, and no one looking at his face, alight from high forehead to sagging jowls, would have questioned the statement.

Then Bert said that his wife would have been glad that her partner in science was her partner in giving, too. He spoke brokenly and softly, his eyes downcast, because he couldn't remember the lines Bryson had fed him a few minutes ago. But that was all right, because finally he was acting the part of a bereaved widower with the dignity that had eluded him up to now.

Bryson himself made no speech. Congreve opened the floor to questions. The first ones were pointed, even hostile: a SLO employee was in jail, charged with the murder of Helen Stromberg-Brand. Yesterday Bert had given an interview in which he revealed their affair and made harsh comments about the opera company. What had happened to change his mind?

This time Bert remembered exactly what he had been told to say: yesterday he had been in shock. Angry. Looking for someone to blame. He'd hardly known what he was saying. Now he wanted his wife's last wishes to be carried out.

Some of the reporters, guessing that they were not getting the whole story, pressed harder. Bert simply repeated his answers, and attention shifted to Congreve. His noble brow furrowing with disapproval, he said that in the days after Helen had finalized her gift, she and Don Radleigh had spent a lot of time together. In the excitement surrounding production of what was now her opera, they had begun a relationship. On Radleigh's part this was not just a personal failing but a lapse of professional ethics. He had been suspended without pay. Of his guilt or innocence of the murder, Congreve would only say that he could not comment on an open case and that he and his employees were cooperating fully with the police.

A man in the front row, bald, fat, and poorly dressed—obviously from the print media—looked up from his notebook and asked, "Mr. Bryson, what are you doing here?"

Bryson stepped forward. A ripple of excitement ran through the media people. The Stromberg-Brand murder had been a big story up to now, but only a local story. Keith Bryson's appearance made it national. The television reporters were thinking that their stories might appear on the network evening news. Famous anchorpersons in New York who had never even known their names would be chatting with them like colleagues while the nation watched. Their professional futures, their move up to Dallas or Atlanta, hinged on the questions they would ask in the next few minutes.

"I'm Doctor Stromberg-Brand's partner in Ezylon, the company that's developing her vaccine. I'm involved in many endeavors, as you know, but I regard this as one of the most important."

"Do you mean one of the most potentially profitable?" called out a young man from the back.

"If all of us at Ezylon do our jobs well and the vaccine reaches the market, there will be large profits." Bryson always handled money questions forthrightly. Reporters could be as snide as they wanted; he knew that being a successful businessman did him no harm with the public.

A woman started to ask a question, but Bryson cut her off with a hand gesture; he hadn't finished his answer. He took a deep breath. Dame Judi Dench had once said that she wished she had Bryson's gift for timing a pause. The room grew quiet.

"The other reason I'm here," he went on, "is the double standard."

Now the room was silent except for the squeaks of still photographer's shoes as they maneuvered to get a better angle and the clicks of their shutters.

"A great scientist has died in scandalous circumstances. For the moment, the scandal is all that matters. Ordinarily, time would redress the balance. The scandal would fade and the person's achievements would be recognized. So, if Helen Stromberg-Brand was a man, I would not be worried. Unfortunately, the old double standard is still operating. This sad incident at the end of her life could do permanent damage to Helen's reputation. Could outweigh the contributions she has made to medicine. Even the good her discovery is going to do for millions of people."

During his speech the silence had given away to shiftings and murmurings and sighs among the media people. Some thought Bryson was trying to write their stories for them. Others had no trouble picking up the implied criticism of themselves. A minority—the women—thought he had a good point.

The instant he finished, a man in the middle of the pack shouted a question: "Mr. Bryson, we know you're gonna make a lot of money from this drug. But do you really think Stromberg-Brand deserves a place among the immortals? I mean, it's not like she cured cancer. Just urinary tract infections. You can't say she's going to save millions of lives. Only that she'll prevent millions of trips to the bathroom."

Bryson left another pause. He did not smile, but he looked pleased with the question. There was another stir among the reporters. The women were whispering to each other that obviously the questioner had never had a UTI.

"The short answer is yes, she deserves a place among the immortals. The long answer is not too long. So bear with me."

Bryson slipped both hands into the pockets of his jeans. His elbows jutted. He gazed at the ceiling for a moment before beginning to speak. It was an attitude familiar to all who had watched his TED talks. On the screen even more than in life, it suggested modesty and candor.

"Here's the story of a UTI. The bacteria want to start a colony in the bladder. But the body washes them out with urine. So the bacteria have developed barbs. Picture them as movie commandos, bad guys in black, with grappling hooks. They embed them in the bladder lining. The body responds by sloughing off the outer layer of the lining. Most bacteria go, but some survive by swinging their hooks and clinging to the next layer. The infection seems to clear up, but the bacteria multiply and the person suffers. And so it goes. Or did for millennia. Until Helen intervened on the body's side.

"What she did was very difficult to pull off, but easy to describe. She taught the body's security guards how to spread glop over the bacteria's barbs. The grappling hooks won't stick, the bacteria can't hang on, and the patient happily pisses them away."

No one laughed outright, but there was a murmur of appreciation among the journalists.

"Helen taught the body how to solve a problem it hadn't been able to figure out on its own, over millions of years of evolution. You take her pill, and you never have to worry about UTIs again. At present, UTIs are treated with antibiotics, the best-known of which is marketed as Sūthene. They're unsatisfactory, but at least they keep the infection from spreading. But as you know, these days more and more bacteria are becoming resistant to antibiotics. If that happens with UTIs, people will die. Perhaps we should wait to develop Helen's drug … if we want to impress *you*, sir."

He was looking straight at the man who had asked the question, his eyebrows raised. Now there were a few chuckles. Congreve brushed a lock of silver hair from his forehead and smiled.

# 21

—

Renata missed the press conference. She left immediately after her interview, drove to Clayton Police Headquarters and asked to see Detective McCutcheon. To her surprise, there was no delay. The young detective with the spiky forelock came out to the desk. His manner was as bland as before. He led her into a big, bright room with four desks. The others were unoccupied.

As soon as they sat down she asked, "Did you get a call from Luis Reyes?"

McCutcheon nodded.

"Oh good!" She waited, but McCutcheon said no more. "Well?"

"Well what?"

"A man was seen walking away from the house … after my brother left. Just before Reyes and Bert found the body. What do you have to say about that?"

"Ms Radleigh, please don't do that again."

"What?"

"Don't go around talking to the other witnesses in your brother's case and pressuring them to change their stories."

"I did not pressure him! I just asked a rather important question that you apparently forgot to ask."

"You're a family member of the suspect. You can't go around questioning people. It could be considered witness tampering. There's a law against that."

"This is the second time you've threatened to throw me in jail."

"Please don't make this personal, ma'am. I have to file a report that goes to the primary investigator on this case, and the lieutenant, and maybe the prosecuting attorney. I'm warning you that any of those people might decide to charge you."

"You've made up your minds my brother is guilty. You won't consider any other possibility."

"The investigation is ongoing."

"Well, what are you going to do about Mr. Reyes's call?"

"I reported it to the primary. I've suggested another canvass of the area. He'll decide if it's worth it."

"If it's worth it! A man was seen walking away from the house—"

"Mr. Reyes did not say that. He said a man was walking along the sidewalk, maybe fifty yards down from the house. And his description was pretty vague. Sorry."

Renata sighed heavily. "You think I'm a rather pathetic case, don't you, Detective?"

McCutcheon shook his head. "It's natural for you to believe he's innocent. He's your brother. But leave the other witnesses alone, okay? If you want to help your brother, the best thing for you to do is go visit him."

# 22

—

IN RESPONSE TO A BREATHLESS summons from his boss Diane, Peter Lombardo jogged down the hall to the conference room. Most of the medical writers were sitting at the long table, looking at a television atop a credenza. The screen showed the well-coiffed and well-dressed anchorpersons of the Channel 2 afternoon newscast sitting at their desk. Diane beckoned him to sit next to her.

"What's going on?"

"Have you ever met Keith Bryson?"

"Stromberg-Brand's venture capitalist? Never. I deal with Jayson, the obnoxious kid he has running the office at Amygdala."

"Well, he's in town."

"Bryson? You're joking."

"Apparently Roger convinced him to speak up for Stromberg-Brand. He did a terrific job, Roger says. It should be on the newscast."

The first story was about a drive-by shooting in north St. Louis. The second was Keith Bryson. The assembled flaks shook their heads over the anchor's setup, which repeated all the unwelcome details of Stromberg-Brand's murder. They cheered up when the poised and handsome Bryson appeared on screen, lambasting the double standard. As Bryson explained Helen's vaccine, they murmured appreciatively. Making bioscience understandable to the public was their métier.

When Bryson ended with "… and the patient happily [BLEEP] them away," the medical writers cheered.

Grinning, Diane asked, "What do you think he said?"

" 'Pisses,' I expect."

"And they censored that? In a medical context? What a bunch of prudes."

"You could call Channel 2 and complain."

"No. I'll call Channel 5 and Channel 4 and dare them to run it uncut." With a gleam in her eye, Diane headed back to her office. The other writers stretched and rose. As they filed out of the room, chatting, Peter reached for the remote to turn off the television.

The screen showed a head-and-shoulders shot of a beautiful woman with thick black hair and piercing blue eyes. She looked worried and tired. The caption "Renata Radleigh" came up. She was saying, "As far as I know, no one has suggested any reason, let alone a plausible one, why my brother would want Dr. Stromberg-Brand dead. The case is purely circumstantial."

She was replaced by the anchorwoman, who said that Ms. Radleigh was appearing in the SLO production of *Carmen*, and that Donald Radleigh had been charged that morning and denied bail. Weather was up next. Peter clicked off. For a long moment, he stood staring at the blank screen.

# 23

—

Visiting time at the county jail wasn't as bad as Renata's movie-fed imagination had led her to expect. It was pretty much like going to the airport: you waited in line, presented ID, submitted to a search, then sat on a hard chair in a noisy room, waiting to be called. She had plenty of time to think. More than she wanted, really.

Two hours ago, she had stood before the cameras and told the television viewers of St. Louis that her brother was innocent. An hour ago, she had talked with Detective McCutcheon, who plainly thought she was delusional. What was she to make of herself?

Renata was always willing to entertain any thought, as long as it was discomfiting. She made her living, such as it was, by pretending to be imaginary persons. Her business was make-believe. Had she made herself believe that Don was innocent?

Ordinarily she reproached herself for the opposite fault: for not being emotional and fanciful enough. Not that she could do anything about it. The life of an aging journeyman mezzo-soprano beat that out of you. It was all schedules and budgets and holding your tongue. Only successful singers could afford tantrums, tardiness, and other forms of self-indulgence.

So she was used to thinking. But it wasn't true, was it?

Yesterday morning, she had seen officers of the law doing their duty, arresting Don, and she had attacked them. She had waded into them swinging, with no more forethought or self-restraint than Lucia di Lammermoor. And within five seconds she was flat on the floor with her hands cuffed behind her.

Renata could feel herself smiling at the memory.

Now that was extraordinary. Regret and recrimination were her usual habits of thought. If she wasted four quid by helping herself to a drink from a hotel minibar, she would reproach herself for weeks afterward. If she made a candid remark to a slovenly makeup artist or forgetful chorister, she would remember it and cringe a hundred times. But she felt no urge to talk herself out of her pride at standing up for her brother. She would do it again.

*If he's a murderer, then I'm a fool, and I'd rather stay that way*, Renata decided. Though she had another quarter hour to wait, she did not give the matter any more thought. Rarely did her mind grant her such peace.

At last her group was led into a long narrow room with a row of chairs on either side of a piece of furniture that was part table, part barrier. The chairs opposite were empty. They would not be able to embrace; in fact, a sign on the wall stated that touching was forbidden. So she would have to find words to console Don, whom she had not seen since his life was smashed up, possibly beyond repair.

Through a wired-glass window in a door in the opposite wall, she watched a group of prisoners being formed into a line by guards. They wore short-sleeved buttonless shirts and long baggy pants of some heavy tan material, with CO JAIL printed on their backs. Don's blond head appeared, peering round the heads of the men in front of him. He grinned and waved as he saw her. When the guard opened the door, he bounded over to sit in the chair across from her.

"Renata, love, thanks for coming!"

This was surprising and heartening. Don set great store by

his social status and possessions, and now he had lost ther possibly forever. She assumed he would be dejected. But sl tended to forget her brother's good points. As a child he'd bee a plucky little chap, cheerily facing up to the dental checku, or the first day of school, while his sister was moping and whingeing. She said that it was good to see him bearing up so well.

"I've been watching the afternoon news. We watch a lot of television in here. I saw what happened at SLO today."

"Oh! Well, I simply told them what I believe, that you are innocent and will be cleared."

"They interviewed *you*? Sorry, I missed that bit. I suppose one can't expect them to give you much screen time when they have Keith Bryson. You were there? You saw him speak?"

"I saw him arrive. He was closeted with Bert and Congreve when I left. He gave a press conference, then?"

"It was absolutely splendid. He had those reporters in the palm of his hand. For starters, he's giving us a gift, matching Helen's. Three hundred thirty thousand is pocket change to Keith, of course, but it's a wonderful thing for us. The timing is perfect."

He would say *Keith*. She was willing to bet he'd never met Bryson. She straightened up and put her smile back on. Today, for once, she was not going to be irritated by her brother. "That is splendid."

"He's also neutralized bloody Bert. Reminded him which side his bread is buttered on, I expect. Best of all, he reminded people of what's important about Helen—what a great scientist she was. He explained her discovery in terms even the great unwashed could understand." Don was almost manic, bouncing around in his chair, gesturing with both hands. "He's turned this whole thing round today. You watch."

"That's brilliant. But I … I'm not sure what you mean."

"He's put the, uh, our affair in proportion. People will stop talking about it now."

"How will that—"

"Not that I'm looking for excuses. Don't accuse me of that, Renata. I made a mistake. We'd been at SLO that afternoon. I'd shown her the sets and costumes. She had lunch with Phil and met Amy Song. She was a bit star-struck, which was fun to see. I drove her back to Clayton, but she simply didn't want to cover the last two blocks to home. To bloody Bert. So we went to a little tapas bar on Central. Had a good deal more wine than tapas and, well, my judgment went out the window. We ended up in bed."

"At the Five Gables. This was the day Bert was talking about on Saturday night?"

"Yes. Little did we know he was peeping in the keyhole, or whatever he was doing. The slimy bugger."

"He said something rather odd this morning. To Phil. He said, 'I know what happened in Chicago.'"

It was as if she had pulled the plug on a neon sign. All Don's ebullience left him. "Chicago," he repeated hollowly.

"Do you know what he was talking about?"

"When I was trying to talk them into making the gift, I noticed that the Lyric Opera was putting on *Carmen*. They'd never seen it, and I thought, they certainly should. *Carmen* will sell itself. It's not like we were asking them to support *Wozzeck*. So I offered to take them to Chicago. Wine and dine them at a top restaurant, stay at the Palmer House Hotel. We agreed to meet at the airport."

"Only Helen showed up. Spitting mad that Bert had backed out at the last moment. What was I to do? Call the trip off?"

"You were alone together? What happened?"

He shrugged. "I took her to the opera, and afterward she signed the check. *Carmen* sold itself. I didn't have to do anything, really."

Renata stared hard at her brother's averted face. Whenever Don said something modest, he sounded insincere. "She slept in her room; you slept in yours?"

"Yes, of course. I can't help it if bilious Bert got ideas. We won't have any more trouble with him now that Keith's here."

That was something else she was wondering about. Bryson had popped up at SLO, as prompt to his cue as the Devil in the first act of *Faust*. "Don, why is Bryson here, d'you think? Why would someone like that drop everything and fly to St. Louis?"

"Just watch the press conference. He and Helen were friends. You must have seen his TED talk about the potential of biomedical research. And there's the money, of course."

"That doesn't matter to Bryson. He's a billionaire."

Don gave her one of his tolerant smiles. "One half of American women suffer from a UTI at some point. A quarter of the population. We're talking about a market of almost a hundred million people for the vaccine. In the States alone. Even to the likes of Keith, that's significant."

Renata sat silent for a moment. A hundred million potential customers. And prescription drugs cost a fortune in America, as she was reminded every time she had to refill her anti-depressants. Not to mention that European women—herself, for instance—got UTIs too. The vaccine would be worth a stupendous sum.

Suddenly she was struck by an inchoate but potent insight. It wasn't the opera and Don that had gotten Helen killed. It was, somehow, the vaccine and Bryson. The police were barking up the wrong tree.

One of the guards who had been walking back and forth behind the prisoners shouted, "Five minutes! You've got five minutes left!"

Don straightened up in his chair and smiled. "Don't look so worried. There'll be good news soon."

"Don, what exactly do you expect Bryson to do for you?"

"Well … not him, not directly. But I have friends. SLO's general counsel is representing me, remember. Dick Samuelson's a Harvard man. College and law school. Very well-connected at the courthouse as well."

His sandy eyebrows had disappeared under his blond
forelock. He was smiling archly, the way he always did when
he talked about his powerful friends. Renata was about to say
that the Harvard man had failed to get him out on bail this
morning, but she clamped her lips shut, reminding herself that
she was here to cheer Don up. Not the opposite. But she was
full of misgivings.

# 24

―

PETER'S COLLEAGUES MEANT IT WHEN they praised the regular schedules of PR, compared to the long hours at a newspaper. Everybody bailed out promptly at 5 p.m. Heading for the elevator an hour later, he walked down a dim, quiet corridor.

The last few hours had been the busiest of his PR career. He had been fielding reporter queries about Dr. Stromberg-Brand's vaccine non-stop. They were calling from all over the country. His boss Diane had looked in to tell him that there was more interest now than there had been when Stromberg-Brand first published her results in *Nature*. Such was the power of Keith Bryson. Peter had even taken a few calls from members of the public, UTI sufferers eager to know when the miracle vaccine would be in Walgreen's. He had to tell them that FDA approval would take several more years.

Peter came to the elevator lobby but did not press the call button. The other half of the floor was the development department. Marian, the fundraiser who could tell him about the Sturm und Drang-Chase history, had an office farther down this corridor. He hesitated. Truth to tell, he was feeling a bit embarrassed about the glee he had felt stumbling on that grudge this morning. Working in PR, you tended to forget that the people and incidents you were writing about were real. Somebody really had broken Stromberg-Brand's head with a crystal bowl. And Don Radleigh really was in jail, facing another twenty or thirty years behind bars.

Seeing the sister on TV was what had sobered him up. Her pale, lined face and intense blue eyes. Her swooping, emphatic English voice: "No one has suggested *any* reason, let alone a *plausible* one, why my *brother* would want Dr. Stromberg-Brand *dead.*"

She had a point: Radleigh and Stromberg-Brand had been cheating on her husband, and he'd found out, so the fundraiser was in big trouble. Killing her wouldn't do him any good. But Peter had worked the crime beat in Springfield long enough to know that cops believed people in trouble didn't think straight. Anyway, cops were not that interested in motive. If they had enough physical and circumstantial evidence against Radleigh, they weren't likely to put a lot of effort into developing other suspects. Should they?

Reluctantly Peter turned away from the elevator and proceeded down the hall. He was tired. With any luck, Marian would have gone home for the evening and he would shortly be behind the wheel of his car, headed for home and a gin and tonic.

Marian, one of the most senior people in development, was still at her desk. A small woman of sixty, she had short gray hair and big blue eyes behind horn-rim bifocals. She had a square chin she was in the habit of sticking out when she made a dry pronouncement about the state of the coffee in the office kitchenette, or the heat, or the tardiness of shuttle buses. All he knew about her was that she had an amusing style of complaining, but that in itself went a long way in office life.

She looked up and smiled. "Pete, come in. I've been meaning to send you an email."

"What about?"

"You're doing the Stromberg-Brand obit, right? Mrs. Blix might like to be quoted."

"The obit has gone to Roger already. So the Blixes are still alive?"

"The widow is. Very gracious, ancient lady. She called this afternoon. Wanted to know if she should say something on the passing of her professor."

"What would she like to say?"

"She didn't know. Could you write up a few possibilities for her? I'll call Roger now and explain."

"Well, Marian, the thing is, Roger walked the obit straight over to the chancellor, and as soon as he approved it, Roger sent it out. I understand that he and the chancellor are currently unwinding with a drink."

"Oh, if Roger is *chez* the chancellor, nothing else matters. I'll mollify Mrs. B."

"Was it you who talked her into giving the chair?" He thought this must have been a considerable feat. He didn't know how much money it took, but the endowment had to be big enough to produce a six-figure annual income for the professor. An endowed chair was the top tier of academic heaven.

"Oh, she wanted to give a chair. No problem about that. The tricky part was that she wanted to give it to the department of surgery. We had a hard time talking her into giving it to molecular micro. She didn't know anything about the department, and she didn't like what we told her. You know: it's all germs and worms that get into people's guts and do disgusting things."

Peter nodded. No, getting around it, there was a lot of pissing, crapping, and barfing in molecular micro. "Why did it have to be micro?"

"Surgery didn't have any candidates right then, and micro had two. Stromberg-Brand and this other guy who had a bit of buzz at the time."

"Would that happen to be Ransome Chase?"

Marion nodded.

"And he lost out. Is that why Roger wants us to ignore him?"

Marian lifted her eyebrows and her chin and said, "No. There was a little more to it." And waited.

Peter said, "Would this have had anything to do with Dr. Patel?"

Marian smiled and beckoned him in. He shut the door—unnecessarily, because the corridor and adjoining offices were empty. But it contributed to the atmosphere. There was nothing cozier than a fundraiser/PR writer end-of-day gossip.

"Patel was a postdoc," Marian began. "At about this time she made a complaint that Dr. Chase had sexually abused her."

"Wow."

"It didn't come to that much. She wasn't saying he touched her or anything, it was oral sexual abuse she was complaining about." She paused and her blue eyes sparkled. She was enjoying this as much as he was. "No, that term won't do, will it? Verbal sexual abuse. I forgot if he was telling her dirty jokes or what. Anyway the complaint never reached the hearing stage. I don't know what happened exactly. It went away, as these things generally do."

Peter thought it over. "So the guy is up for a named professorship, and he picks this moment to harass a postdoc?"

Marian's smile broadened. She was pleased with him. "Actually, the incidents she complained about had taken place six months to a year earlier. There was some comment about the timing of her complaint."

"What did she say?"

"That she had decided to sit quiet and take it, but that later she decided she owed it to other women in medicine to speak out."

"And is there an alternative explanation?"

"The lab she was a postdoc in was Stromberg-Brand's."

"Stromberg-Brand put her up to it, to sink his candidacy? And rewarded her with a tenure-track position?"

"That's Chase's version, anyway. He's never stopped complaining. Very loudly. That's why Roger declared him a nonperson. Of course, nobody's much interested anymore. Six years have passed, and Chase's research hasn't gone anywhere. Stromberg-Brand's has."

Peter nodded. "What do you think, Marian?"

"Oh, I think the timing of the complaint is a little suspicious. But, to be fair to Patel, nobody who knows Ransome Chase doubts that he did what she complained he did. He's a wild man."

"Really? How wild?"

Marian stuck out her chin. "Let's just say, I'm glad he doesn't bear a grudge against me."

# 25

—

RENATA ARRIVED HOME AT DUSK. There was much to fault Don on, but he had excellent taste. He lived in the green heart of Webster Groves, less than a mile from SLO. His house had been added on to over the years but was still a cottage, a charming jumble of brick, stucco, and wood perched on a steep bank above a narrow lane. As she stood gazing up at it, she remembered a party at which some American had complimented him on the house and asked if he'd bought it because it reminded him of his old family home in a Cotswold village. Don had confirmed it with a fond, reminiscent smile. He did it so well that Renata almost believed him, even though she remembered perfectly well that they had grown up in a flat in a tower block in north London.

He hadn't been half so convincing this afternoon, saying that all he'd done that weekend in Chicago was take Helen to the opera. Her certainty that he could not kill anyone remained unshaken, but it would be much easier to champion his cause if he didn't lie to her.

She went in the front door and switched on the light. The living room was a mess. The police must have come back. They'd searched the place Sunday and decided to have another go today. Tired and hungry as she was, she went around the house, putting books back on shelves and cushions back on furniture, and wiping some nasty pink sludge off countertops and doorjambs. She supposed it was fingerprint powder. When she looked in the laundry hamper, her temper got the better of her. Digging Detective McCutcheon's card out of her purse, she called his cellphone.

The line opened and she heard the roar of sports fans from a television. McCutcheon was relaxing, probably with the St. Louis Cardinals.

"Hello?"

"Detective McCutcheon, this is Renata Radleigh."

"Yes?"

"I have a question. When are the Clayton police going to return my knickers?"

"Your what?"

"My panties. The people who searched the house took every pair of panties out of the laundry hamper. They must have been hoping they were Helen Stromberg-Brand's. They're not; they're mine."

She was rather hoping that McCutcheon would make a ribald joke or at least snigger in a dirty way, giving her a chance to rip into him. But he was as bland as ever. "I'll look into it. Sorry for the inconvenience."

"You're looking for evidence that she was here, aren't you? Why are you doing that?"

"I can't discuss the investigation with you."

"Right. Then I'll just assume The Clayton PD collects lingerie." She waited, but McCutcheon chose to leave that one alone. "Did your superior okay another canvass?"

"What?"

"You said you requested another canvass. To look for the man Reyes saw. The man who was not walking his dog. Don't tell me you've forgotten."

"Ms. Radleigh, please. I can't discuss the investigation with you."

"You're not really investigating anymore, are you? I mean looking for the person who actually killed Helen. You've made up your minds my brother did it. You're only looking for more evidence against him."

The background noise dropped. McCutcheon was dialing down the remote to give her his full attention. "Ma'am, do you mind if I give you a piece of advice?"

"What? Of course I mind! I don't want any of your condescending—"

"Please, ma'am. This thing is gonna drag on. The prelim, the trial, maybe the appeal. We're talking years. You've got to calm down."

# 26

—

PETER LOMBARDO HAD BOUGHT THE condo north of Forest Park when he was hired by Public Relations. It was still rather under-furnished. The tedium of his days at the office sucked up all his energy, and he spent his evenings drinking too much beer and eating microwaved meals in front of the TV, watching a movie—if possible with Natalie Portman, who was the woman in his life at the moment.

Tonight, though, he was sitting at the computer, drinking iced tea. In his first day at PR, Roger had told him something interesting: more people got on the Web looking for medical information than for anything else, even porn. Once upon a time, Roger had said, people who worked miracle cures were called saints. The afflicted built shrines in their name and made pilgrimages to them. Today, the healers were big shot research docs, and the shrines and pilgrimages were on the internet.

Peter typed "Helen Stromberg-Brand" into the search engine, which promptly returned eight and a half million hits. Even when he eliminated the ones for Stromberg Machine Tool Co., Ibsen's *Brand*, and Helen of Troy sex aids, there were still millions.

Topping the list were scores of Adams University hits, in which Peter and his colleagues sang Helen's praises. He skipped those, as well as the glossy site of the Amygdala startup. Plowing through the medical journals her papers had appeared in and the professional associations she belonged to, by-passing *Mademoiselle* and *Redbook* and *Oprah*, which had all profiled her, he finally reached the patients' level. This was the phenomenon Roger had told him about: chronic UTI sufferers by the hundreds, condoling with each other, hallowing the name of Dr. Helen Stromberg-Brand, whose vaccine was almost in human trials and only a few itchy years away from the market.

He clicked on new search and typed "Ransome Chase" into the search engine. He had almost as many hits as Helen, but they were of a different kind. Adams University admitted that he was on the faculty, but that was all. No pharmaceutical companies, no glossy magazines, only second-tier scholarly journals. Peter found himself on the hopelessly unslick websites and Facebook pages of international aid workers and developing world health organizations. Chase was an expert on Chagas Disease and other infections that had been wiped out in America, but continued to be scourges in countries with primitive sanitation and—unfortunately for Chase—equally primitive public relations firms.

He soon encountered the man himself. Helen was a remote and glorious presence on patients' sites, but Chase was all over the sites devoted to his diseases—suggesting, arguing, complaining, advocating. He came across rather well. He was tough with bureaucrats, demanding more funding and facilities, compassionate with sufferers, whom he responded to directly. Peter wondered if Sturm und Drang had ever sent a consoling message to a UTI sufferer. He doubted it. Chase did have more than a touch of the white coat syndrome. He started posts by apologizing for spelling errors he might make because he had been up for the last twenty-seven hours, saving lives in a slum clinic in Mexico City or Lima.

There were pictures, too. Now Peter saw why Marian had

called Chase a wild man. He was big, taller and broader than everyone who was shaking hands with him or hugging him. He had a head of tousled, graying dark hair and a beard that covered his face from his collar to the rims of his oversize glasses. Peter found a portrait-size shot and printed it.

Why? Who was he planning to show it to, the cops?

He sat back from the screen and drained his tea. What did he have? Helen and Chase had competed for a named professorship. She had beaten him, probably by underhanded maneuvers. Result: she was hobnobbing with Keith Bryson while he was in some south-of-the-border clinic, being bled on and barfed on.

According to Marian, he was a sore loser. But angry enough to murder Stromberg-Brand? On the web, colleagues and patients spoke affectionately about Chase. He was a grouchy, plain-spoken, old-fashioned physician. A healer, dedicated to his patients. Like Bones on *Star Trek*. Not the murdering kind. Peter wished he could meet him, interview him about the Patel business.

For a few minutes, Peter toyed with pretexts for going to see Chase. But every scenario he imagined ended up with Chase indignant, Roger angry, and Peter himself embarrassed. And possibly unemployed.

"Nope," said Peter aloud. That was the problem with living alone—sooner or later you started talking to yourself. If he had even a scrap of evidence, he would have gone to the police. But all he had was suspicion, or as Chase would probably call it, slander. Peter closed the search engine. He took off his glasses and rubbed the bridge of his nose. Time to search the freezer for something to microwave for dinner.

But he wasn't hungry. He sat down again, fingers poised over the keys. Someone had told him that every musician in the world had a video on YouTube. He went there, and typed in "Renata Radleigh."

There was only one clip of her. It had 599 views in five years,

compared to Frederica von Stade's 261,000-plus and Cecilia
Bartoli's 445,000. He went to the beginning of it. It was from
a production of *Le Nozze di Figaro* by Mozart at the Liverpool
Opera. The number was "*Voi Che Sapete*."

Mozart he'd heard of; otherwise he was clueless. Sure, Peter
was Italian, and he'd had a grandfather who listened to the
Metropolitan Opera on the radio every Saturday afternoon.
But the opera gene must have been recessive in his case.

The still showed Renata Radleigh wearing an eighteenth-
century wig with a pigtail, a long waistcoat and breeches.
She must be playing a woman pretending to be a man, à la
Shakespeare—though in the Bard's day those were young men
playing women playing men. Renata was gazing off to the side,
smiling shyly. She looked much more than five years younger
than the careworn woman he'd seen on TV this afternoon.

Peter put his hand on the mouse. Hesitated. Something
told him it would be a mistake to listen to her. He thought
about dinner waiting for him in the freezer. It was late. He was
hungry.

No use. He clicked on play.

# 27

—

A S IT HAPPENED, RENATA WAS also watching YouTube.
Someone had taped that afternoon's press conference at
SLO on their cellphone and posted it. She didn't get far enough
to see Bryson himself. What stopped her was the moment when
Congreve disowned Don. "Suspended without pay," he said,
with brow furrowing and jowls flaring. "We are cooperating
fully with the police investigation."

Renata got up. Muttering to herself, she walked in circles
through the downstairs rooms, her head bowed, arms folded
across her middle. It was difficult, having a filthy temper while
being obliged to kowtow to everybody in the opera world if
you wanted to stay employed. It was taking all her strength to
hold herself back from ringing Congreve and shouting down
the line, "He got your bloody money for you, didn't he?"

Presumably Congreve's comment had not made the newscast
Don had watched this afternoon. With Bryson on tap, what
news producer would bother to show Congreve? Poor Don,
babbling to her about Samuelson the Harvard man, so well
connected at the courthouse. Perhaps it was just as well he was
ignorant in jail. He stood a better chance of sleeping on the
hard bunk in his cell if he thought he still had friends in high
places. How it would appall him to know that the only person

he could depend on was his sister, the aging journeyman mezzo-soprano, and that all she'd been able to do for him was bring the man who was not walking his dog to the attention of the police—who weren't interested.

She flopped on the sofa and blew out her breath. *Carmen* opened tomorrow. She ought to be going over the score, making sure of the tricky bits in the role, the card song and the quintet at the end of Act III.

Years ago she'd played Carmen in a student production, and those roles you learned when you were very young stayed with you, or at least they did if you ran through them once in a while. Carmen's part was so fun to sing that those run-throughs were no chore. Of course with everything that had been going on, it had been all she could do to rehearse the role she was actually going to perform.

She opened up the score, but she couldn't concentrate. She was distracted by her memories of the moments before Bryson's arrival: the coldly angry Bert, threatening to tell the world what had happened in Chicago, Congreve wheedling and placating, the usually glib Samuelson silent. What a transformation Keith Bryson had worked upon Bert in a few minutes upstairs in the office. Chicago had dropped entirely from view. Again she wondered at his perfect timing. What had brought one of the world's busiest men so swiftly to St. Louis?

She listened to his own explanation: a great scientific discovery, a boon to millions of women, a fortune to be shared with Adams University, Bryson, and Bert. Her conviction strengthened that the police were looking in the wrong direction. It was the vaccine that had gotten Helen killed. But how?

It would be interesting to ask Keith Bryson.

She laughed aloud when that idea popped into her head. By now Bryson was probably aboard his executive jet, winging to one coast or the other. If he was still in town, he was staying at some luxury hotel, hidden behind layer upon layer of flunkies.

And yet, this afternoon she had been standing close enough to him to read the tag on his jeans. His waist was 30, his inseam 32. That emboldened her somehow. She thought that she could take it as read that he was staying in town for a while, having come so far. She could even go a little further, and assume that he had a pied-à-terre in St. Louis. It was even possible that her brother had the address. Whether he had ever met them or not, Don collected the addresses of important people.

She went into his office. The police search had been especially thorough here. His files and books were scattered about the floor. His computer was gutted; no doubt Detective McCutcheon and friends hoped to find electronic billets-doux from Helen on the hard drive. Renata could do without it, because fortunately Don was old-fashioned in some respects. His contacts being the most important thing in life to him, his address book had totemic status.

She opened the bottom drawer and there it was, the thick book with well-worn leather binding and gilt-edged pages that he'd had for years. Business cards and scraps of paper that had been tucked in slipped out as she lifted it and put it on the desk. The pages were full, and alphabetical order had gone by the board, but eventually she found what she was looking for:

BRYSON, Keith (partner of HSB) 4909 Laclede St L 63108

# 28

―

Even if it hadn't been the neighborhood of Adams University Medical Center, Bryson's realtors probably would have chosen the Central West End for him. The city of St. Louis was the most battered and depressed of the American cities Renata had visited, but the Central West End, abutting the town's nicest park, made a credible attempt at Manhattan-style urban glamour. It was a mix of old townhouses and stylish apartment buildings. She passed by sidewalk cafés where people were lingering over dinner on a balmy night and turned onto Laclede Avenue.

She spotted Bryson's street number as she went by, but had to go down the block a ways to find a parking space big enough for Don's absurd car. It was an ancient Jaguar saloon with a wooden dashboard, leather seats, a chugging, smoking engine, and a rusty, rattling body. She hoped it would remain in one piece long enough to get her back to Webster Groves.

Bryson's building was a new one, with walls of granite and glass. It was tall enough to be topped with a flashing red light on a mast to warn off the helicopters approaching Granger Hospital's rooftop, a couple of blocks away. The lights were on in the floor-to-ceiling windows of the penthouse. She guessed that was where Bryson lived—why wouldn't he choose the penthouse? It crossed her mind that her best chance of getting up there would be to climb the side of the building. Shrugging away the hopeless thought, she stepped into the revolving door.

A man entered from the opposite side. She wouldn't have paid any attention to him, if he hadn't given the door such a push that she had to hasten her own step. She gave him an irritated glance, but his head was bowed. His dark hair was cropped so close his pale scalp showed. He was wearing a T-shirt that revealed a left arm covered with swirling tattoos from shoulder to wrist. As they passed, she just had time to register on his bicep the face of a beautiful girl, crying black tears and drooling a rosary, the crucifix between her teeth.

She stepped into a lobby of spare elegance, whose main feature was a vase of exotic flowers on a marble table shiny enough to reflect them. She walked past it to the reception desk. There were two young men in uniform, one sitting at the bank of television monitors, one standing with his hands on his hips. They were grinning, or rather their teeth were bared, because they didn't look happy at all. Their faces were flushed, and they were shaking their heads and muttering.

The standing one noticed her. "Yes, ma'am, can I help you?"

"I want to see Keith Bryson."

"Another one!" said the young man to his mate. He turned to her. "That guy wanted to see Keith Bryson too, which is funny, because he doesn't live here."

"I know he does."

"No. Sorry."

"I'll pay you fifty dollars just to call up to his flat and give my name, Rad—"

"The other guy offered twice that. But Mr. Bryson still doesn't live here."

"Look, this is terribly important. I'm just asking—"

"You're wasting your time."

"We don't have to put up with this," said the sitting man, who surged to his feet. The expression on his face made her back up a step. "This is private property. Go *now*, or we will escort you out, you got it?"

Renata turned away, her cheeks burning. She'd thought that at least it would be Bryson himself, on the phone, who refused to see her. No chance even to use any of the arguments she had thought up. Hard luck that tattooed bloke had put the guards in such a filthy mood.

Pushing through the door to the street, she was just in time to see a smudge of white across the street—the tattooed man's T-shirt. It disappeared as he got into his car. The engine started up.

Who was he? He seemed to want to see Bryson as badly as she did. As the car passed she had a good look at it: a four-door sedan, light gray or tan.

The car's taillights brightened as it reached the next intersection, where the signal was red. Renata found herself running. She jumped into the Jaguar and twisted the key. Amazingly, the decrepit engine awoke on the first try. The signal turned green and the gray or tan car turned right.

She followed. This was Kingshighway, a six-lane road, and traffic was fairly heavy. She couldn't see the other car. But then the truck in front of her changed lanes and there it was, last car in a queue stopped at a light. She lifted her foot off the accelerator, realizing she was closing in much too fast. She was going to pull up right behind him.

What did she have in mind? Jump out, run around to his window and knock on it, suggest they compare notes about how to reach Keith Bryson? The decision was taken out of her hands. The light changed and the car pulled away.

Keeping the car in sight occupied her fully, leaving her no time to plan. Driving on the right side of the road was difficult enough. Following somebody was beyond her. A car got in between her and the gray or tan car, and it would have to be one of those enormous SUVs St. Louisans were so fond of. She could not see ahead at all. She swerved left and the car in her blind spot honked its horn. Now there was room on the right. She changed lanes and stamped on the accelerator, startling the aged Jaguar. It coughed and surged forward. Again, the gray or tan sedan was pulling away as a light turned green.

As she was prone to do, Renata was having second thoughts. Even if she managed to get close enough to draw his attention by honking and waving, and induced him to pull over and talk, he was probably going to turn out to be a reporter who knew no more than she did. Assuming he didn't have some other business with Bryson completely irrelevant to the murder. Assuming it was even the same gray or possibly tan sedan that she was following.

Traffic was thinning out. The character of the neighborhood had changed, something that happened fast in St. Louis. The streetlights were dimmer. There were fountains of neon and arc-light marking gas stations, but only darkness elsewhere. She was passing vacant lots and abandoned buildings. Groups of young black men, wearing hoodies even on this warm night, were standing around on the street corners.

*Enough of this*, Renata decided. She slowed and put on her turn signal, preparing to turn around and head back to Webster Groves. Before she could, the gray or possibly tan car displayed its boxy profile again as it turned right. She had been following the right car, then. She couldn't resist taking the same turn.

There were no taillights ahead of her. Then she noticed that the car was parked at the curb. Here was her chance. She drew up beside it. But there was no one in the driver's seat.

She looked around. Where could the man have gone? There was nothing here: a chain-link fence surrounding a vacant lot on one side, a building with empty holes for windows and a collapsing roof on the other. This was very odd. She considered parking and waiting to see if the man would reappear. But it was damned scary around here and she didn't want to linger. She would take down the car's license number and go home.

Leaving the engine running, she climbed out and went

around to the back of the car with her notebook and pencil. There was no streetlight here and her headlights were no help. She bent down, squinting at the plate.

A sudden pain at the back of her head and blackness closed in.

# 29

—

THE GRAY OR TAN CAR drove along the access road across the highway from Lambert St. Louis Airport, passing a row of chain motels. It turned into the cheapest of them and parked under a security light on a tall pole, which revealed it to be a faded silver, with a few freckles of rust.

The driver got out and tucked Renata's purse under his tattooed arm. In addition to the girl biting a rosary that Renata had noticed, the swirling ink also depicted a skull, a red rose, and a leafless tree silhouetted against a sunset. The man ran to the building and pounded his fist on one of the guest-room doors. A jet was passing low overhead, drowning out his knock. He shouted, "Bistouri! It's me!"

The door was opened by a tall, narrow-shouldered man, wearing a T-shirt and the pants of a dark suit. The tattooed man rushed past him into the room. "Something's going on. We gotta … gotta reconsider this situation."

Bistouri shut the door. "Did you get in to see Bryson?"

"What? No."

Bistouri sighed. He was in his forties, with a long face under a dark widow's peak and a graying moustache. There were heavy bags under his eyes. "So how hard did you try, Shane?"

"Never mind about that. Somebody tried to follow me."

"Is my car okay?"

"Your fuckin' limo is *fine.*" Shane dug in the pocket of his jeans and threw a set of keys at Bistouri, who deftly caught them.

"What is that?" he asked, indicating the purse under Shane's arm.

"It's hers."

"Hers?"

"It was a woman following me. I didn't realize that till after I hit her. She was real tall."

"You hit her? How hard?"

"She was still breathing. Will you just shut up for a minute and let me tell the story?"

Bistouri sat down on the end of the bed. The small room was very neat. The only signs of occupation were a suitcase on a rack and a copy of the St. Louis *Post-Dispatch* on the night-table, with a pair of reading glasses on top. Shane looked around for a chair, but there wasn't one. He evidently didn't want to sit next to Bistouri. He remained standing, clutching the purse, as he told the story. He was breathing hard and his dark eyes were wide with alarm. They looked enormous in his bony, pale face.

"And the purse?" Bistouri asked. He reached into his suitcase and took out a pair of cheap latex gloves.

"Her car door was open. I could see the purse lying on the seat, so I grabbed it."

Bistouri put out a hand, now gloved. Shane gave him the purse and he opened it and extracted the wallet. Shane moved to look over his shoulder.

"That's some weird license. You ever seen anything like that?"

"It's British."

"*British?* What's some British person doing here?"

"Well, she must be from Scotland Yard," said Bistouri in a mocking, sing-song tone. "Christ, you're dumb. See the name? Radleigh?"

Shane looked blank.

"Like the guy they arrested for the Stromberg-Brand murder."

"So she's trying to help him? She's his wife?"

"If she was, she probably wouldn't be trying to help him. Not after he balled Stromberg-Brand. His sister, maybe."

"Why would she want to see Bryson?"

"Everybody wants to see Bryson. But she had no more luck than you did, obviously. I'm not worried."

"No? Well, I am. Why did we have to come to St. Louis to see Bryson, with this murder investigation going on?"

"It's not going on. The cops arrested the Radleigh guy. Case closed."

"We could wait for Bryson to go back to California. Talk to him there."

"You're in no hurry for your money? I am. Take some of your calm-down pills and go to bed. You're gonna try Bryson at his office tomorrow morning. And wear a jacket or something. That fucking tattoo. You might as well have your name written down your arm."

"Why me?"

"We're holding me in reserve."

Bistouri was continuing to inspect Renata's wallet. He took a five and two singles out of it and tucked them in his pants pocket, then dropped the wallet back in the purse.

"Right now, though, you're gonna get rid of this."

"The trash can is right there."

"Go at least ten miles from here. And don't throw it out the window. Stop, get out, drop it in a storm sewer." He lobbed the car keys to Shane, who let them bounce off his chest and drop to the floor.

"Hey. I'm tired. I'm not doing this."

Bistouri pulled a cellphone out of the purse and shook it at Shane. "These things can be tracked."

"By the NSA maybe. Not the local cops."

"You waste your time worrying about the wrong things, Shane. Some risks you got to take, but don't get sloppy. It's little shit like this that will screw you up." He dropped the phone in the purse, zipped it, and held it out to the younger man. "Just do what I tell you for the next couple of days. All we need is a few minutes face to face with Bryson, and you'll never have to peddle pills again."

Shane glared at him but said nothing. After a moment he snatched the purse from Bistouri's hand and bent down for the keys. Then he went out, slamming the door.

He stalked across the parking lot, still scowling, to Bistouri's car. Reaching it, he hesitated, looked back at the room, and walked on. He passed a low steel barrier that demarked a lot for larger vehicles. Passing an RV, a four-door pickup, and a couple of cargo vans, he stopped beside a delivery truck—rectangular, flat-roofed, about twelve feet high. Bending at the knees, he gave Renata's purse an underhand lob. It landed with a clunk atop the truck. Smiling at his triumph over Bistouri, Shane walked back to the motel.

# PART IV

—

## TUESDAY, MAY 25

# 30

—

R ENATA WAS AWAKENED BY THE telephone. It was the general director's secretary, saying he wanted to see her. They were sending a car for her. It would arrive in fifteen minutes. The coercive courtesy was typical of Phil Congreve, she thought as she fumbled the receiver back onto its cradle.

It was impossible for the moment to get out of bed. She strove to gather her thoughts. What did Congreve want with her? To tell her off for the television interview yesterday, probably. On Sunday he personally had ordered her not to speak to the media. It was especially inappropriate that she should protest her brother's innocence while Congreve was disowning him. How odd, how unlike her it was that the immediate prospect of being chastised by the head of SLO did not make her anxious. There was nothing like a spot of assault and battery to put one's fears in proportion.

She'd had a bad night. When the shot they had given her at the emergency room wore off, she awakened in agony. Oddly it was not the wound in the back of her head that hurt the most. She had fallen hard, on the right side of her face, and her cheek and forehead were afire. Fortunately the doctor had given her some pills, and she was eventually able to get back to sleep lying on her left side.

In the interval there had been a revolting episode of self-pity. Tears ran freely from her closed eyes, making a damp spot on the pillow, and she was sobbing and moaning in the most appalling way. The feeble sounds inspired feeble thoughts: *I don't want to be in the middle of America, alone in this bed, with sole responsibility for my jailed and disgraced brother.*

*Alone.* She imagined how lovely it would be to have someone lying beside her, stroking her hair and murmuring consolation. But did men even go in for that sort of thing? Not the ones who'd shared her bed. They'd been roll-over-and-snore types.

This morning she was better, she told herself. The pain in her face was down to a dull throb. But her whole head felt wrong. Her teeth did not seem to meet the way they used to. Her eyeballs didn't quite fit their sockets. She was aware all the time that the pain had been caused by the deliberate action of another person, which made it twice as bad. She supposed that if you were a policeman or a soldier, someone who dealt in violence, you got used to it. But it was a new thing in the life of a mezzo-soprano, and Renata was frightened.

Exhausted as she had been when she got home last night, she had gone round the house to make sure all the windows and doors were locked, and turned on the security system that Don usually ignored. She feared that her assailant was going to come after her.

A uniformed policeman had questioned her in the emergency room. Woozy as she felt, she knew that if she told him the truth, she would initiate a chain of events that would end with being questioned by a sleepy and bad-tempered Detective McCutcheon: *What makes you think this has anything to do with the Stromberg-Brand murder? What do you expect to happen when you follow a strange man into north St. Louis?*

So she told the policeman that she had been lost and had pulled over to read a street sign. She had not seen the man who hit her. There was nothing valuable in her purse but a cellphone, a few dollars, and a Visa card. The policeman said her assailant would be disappointed with the haul, if it was any consolation to her. Then he lent her his phone to cancel the card.

A horn honked. The company car was here already. Gritting her teeth, she pushed herself upright and swung her feet to the floor. It belatedly occurred to her that tonight *Carmen* would open. On every previous morning of an opening night in her life, the evening's opera had been her first thought, before she even opened her eyes.

# 31

⸺

ARRIVING IN HIS OFFICE AT Medical PR, Peter Lombardo hung up his sports jacket and turned on his computer. A couple of hundred emails had come in overnight from reporters in Europe and Asia, wanting to know more about this wonder drug in which Keith Bryson had invested. He sat down and tackled them. He had resolved that he was going to be the impeccable PR man today. He would waste no more company time on Ransome Chase. He had no evidence against the hot-headed doctor, and he wasn't going to look for any. If his conscience bothered him, he would go to the payphone across the street, call in an anonymous tip to the Clayton police, and consider his duty done. Of course they would ignore it, but that was their problem.

He worked his way efficiently through twenty-seven emails. Then something unaccountable happened. His mouse dragged his hand down to the icon for his browser, and within seconds he had his headphones on and was listening to Renata Radleigh sing *"Voi Che Sapete"* on YouTube one more time.

Peter was an expert internet researcher, and by now he knew a lot about her. He knew, for instance, that she was playing Cherubino, who was not a woman pretending to be a man as in Shakespeare, but simply a man. There were a lot of parts like that, called "trouser roles," in opera, and they were played by mezzo-sopranos. The joke was that a mezzo's career was "britches, bitches, and witches." When not playing men, they generally played villainesses. The stars of the show, the heroines who sang of love and died in a weeping tenor's arms as the curtain fell, were played by sopranos.

This was the nineteenth time he had listened to her sing "*Voi Che Sapete*." Unlike most of the arias he'd heard, it was short and didn't involve a lot of wailing. Cherubino, a teenager whose hormones were seriously out of control, asked two older women to teach him about love.

The earphones here were higher quality than his speakers at home, and her voice sounded even richer, deeper, and smoother. She acted a swaggering young man very plausibly, but that didn't prevent him from seeing that she was a beautiful woman. Her blue eyes sparkled. Her smile got to him—more than once he had caught himself idiotically grinning back at her.

It was a good thing that nobody had uploaded to YouTube the interview she had done on the local news yesterday. The contrast would be too painful. How worn and tired and worried and sad she looked. It must be pretty tough to stand up for her brother, when everybody else in the St. Louis metropolitan area thought he was guilty as sin ....

"Except Peter Lombardo," Peter said aloud. "Oh, *crap.*"

Shucking the headphones, he got up and went down the hall to the file room. There were filing cabinets full of old papers and reports, which people tended to neglect as the office went more and more digital. There might be some good stuff about Patel and Ransome Chase in there.

# 32

—

CONGREVE STARED AT HER AS she approached his desk across his vast office. In the bathroom mirror she had seen that she had developed an impressive black eye, swollen and empurpled. She didn't wait for him to ask. "I tripped and fell. Don't worry, makeup will cover it tonight."

He came around the desk, waving her to sit on the sofa and taking a seat beside her. He brushed back a lock of silver hair and smiled. This was better than the reception she'd expected. "How are you bearing up, Renata? I'm sorry I've had no chance to talk to you since this nightmare began."

"Oh, I'm all right. About that interview I gave yesterday. I know you told me not to talk to reporters—"

"Don't worry about it. No one would expect you to say anything else."

Meaning no one was going to take her seriously either. "I went to see Don yesterday."

"Ah, poor Don," said Congreve. "And how is he?"

Renata shook her head, which she immediately regretted. Pain ricocheted between her ears. As soon as she was done wincing she said, "Sorry, but I don't understand your concern. Yesterday you as good as sacked him."

"I was talking to the media. There was nothing else I could

say. Renata, we have to ask people for money every day. And if the first thing they think about is Don and Helen Stromberg-Brand …. The local media are taking a very negative attitude. Did you see the *Post* this morning?"

"No."

"The headline of Bill McClellan's column is, 'Don Giovanni?'"

"Oh. Yes, that is unfortunate. Could have been worse, I suppose. I mean if Bert Stromberg-Brand had told the reporters that Don swept Helen off to Chicago and seduced her to make her give the money."

Congreve's sympathetic expression abruptly hardened. His noble brow furrowed and his dewlaps drooped. "Did Don tell you that?"

"No. I was there yesterday when Bert made his threat."

"Oh. That's right. I forgot."

He continued to gaze at her, but he wasn't seeing her. Behind the eyes the brain was busy. Talking to Congreve at such moments was as useless as tapping the keys of a computer that was displaying the little hourglass on its screen. So Renata just waited.

He got up, went to his desk and picked up the telephone. "Mike, could you come over? Yes, *now*." This wasn't too ominous; Mike Joyce was her favorite person at SLO. Unlike most heads of production, he took understudying as seriously as she did, and had arranged extra sessions with the repetiteur and stage manager for her to rehearse Carmen, a very long part. He'd even paid her overtime.

Congreve returned to the sofa. "You'll visit Don today?"

"Yes."

"Tell him we wish him well. That we still see him as one of us. We'll do everything to help … behind the scenes."

"I'll tell him." She hoped it would comfort Don more than it did her.

Mike ambled in and gave her a smile as he sank into a chair facing them. He was a tall, loose-limbed, fit-looking African American in his forties whose gift was for looking well-rested and unhurried when in fact he was neither. As production head he had ultimate responsibility for the countless details involved in putting the operas on stage. With the world premiere of *Catch-22* and the gimmicky production of *Carmen*, this was an especially nerve-wracking season for him.

"Mike," Congreve said, "I think we should let Renata out of her contract."

She jumped. "What?"

He turned to her. "With all the strain you're under, you don't want to be bothered with an opera."

Renata said nothing. The thought that *Carmen* would go on at 7:30 tonight and she would not be there appalled her.

"You can find somebody else to play Frasquita, can't you, Mike?"

"Mercédès."

"Right, Mercédès. How about it, Mike?"

Mike was watching Renata. His gaze shifted to his boss. "Iris knows the role."

"Well then."

"The problem is, Renata's also understudying Carmen."

"Problem? But Amy's fine."

"I just got off the phone with her. I'm taking her to our ear nose and throat guy."

Congreve had another of his little-hourglass moments. He was probably wondering whom he could blame if the star bowed out and—disaster of disasters—Renata sang the lead. Renata was thinking about the possibility too, with very different emotions.

"My God. What's wrong with her?"

"Sinuses. Her head feels like a cinderblock, she says."

"Well, the doc can give her something, can't he? I mean, what are we keeping him on retainer for?"

"I would feel more comfortable if we had Renata on hand, Phil."

Everyone at SLO was familiar with the production head's understated style. Even Congreve recognized that he was stating a non-negotiable demand and backed down. He rose to return to his desk. "Okay. Keep me informed."

Renata followed Mike across the corridor into his office. He shut the door and said, "Amy's fine. Sorry."

"Oh!" Renata sagged against the door. What a bizarre creature I am, she thought. My brother in jail. Myself battered and bruised from a criminal assault. Half an hour ago I could barely drag myself out of bed. And yet my blood was singing in my veins at the thought that I might play Carmen tonight.

"I wasn't exactly lying," Mike went on. "Amy is complaining, and I am taking her to the ENT. But he will convince her that she can sing tonight. There's nothing wrong with her except it's her first time singing in St. Louis and she has the jitters."

Renata nodded. Mike had years of experience at diva-wrangling, and knew whereof he spoke. Opera singers' careers depended on the state of their mucous membranes. They were notorious hypochondriacs. St. Louis, being downwind of the Wheat Belt, had an evil reputation. Even singers who had never suffered from allergies imagined that they would lose their voices.

"I'm sorry, Renata. I hate to disappoint you. But it was the only way I could think of to head off Phil. I hope I did the right thing?"

"Oh God, yes. Thank you, Mike. If I didn't know I'd be singing Mercédès tonight, I'd fall apart. But why is he trying to get rid of me? What good will it do?"

"Phil finds it soothing to fire people. And he's nervous as hell right now. We all are. You have to understand, we've sold every seat in the house tonight, and that still only pays one-third of our expenses. The rest we have to beg for. I like Don, I feel bad about what's happened to him, but he's put us in a very difficult position."

She sighed heavily. That was the most temperate statement she was going to hear about her brother from an SLO employee today.

Mike patted her shoulder. "We have to make this look good or Phil will get suspicious. Go over to wardrobe and tell them I said to measure you for Amy's costumes, just in case. And keep your cellphone in hand, like you're expecting an important call from me."

"Oh! I've, uh, lost my phone."

He went to his desk, opened a lower drawer, and handed her a cellphone. A sensitive man, he read her face and smiled sadly. "I wish it could be you singing *Carmen* tonight."

She shrugged. "I sang her my last year at the Guildhall School of Music and Drama. I was twenty-three. I thought it was going to be the first of many times. But that was it."

"So far," said Mike as he hugged her.

Crossing the Emerson Electric Picnic Lawn, she entered the Jane B. Pritchard Theatre. As she was descending the steps to the costume room, a voice called out, "Hi, Renata." It was Ray, the irascible super.

"Oh, good morning."

"That's some shiner. What happened?"

"I fell. It's nothing. What are you doing here so early?"

Ray rolled his eyes and indicated his T-shirt. "The Commie had a last minute inspiration."

This was his nickname for Bernhard von Schussnigg, who had been born in what was then East Germany. During rehearsals Ray had grumbled frequently and a bit too audibly about the director's lefty ideas. Renata had him turn around so she could appraise his costume change. The crowd scenes in *Carmen* made for a full evening for the supers, and Ray was playing a soldier in Act I, a barfly in Act II, a smuggler in Act III, and a bullfight spectator in Act IV. The T-shirt was obviously for the smuggler, who in von Schussnigg's production had become an illegal immigrant. It had "Home of the Brave, Land of the Free" on the back and an American flag on the front.

"Brilliant," she said. "You can't top von Schussnigg for subtlety."

"What brings you here this morning?"

"Costumes. Just in case Amy can't go on tonight, they're seeing how many feet they'll have to lower her hemlines to fit me."

Ray's eyes widened. "You mean you might play Carmen tonight?"

"Not a chance. It's just a precaution."

"Too bad. I'd like to see you as Carmen."

"Thank you, Ray. I'm afraid the audience would not agree with you." She turned to go.

"What's that at the back of your head?"

In the ER last night, they had shaved a small area to staple her wound. "I told you, I fell."

"You fell on your face *and* on the back of your head?"

"Long story. Really, I'll be fine tonight."

But Ray caught her arm and stepped in front of her. "You're not being honest with me, Renata."

His grip was almost painfully strong. The look in his eyes made her heart lurch. During the weeks of rehearsal, she had discovered that he had a short fuse, but she had no idea what had set him off this time.

"Easy, Ray," she said. "Only divas and directors are allowed temperament."

It was a line she had used on him a few times in rehearsal, and as always it had a calming effect. He let go of her arm and backed off a step. "Okay, it's none of my business. But I hate to see you taking stupid chances for your brother. And that's what you were doing, wasn't it?"

"Well … yes. That's a fair description."

"What did you find out?"

"Nothing helpful."

"You know, Renata? I think you better start getting used to the idea that your brother is guilty."

"No. The news reports make it sound a good deal worse than it is. And there are some things that haven't made the news."

"Like what?"

She told him about the man Luis Reyes had seen on Helen's street, the man who was not walking his dog.

"You told the police about this man? What did they say?"

"They weren't impressed. They said he was just a man walking down the street. But people don't walk down residential streets in Clayton at that time of night unless they're walking their dogs."

"He didn't have a dog so he must be the killer?" Ray was shaking his head. "The newspaper said the police can prove your brother was in the house with her."

"Yes. But she was alive and well when he left."

"So he says. But how long was it between the time your brother left and the gardener and her husband arrived?"

"I don't know," said Renata, thinking it was odd that he had given the matter so much thought.

"Well, we're talking about a pretty narrow window of opportunity for this other guy who just happened to want Dr. Stromberg-Brand dead, to just happen to come along. And he was real lucky that she was alone in the house, and that your brother took the blame for him."

"Well, when you put it like that, it sounds far-fetched."

"How else could you put it, Renata? That's what you're saying happened."

She took a deep breath. "Please, Ray. I'm on my way to see my brother in jail, to try to cheer him up. This is not what I want to listen to right now."

"Maybe it's what you ought to listen to. Before you get hurt any worse."

# 33

—

IN THE FRONT OFFICE OF Ezylon, at Amygdala, Jayson was sitting at the reception desk, leaning back so far in his chair that the front legs were off the ground. He was talking on the telephone, discussing restaurants with his luncheon companion. At length. In the waiting area, under the huge picture of Helen Stromberg-Brand and Keith Bryson in her lab, Shane was pacing, turning his head from time to time to scowl at Jayson, who was blissfully unaware of him. He was wearing a long-sleeved denim shirt that covered his tattoo. Jayson leaned forward and replaced the phone.

Shane walked up to the desk. "I want to see Bryson. I know he's in town, and I know this is his office, so don't give me any shit."

"Tell me, does this approach open a lot of doors for you?"

"Just tell me when I can see Bryson."

"As soon as you can convince me you're worth his time."

"It's way too important to tell you about."

Jayson folded his hands in his lap and rocked onto the back legs of his chair. "You're going to have to do better."

"You don't let me in to see Bryson today, he's gonna fire you tomorrow."

"Keep trying."

"I got no time for this."

He walked past the desk and opened the door.

"He isn't actually here right now. But go look around if you want. Don't steal any staplers, okay?"

Shane returned to stand in front of the desk. "I want an appointment to see him."

"Let's have a look at the sked." Jayson tapped keys. "He's heading for Ladue now, to play tennis with the CEO of Granger Hospital. Later he'll be downtown having lunch with the mayor. Then he's going home for a conference call with the secretary of health and human services. Which one of those do you think he'll want to cancel to meet a man with a cheap haircut and bad manners?"

"You are gonna be so sorry tomorrow. You are gonna be out of here on your ass."

"This is sounding familiar. Are you the gentleman who tried to get in to see Mr. Bryson at his condo last night?"

Shane straightened up and backed away from the desk. "Nah, wasn't me."

"I've heard about your act, and I'm not about to sit through it." He picked up the telephone. "I'm calling security. They're right downstairs and they'll have two big guys here in one minute flat. They've done it before."

"Now listen—"

"No. We're through. You can walk out or security can drag you out."

Shane spun on his heel and left, leaving the door swinging on its hinges. Jayson let it swing. He replaced the receiver and turned to his computer.

# 34

---

RENATA WAS IN A CORRIDOR of the county jail, waiting in a long queue for the metal detector. It was noisy and stuffy and now somebody's cellphone began to play a particularly irritating tune. It went on and on. She turned and glared at the woman behind her, who glared right back. Oh—it was the phone Mike had lent her. She hadn't heard its ringtone before.

"Hello?"

"Renata, it's Hannah at SLO. We just got a call for you. Kind of a strange one."

"Who from?"

"His name is Archibald Henderson. He said he found your purse."

"Oh!' She was astonished; she had taken for granted that it was gone forever. "Where did he find it?"

"He didn't say. Do you want his number?"

"Well … I suppose so." She tapped the number into her phone's memory as Hannah gave it. Then, since the line was not moving, she tried it. A velvety drawl said, "Hello, this is the number of Archibald Henderson. I'm sorry you reached this recording and wish I was speaking with you. But I am in all probability at the wheel of my truck. Whatever the laws of the jurisdiction in which I find myself, I do not talk on the phone while driving, which I regard as unsafe."

Mr. Henderson was one of those people who regarded the outgoing message as a performance art. She wondered how people who called him often could bear it. To compound the irritation, he had a slow, drawling voice from the American South. She was standing in a queue anyway, and she still felt like pressing the End Call button. Finally he wound up his oration and she left her number.

There were more visitors this morning, and they were noisier. By the time she reached the long table, only one seat remained. The prisoners didn't file in but pushed through the door in a bunch. Don emerged from behind other heads and shoulders and sat down opposite her.

He pointed to her black eye. "Good lord Renata. What happened to you?"

"I tried to get in to see Keith Bryson last night. Couldn't. There was somebody else who'd failed to get in, so I followed him."

"Followed him?"

"I just wanted to talk to him. He obviously didn't want to talk to me."

Don was slowly wagging his head. "Someone like Keith is always being pestered by whack jobs. Stalkers and paparazzi and conmen and what-not. Renata, I am sorry. If I'd known you wanted to see Keith, I could have called someone."

Renata sighed. In the car on the way over, she had formed her resolve to make Don face reality. It was absolutely essential now. The problem was, she had been trying to do it for a quarter-century or so, starting with advising him not to press Mummy and Daddy to buy him that Italian racing bike because it was sure to be stolen. But he had, and it was. She'd had no better luck since.

"Why did you want to see Keith, anyway?"

"I think that whoever killed Helen, it must have been

connected to her billion-dollar vaccine rather than the opera. And the police haven't thought of that."

He was looking at her blankly again.

"That's as far as I'd got. Obviously following the bloke wasn't very clever. But I'm beside myself, Don. I'm very worried about you. I'm afraid you're—"

She pulled up short, because Don was grinning. "Good lord, Renata. You're amateur sleuthing, aren't you? You think you're Miss Marple. Or it's amateur-*ish* sleuthing, more like."

A white-hot bolt of fury shot up Renata's spine and exploded in her brain. "*That's* what you have to say? How about *thanking* me? How about apologizing that I got my head split open because of *you*?"

She found that she was on her feet. The couples on either side of them had stopped talking and were staring up at her. A guard was striding toward her.

"Renata, love, I am sorry of course. Now please don't storm out of the room the way you usually do, because I can't follow you and pet your shoulder and apologize to your back, the way I usually do."

She sat down, with a nod to the guard that she hoped was reassuring. "Right. I shall be calm. I've realized what I'm doing is not helping you and I'm going to stop."

"Agreed. Go on."

"I'm going to leave you with one piece of advice. It's incredibly good advice, so please listen. It's time for you to get your own lawyer."

"That's being sorted as we speak. Dick Samuelson rang this morning. He said he can't represent me anymore, obviously, but he is ringing people—colleagues—on my behalf. He mentioned some very impressive names. Some of the top criminal attorneys in town. Very experienced, very well-connected. Of course they're terribly busy and it'll take a while, but—"

"No, Don. Get your own lawyer, straightaway. Someone who has nothing to do with Dick or SLO."

"Dick can get me someone who's much better than I could find on my own."

"Your interests are not the same as SLO's. Phil Congreve has announced to the media that he's suspended you without pay."

"Right. To the media. He had to, with this 'Don Giovanni' nonsense going on. Dick explained."

"Don't count on these people anymore."

"Ah, you've come to spread doom and gloom as usual. Inject a little paranoia. Thanks awfully."

Renata had only one more thing to say. Get it out, and then she could leave before she threw her car keys at him. "Once you have your own lawyer, tell him everything. The whole truth."

"I don't know what that's supposed to mean."

"I mean tell him what you're not telling me."

"I am telling you the truth."

"Then answer me this: has Dick Samuelson made you promise to keep silent about what happened in Chicago?"

"I took Helen to an opera. That's all that happened in Chicago."

"All right. I've had my say and I'm going. Is there anything you want?"

He was silent a moment, staring down at the scarred Formica tabletop. "D'you really think it'll help my case if I say, 'Well, yes, I am Don Giovanni as a matter of fact. I deliberately set out to seduce her and get a third of a million dollars out of her.' "

"Is that the truth?"

"D'you think it would help my case?"

She pushed her chair back. "I think I'm having one conversation and you're having another, and when we reach that point, it's time to stop."

"Look, just because I'd rather take legal advice from a Harvard-educated lawyer than a mezzo-soprano—"

"You say the truth about Chicago won't help your case. Well, you better find *some*thing to help your case. The police can prove you were in the house that night. They've found your blood there."

"I've already explained all that," he said wearily. "You may not know it, but they have the presumption of innocence here, just as we do back home."

"Somebody said something to me this morning. I wasn't going to tell it you. But now I think I should."

"I thought you were going."

"He said that to believe you innocent, a person would have to believe that after you left, and before Bert got back, a person just happened to come along who just happened to want Helen dead. And happened to find her alone in the house. And there you were to take the blame for him. That's what the presumption of innocence is up against in your case."

"I can't say I'm going to miss your visits. I was actually feeling a bit optimistic before you got to work on me."

He was slumped in the hard chair, his head hanging. He looked as if he'd run ten miles, and that was how Renata felt, too. It always took a few hours to recover after one of their rows.

She got up, went to the door, and rang to be let out. The guard was slow in coming. She turned and walked back. Don hadn't moved. He looked up at her balefully.

"I didn't say I wasn't going to visit. Just that I'm through amateur-sleuthing. I will be back tomorrow. And the next day. And so forth."

Don did not reply but did not look away, either. She turned to go.

# 35

—

Jayson looked up from his computer as the door opened. He grinned and tossed a left-handed salute. "Sergeant Schaefer, how nice to see you."

The man coming in the door was average height but seemed taller because of his physique and posture. He was wearing a white polo shirt without a logo, tucked into khakis with sharp creases. His close-cropped hair was graying but his brow was unlined. He said, "Hello, Jayson. Enlisted veterans don't retain their rank, so it's just Schaefer. I believe I've mentioned that before."

"Yes, and you've made it clear you don't return salutes from civilian scum like me. Is Keith on the way?"

"Not that I know of."

"C'mon. You're the forerunner. Fifteen minutes before he arrives anywhere, you come check the place out."

"I doubt he'll be in today."

Jayson stopped smiling. "He's been in St. Louis since Sunday, if not before, and he hasn't come into the office yet. Could you pass on to him that I have a lot to talk to him about?"

"He's aware of that." By now Schaefer was standing before the desk. The toe ends of his shoes were aligned and his thumbs were on the seams of his khakis. Old habits died hard. "You had a walk-in this morning."

Jayson raised his eyebrows. He seemed to be slouching more now that Schaefer was in the room. "I just filed the report half an hour ago."

"Your report is inadequate. You left the whole description section blank."

"You have no idea how many bozos come in here asking to see Keith. If I filled out every blank on every form, I wouldn't have time to do anything else."

"Complete this one and send it to me by the end of the day."

"I already forgot what the guy looked like."

"I'll be in Keith's office. If the guy comes back, or if there's another walk-in, buzz me."

"You, bothering with walk-ins? Something must be up. What?"

Schaefer was opening the inner door. He paused before passing through it. "Jayson, I'd like you to pay attention to your job. And I'd like you to not pay attention to what is not your job."

# 36

—

WHEN RENATA GOT BACK FROM Clayton, she returned to SLO. She had intended to go home for a bit of a lie-down before the evening's performance, but tired as she was, she knew she wouldn't sleep. She had just promised to keep visiting her brother in jail, and she had the awful feeling that she would be doing so for the next twenty years.

Entering the Jane B. Pritchard Theatre, she looked into the Charles MacNamara III Auditorium. Aside from a few technicians in the wings, adjusting the stage machinery, it was dim and empty. Curtain time was eight hours away. She could use them to make up for lost time and review every note, word, and gesture of her part as Mercédès. But her heart would not be in it.

She went downstairs to the little dressing room she shared with two other minor soloists. Sitting down, she put the phone Mike had lent her on the table. She wished he would ring and say that Amy still looked doubtful for this evening.

Then Renata would be plunged into a happy flurry of costume and wig fittings, meetings with the stage manager to run over the blocking, sessions with the repetiteur to review the score. A couple of times in her career as an understudy she had made all the preparations, only to have the star announce that she would sing after all. It had been infuriating then, but today she would have welcomed a bit of backstage panic to take her mind off things.

Her brother's situation was a grim novelty, but having an empty afternoon to while away before a performance was routine. Ordinarily she kept busy sending off emails begging for work. And envying people who were Skyping with their families back home. It got so lonely, having no one to miss.

She had only her brother. Not the best of brothers, but better than Enrico in *Lucia di Lammermoor,* anyway. He was in terrible trouble. How could she have lost her temper with him this morning? That had poisoned the whole conversation. He hadn't taken her advice seriously.

The phone began to play its annoying tune. She looked at the screen: it was not Mike but Archibald Henderson.

"Hello, Mr. Henderson. I was told you'd found my purse?"

"That's right, ma'am. And I'm happy to be of service to a visitor from the mother country."

She had the feeling that he was the sort of man who would resent a brusque getting down to business. "I'll bet you're a stranger in town, too."

"From Fayetteville, North Carolina. I'm delivering chairs. We make a lot of furniture in North Carolina."

"Yes, I've heard."

"Very fine furniture."

"Indeed." Was that enough? She hoped so. "Tell me, Mr. Henderson. Where did you find my purse?"

He chuckled. "Well, that's kind of a long story. But I want to assure you first off, there was no money in it."

"I wouldn't expect there to be."

"I did not take any money out of your purse. I hope you'll accept my word on that."

"Yes, of course."

"Then you won't be offended if I ask for a little recompense for my time and trouble?"

"Oh. No, I suppose not. How much."

"A hundred."

"Dollars? You're barking!"

"I'm what, ma'am?"

"Barking mad."

He was not offended. In fact he was chuckling richly. "I do love your colorful expressions. That's a new one to me, and I watch *Doc Martin* every week."

"Mr. Henderson, I will not pay one hundred dollars."

"I'm sorry you were robbed and wish I could just give the purse back—"

"Then do!"

"But I've already been put to considerable trouble to retrieve it, and I'll lose more time meeting you, and I'm on a tight schedule, or shed-*ule* as you folks say in the mother country. I can't go below a hundred."

"Then you can keep the bloody thing."

She shouldn't have said "bloody." He was chuckling again. It was so annoying, trying to offend someone and not being able to.

"Now, don't get your knickers in a twist. Your purse has your credit card in it."

"Cancelled already."

"And your phone … I mean your mo-*bile*. And your driver's license. You may not be able to replace that till you get back to your side of the pond."

"I have my passport."

"Lot of good that will do you if you're stopped for speeding. And then there's the purse itself. Genuine leather. A little worn, but—"

"Glad you like it. It's yours."

His stately voice sounded unperturbed. "I'll be in St. Louis until about five p.m., ma'am, in case you change your mind."

"Not likely."

She clicked off and sat shaking her head. She would prefer not to see her purse again anyway. Not after her assailant had poked his fingers into all its folds and crevices, seeking all the information it could disclose about her. Come to that, Archibald Henderson seemed to have given it a good going over, too.

"Mother country indeed," she muttered.

The phone emitted its little ditty again. It had gone half past eleven; this had to be Mike. But the screen showed only an unfamiliar number, no name. A recorded voice said that if she was willing to accept a collect call from a detainee in the St. Louis County Justice Center, she should press "1" now. She did.

"Renata, love, this is a happy call," said Don's excited voice. "We've been utter fools, thinking the situation was hopeless."

She could hardly hear him. Shouts were echoing down a long corridor. "Don, are you all right? What's going on there?"

"Oh, this is normal. But listen. I've had a revelation. A thought that's absolutely brilliant."

She waited in befuddled silence.

"It's that thing old Thingummy said. Your friend, I mean. How it was totally implausible that the real killer just happened to come along right after I left. And was lucky enough to find Helen alone. It's all too much of a coincidence."

"Yes, I remember."

"And you got totally down in the dumps about it."

"Well, yes. I did."

"Typically, if you'll forgive my saying so."

"I'm sorry Don, but I don't see how you can dismiss it."

"I don't. That's the point. Thingummy's quite right."

"Go on."

"The real killer didn't just happen to come along. Think back to Carmen's Cornucopia. We're under the pavilion at SLO. The argument. Bert was raising his voice. So was Helen. Then she stood up and said something like, 'Get on your bike and ride off. I want my house to myself tonight.' Remember?"

"Yes."

"Well, someone heard. And saw his chance. Or hers."

"You're saying the killer was at the party."

"Yes. Sitting within earshot of us."

"Don, I can't remember who was sitting at the tables near us."

"No. It was pretty riveting, what was going on at our table. But there had to be somebody who hated Helen. He heard her say she was going home, and she was going to be alone. On the spur of the moment, he made up his mind to kill her.

"And here's the part that gives me the shivers. He was probably sitting on her street in his parked car, waiting for me to leave. He knew I'd be suspected."

It gave her the shivers, too. "Yes," she said. "Yes, I see. But Don, how does all this help you?"

He gave a low, rich chortle of happiness. "Because we have his name. The killer's name."

"We do? How?"

"On the guest list. There's a file on my computer at home called—"

"The police took your hard drive."

"Oh. Well, there's another copy on the system at work. Filename carmenscornucopia, no spaces."

"There were a lot of people there."

"All you have to do is find someone who hated Helen."

Renata nearly dropped the phone. "All *I* have to do?!"

"Yes. We didn't have assigned seating, unfortunately, which would have narrowed it down. But it's still doable."

"No, Don, listen to me. You have to hire a lawyer of your own who will do what you tell him, who has a competent professional investigator working for him—"

"Oh we're back to that again. As if nothing's happened. Have you even been listening to me?"

"I'm not doing any more investigating. I nearly got my head bashed in."

"I'm not asking you to follow a car into north St. Louis at night. Just go to my office. Identify the people who are connected to Helen. A lot of the information will be in my files. My secretary can help. The rest you can get on the internet. There's no danger at all."

Renata was distracted, wondering if Keith Bryson had been at the party. No, of course not. He would have caused a sensation. Meanwhile she had let the pause go on too long. Don was not a sensitive person, but he knew when he had made a sale. "You'll do this for me, won't you? And come see me, soon as you can. I'll be on tenterhooks."

Renata made promises and rang off. With a sigh, she stowed her phone and got up. A moment ago she had been wishing for something to do, and here it was. She climbed the steps and went through the doors into the noontime heat. Halfway across the Emerson Electric Picnic Lawn, she saw Mike Joyce and Amy Song.

They were coming up the path from the parking lot. He had his suit coat slung over his shoulder. She was talking on her phone. She looked the picture of health, Renata thought, her black hair gleaming under the sun, her gait quick and springy. Mike saw her and put her out of her misery with a frowning headshake.

She walked toward them. Amy Song, who was having an intense conversation in Korean, walked past without seeing her. Mike greeted her with a rueful smile and a shrug.

"The doctor convinced her she can sing?" Renata asked.

"He said her vocal equipment is in tip-top shape. Since we left she's been talking to her wife in San Francisco, her mother in Seoul, and her manager in New York. And some other people. They're all encouraging her to be brave and get out there. Sorry, Renata."

"It's all right. At least I've still got Mercédès."

He put an arm around her shoulders. He was tall enough to do it comfortably. "Let me take you to lunch."

"Oh, Mike, you've a thousand things to do more important than cheer me up. Anyway I need to go see Don's secretary. Remind me … is it Barb or Karen?"

"Barb." Michael withdrew his arm and gave her a look. "Let's go to my office first."

Renata didn't know what that meant, but she followed him into the Peter J. Calvocoressi Administration Building. Hannah at the reception desk looked up. "Oh, Renata, there's someone waiting to see you. At the parking lot entrance. He says he's a fan."

"A fan?" Mike grinned at her.

"I'll have you know I'm approached by an appreciative opera-goer from time to time. Say, once every couple of years. Usually they're little old ladies."

"This is a young guy. And not bad looking," said Hannah.

"A reporter, obviously," said Renata. "Trying to get something indiscreet from me. Well, if he's going to be sneaky with me, I needn't be polite to him. Let him sit there till he decides to go away."

She and Mike went upstairs and into his office. He closed the door and offered her a chair. "Why do you want to speak to Barb?"

"Don just called from jail. He has an idea." As Renata explained it, she reflected that though it sounded far-fetched, Don's logic was sound. The killer's name might very well be on the guest list.

Mike was unimpressed. He listened somberly, then said, "I'm afraid Barb won't cooperate with you. Orders have come down from Congreve: you are not to be assisted in anything but singing."

"Bugger." Renata slumped in her chair. She didn't know why she was even surprised. "Well, maybe I can log in remotely. I know Don's username, and I can probably guess his password. He always uses kings of England."

"The passwords have been changed. I'm afraid you don't get it yet, Renata. With the media hot on this Don Giovanni thing and the season starting today, we're walking on eggs around here. You saw how nervous Phil is."

Renata nodded. But there was nothing to think about. She took a deep breath and straightened up. "Right. I'll go see Barb."

Mike narrowed his eyes, puzzled. "Renata, she won't give you that list. Her job is on the line."

"I don't expect her to. But I have to demand it. My brother in jail has asked me to do this for him, and I can't not do it. I'm afraid I shall have to make a scene. Shouting and accusing, effing and blinding. I'm sorry for Barb, but there it is."

"You do remember, a few hours ago Phil tried to ease you out."

"Yes. And in about fifteen minutes he'll sack me. Without hesitation. But that's the point, you see. When I tell Don what happened, he may finally be convinced that he's no longer part of the SLO family, and he'll hire a lawyer of his own, who will give you lot a great deal of trouble, which I'm afraid is what's going to be necessary to defend him properly."

"But Renata—"

She stood up. "I'm sorry about not being there tonight. I hope Iris can cover Mercédès."

"She'll be fine."

"Give her the good news. I'm glad someone is moving up today."

She turned and went out. She could feel Mike's gaze on her back, but he didn't speak. There was nothing more to say, really. She walked down the corridor and descended the stairs. Don's office was on the ground floor.

A man was sitting in one of the row of chairs next to the parking lot entrance. He was looking at her. He stood and walked toward her. He had thick, reddish-brown hair and gold-framed spectacles, and he was smiling. They met at the foot of the stairs.

He said, "Hello, Renata. My name is Peter Lombardo."

# 37

---

FUNNY HOW AS SOON AS he saw her left foot on the top step, he knew it was Renata.

The staircase was one of those minimalist jobs, just descending faux-marble slabs and a handrail on steel poles, affording Peter an excellent view: first the feet clad in flat-heeled sandals, then calves shapely and rather pale by St. Louis summertime standards, disappearing into a long flowing skirt of light-blue cotton. Next a deep-red blouse, the sleeves rolled below the elbows. Finally—my, she was tall—her head. He'd seen the thick black hair tumbling to her shoulders in her interview, but since then he had gotten used to her Cherubino wig. Her profile looked austere and purposeful. She was altogether rather forbidding, and when they met he did not put out his hand, and she did not smile.

"You're the one claiming to be my fan. But you're a reporter, aren't you?"

"Well … yes. But not in the bad sense," he answered carefully. He was trying not to stare at her black eye. He figured everybody else who had spoken to her today must have asked about it, so he wasn't going to. "I work at Adams U Medical PR. I was flack to the late Dr. Stromberg-Brand."

"Oh." In British, the word had two syllables, and sounded

very skeptical. "Well, what do you want with me? I'm afraid I'm rather busy."

"Of course you are. It's opening night tonight." He was hoping this would elicit a smile from her, but oddly it did not. He felt intimidated standing before her. For one thing, she was taller than he. Better plunge right in. "I heard you on television yesterday, saying you believed your brother was innocent. Well, I do, too."

Her brows drew together, furrowing her pale forehead. "Do you know Don?"

"No. But I have an idea who did kill Dr. Stromberg-Brand."

The blue eyes widened. She reached out and grasped his biceps. "Come sit down and talk to me, Mister Peter Lombardo."

They sat side by side in chairs under the big windows. Despite the chill of the air conditioning, he could feel the sun on his shoulders and the back of his head. Only now did Renata release her grip on him. "You're quite sure you're not a reporter? Trying to make me say something stupid?"

He handed her his Adams U identification. She bent her head to examine it. He noticed a shaved spot and staples at the back of her head. The sight disturbed him, but it was not the right moment to ask questions.

"Is the person you suspect at the medical school?"

"In the same department as Stromberg-Brand. His name is Ransome Chase. Six years ago, she beat him out for a named professorship."

"Do people at the med school kill for that sort of thing?"

"It isn't just prestige. A named professorship gives you an income separate from the department budget. So you aren't dependent on your department chair. It can make the difference between success and failure in reaching your research goal."

"And did it in this case?"

"Well, Stromberg-Brand you know about. Chase has been researching Chagas Disease. He hasn't published any world-shaking results."

"Chagas Disease? I've never heard of it."

"A parasite-born infection. We don't have it here. In equatorial countries it kills tens of thousands every year."

"And you think he killed Helen out of sour grapes?"

"There was a postdoc in Helen's lab named Patel. She filed a sexual harassment complaint against him at the worst possible time."

"You think Helen put her up to it?"

"Yes."

"Does Chase know that? Because if he didn't, he'd blame this Patel person, not Helen, wouldn't he?"

"I'm not sure. We'd have to ask Patel."

"What sort of person is Chase?"

"I have a picture." He reached in his coat pocket and handed over the head and shoulders photo he had downloaded last night of Ransome Chase, with his out-of-control beard and hair and oversize glasses.

Renata stared hard at it. "Oh my God. I've seen this man. Unless ... no, it's him. I'm sure. He was there."

"Where?"

"At Carmen's Cornucopia."

"What?"

"The donor party here, Saturday night. I didn't speak to him, but I saw him. I'm sure."

"It's a face you don't forget."

She let the hand holding the photo fall to her lap. For a moment she was silent, thinking. "This fits Don's theory. It couldn't be coincidence, that Helen's murderer just happened to come along right after he left her house. He said the murderer must have been at the party. Helen stood up and told her husband not to come home, that she wanted the house to herself. And the murderer heard."

"Someone who'd been waiting for years for the chance to kill Helen, and here it was. Yes, Chase fits the bill."

She slumped back, shaking her head. "But Peter, what am I

to do? If I take this to the police, they'll say it's not evidence. It's not even a motive, really, because we can't say for sure that Chase knew Helen had done the dirty to him with this Patel person."

"I have an appointment with Patel in," Peter glanced at his watch, "just under an hour."

"You made an appointment?"

"Under false pretences, of course."

"But you'd get in trouble, wouldn't you? No, I should do this on my own."

"I'm going with you," he said.

"Peter—"

He was really getting to like the way she said his name. *Pee-tah*. "My car's outside. Let's go. "

"Just a minute." Taking out her cellphone, she tapped in a text message. Waiting, he noticed her scent: not floral but a mild, sweet spice. Something like cardamom. "I'm notifying our production head that I'll be in the show tonight after all." She glanced up at him. "It's odd. I was on the way to attempt a bit of detective work that was going to cost me my job. Instead I'm going to cost you yours."

"Don't worry, they won't fire me for this," said Peter, though he was far from sure. It all depended on what sort of person Anisha Patel turned out to be. And, of course, on whether Ransome Chase had murdered Helen Stromberg-Brand.

# 38

—

IT WAS A GOOD THING that Peter Lombardo had volunteered
to come with her. On her own, she would never have found
Dr. Patel's lab.

"Granger Hospital, main floor," said a recorded voice as the
doors of the lift that had brought them up from the underground
garage opened. They stepped into a scene that reminded her
of Heathrow Airport at Christmastime. Here was something
to remember—something banal but important. Though her
life was unsatisfactory in many ways, she had her health. So
many did not. This vast lobby was packed, a cistern into which
people flowed from all directions, eddying, swirling, draining
down one corridor or another. It sounded like an airport, too:
the general roar of footfalls and talk, the announcements over
the PA, the curlew-like cheeps of people-moving electric carts,
the mysterious tones and chimes.

Peter set off and she followed him. She passed a young
man in shorts, with a bandaged face and stricken expression,
an old woman leaning on a walker and wincing with each
step, a mother holding a baby on one arm and a toddler by
the hand. They all shuffled along, eyes lifted to the overhead
signs: to radiology, to obstetrics, to oncology. It was the faces
that reminded her most of an airport, Renata thought: the

expressions of mingled boredom, hope, and anxiety. The sick, like travelers, were shorn of home and routine, aware that though their immediate fate was to walk down corridors and sit in waiting rooms, beyond this banality, they were on a journey. They did not know what would happen to them and whether or not they would return.

They took another lift and crossed a glass-enclosed footbridge over a street to a much quieter building. Its corridors were painted light green and smelled of chemicals.

"Welcome to the forefront of biomedical research."

"Rather a letdown."

"Well, most of the exciting stuff is going on at the molecular level."

She glanced sideways at this unlikely would-be savior. Peter had one of those flat, middle-American voices that told you nothing about his background. So far, all she knew was something he had let drop in the car, that he'd worked for a newspaper once and wished he still did. She could believe that. He reminded her of other print journalists she'd met. There was the usual naff turn-out: pinstripe shirt, plaid jacket, paisley tie, and baggy, wrinkled trousers. They looked like he'd slept in them, after swimming the Channel in them. He also had the occupational knack of putting a stranger at ease. In the car he had chatted pleasantly, as if he was happy to be with her, as if inviting strangers down to the medical center to investigate a murder was routine for him. He seemed to know a bit about opera, and about her.

They entered a lab. Two women in white coats and blue jeans were standing over a stainless-steel drum with a lot of dials on it. The taller one was almost Renata's height but very slim, with short black hair and dark-brown skin. This must be Anisha Patel. She was explaining the machine to the younger woman. She had the same sort of middle-American voice as Peter.

Glancing up, she said, "Peter from PR? Right on time. Let's go to my office." She didn't notice Renata behind him. They went into a small room and she stepped around a cluttered metal desk and turned to face them. Seeing Renata, she looked a question at Peter.

He said, "In fact, Dr. Patel, I'm not here to interview you about your latest NIH grant."

"So what is this about?"

"Your sexual harassment complaint against Dr. Chase."

Patel hesitated, caught between amusement and outrage.

"Let me get this straight. I called you yesterday, concerned that Chase might be quoted in Helen's obit, and your response was to go digging around in the past for the reason?"

"Yes. By the way, Doctor, if you thought there was any chance of Chase being quoted in the obit, you don't know how my department works."

"I wonder if you know how your department works, Peter from PR. Suppose I call your boss—what's his name, Roger? And tell him what you're trying to pull?"

"You'd be perfectly justified. But the quickest and most painless way to get rid of us is to answer our questions."

Patel's eyes met hers. "Who are you?"

"Renata Radleigh."

"Radleigh?"

"Yes. His sister."

"So you're trying to help him with his case. Dig up some old scandal to confuse the issues and make Helen look bad."

"No. I believe in my brother's innocence."

"Ah. I see. Well, I suppose if it was my brother, I would be making a fool of myself, too."

Patel shut her eyes and gave two vigorous shakes of her head. "This is amazing. I have to admit I'm curious. All right, Peter from PR. I'm not promising to answer all your questions. And I'm not promising I won't call Roger. But you can sit down. You too, Ms Radleigh."

They sat in metal chairs in front of the desk. Patel sat too and folded her hands on the desk in front of her. "Let me make this clear. The sexual harassment complaint was between Dr. Chase and me. Helen had nothing to do with it."

Peter smiled. "I like the way you stand up for your late boss, Dr. Patel. It shows real class. Which is consistent with what I've heard about you."

"Oh, you've been asking around? How gratifying."

"I'm kind of surprised that someone like you would file a complaint like that. The remarks you cited—"

"You've read the complaint? But it's supposed to be sealed. How—"

"Dr. Chase says you're irritable, you must be in purdah. Or he thinks you're tired, and he says you must have been through at least one hundred eighty-seven positions from the Kama Sutra with your boyfriend—"

"These are racist and sexist remarks under the faculty code. And I had witnesses."

"You could have let it go."

"I had a right to protect myself."

"Okay. Then why didn't you file the complaint right away?"

"I was hoping it would stop."

"It did stop, Dr. Patel. All the incidents you complained about were old. The most recent was eight months before you filed the complaint."

"There was no statute of limitations problem. I don't know what you're getting at."

"Just that you filed the complaint at the time Chase was under consideration for the Blix professorship."

"It was entirely relevant for the Dean's committee to consider."

"Okay. But the truth is, Chase stopped making these dumb jokes, and you were going to let the matter drop, until Helen talked you into filing a complaint. For her own purposes."

Renata was expecting an angry retort, but Patel's expression changed. She gazed at Peter in silence for a long moment. "Oh my God. You think Chase killed Helen. That's why you're here."

"Yep," said Peter. "What do you think?"

Another long moment of reflection, and she surfaced to say, "You're wrong. You've got to be wrong."

"You don't sound too sure."

"Chase is a madman. But murder—"

"He bears a grudge about losing the professorship."

"Helen got the professorship because she deserved it. Her research was looking so promising. And now, of course, it's paid off. Chase's was going nowhere. That's why he was always running off to do clinical in South America. He wanted to get out of his lab because nothing was happening there."

Peter nodded and waited. He was very good at silences that encouraged the other person to speak, Renata noted. Another trick of the reporter's trade.

"I kept telling her, you're a sure shot. You don't need this harassment thing."

"But she insisted."

"Helen was wonderful to me. Nobody could have had a better mentor. But there was this side to her … she pushed too hard. She said, 'If I lose the professorship, I don't want to look back and think I left something undone.'"

"You thought she was making a big mistake."

"I wouldn't say that Chase is popular around here. But his supporters love him. They're fanatically loyal. And his patients adore him. He's the crusty old-fashioned doc who shoots from the hip. And no matter how many times he shoots himself in the foot, there's always someone there to help him limp away."

"You weren't really threatened by his racist and sexist remarks. You've tolerated a lot worse."

"I have, as a matter of fact. You're a shrewd guy, Peter from PR. Chase actually liked me. In his Neanderthal brain, these jokes were just some kind of hazing ritual. He was treating me like one of the boys."

"And since the complaint—"

"He hates me. His feelings are as raw as they were six years ago. I always take the stairs in this building. Walk up seven flights. People think I'm a fitness nut, but the truth is I don't want to meet Chase in the elevator." She smiled ruefully. "It's one thing if you're Helen. Confident and strong like her. But for somebody like me, it's tough being hated."

"So Chase knew? That Helen put you up to filing the complaint, to knock him out of the professorship?"

"Oh yes. He knew. That I dropped the complaint as soon as Helen let me—that made it even worse, as far as he was concerned." She pushed back in her chair. "God, what a mess. How I wish you hadn't come here. It was horrible enough, Helen dying. And this … this *scandal*. People treating her death like a dirty joke. And now …." She looked at Renata. "Do you have any reason for thinking your brother didn't do it? I mean, aside from he's your brother and you love him?"

"Yes. He told me what happened between him and Helen in her house on Saturday night, and it sounded plausible to me."

"What did he say?"

"He said she was perfectly calm. She'd gotten over the scene with her husband. She told Don she wasn't going to let Bert demand the money back. If he delivered on his threat to go public, that was his problem. She was going to divorce him anyway. Don said he was out of the house in less than fifteen minutes. Well, from what I saw of Helen Stromberg-Brand, that sounds like her."

"Yes. It does sound like her." Patel sighed and shook her head. "Bert. What a piece of work he is. Do you think he'll be … going public, as you put it? Defaming Helen's memory any more than he has already?"

"I don't think so. But it was a narrow escape yesterday. He was planning on telling the media that the affair started earlier than people thought. That Don seduced her to make her give the money."

"What a disgusting mind he has. That can't be true, can it?"

Renata shrugged. "They were all three supposed to go to

Chicago about ten days ago to see *Carmen*. Bert dropped out, so Helen and Don went on their own."

"To Chicago?" Patel asked.

"Yes."

"What happened? Was Bert right?"

"I don't know," said Renata.

"Do you have an idea, Dr. Patel?" asked Peter.

"No idea at all. How would I?" She got to her feet, looking at her watch. "I have a lab meeting in fifteen minutes and that's nowhere near long enough to pull myself together. I will not snitch on you, Peter from PR, but I will not talk to you again. It will have to be the police."

"Fair enough," said Peter, also rising.

In the corridor, Renata started back the way they had come, toward the elevators. He caught her arm and pointed to the stair door. "It's just one flight."

"To where?"

"Dr. Chase's lab."

"Oh no."

"He shoots himself in the foot a lot, Patel said. Maybe we can take him by surprise and make him do that."

"But we can't talk to him. He ... he could be a murderer."

"I interviewed a few murderers, when I was on the paper. They were pretty much like anybody else."

# 39

—

SCHAEFER ENTERED THE EZLYON RECEPTION room. Jayson was sitting behind the desk. Bistouri was standing in front of it.

"Mr. Schaefer, meet Mr. Won't-Give-His-Name. He wants to see Keith Bryson, and that's about all I can tell you."

Bistouri looked Schaefer up and down and seemed to recognize him, but said nothing. Schaefer closed the door and leaned against it, folding his arms.

"Are you connected to the guy who came in this morning?" asked Jayson.

"Forget about him. I just sent him to test your set up. You'll be dealing with me from now on."

"You're not gonna have any better luck than he did, unless you tell us more than he did. So let's try again. Why do you want to see Keith?"

Bistouri said nothing.

"What's your name?"

Bistouri said nothing.

"Where are you from?"

Bistouri said, "Chicago."

Schaefer straightened up and let his arms fall to his sides. "Okay, Jayson. We're gonna need the room for a minute."

Jayson turned to look at him. "What?"

"Give us the room, please."

"The room you're talking about happens to be my office."

"Get the fuck out of here, now."

Jayson rose grudgingly and went out, slamming the door behind him.

Bistouri said, "The kid is very slick. He's got a switch under the desk that turns on a recorder. You probably want to turn it off now."

Schaefer went to the desk, opened a bottom drawer and reached in. There was a click as the recorder went off. He straightened up. "What have you got?"

"A video recording made between nine seventeen and ten oh four p.m. May twentieth, at apartment B-218, 1396 Kominsky Avenue, Chicago, Illinois. Picture and sound quality are very good."

Schaefer's face showed no reaction, but he was silent for a long time. Finally he said, "I'll need to see it, eventually. For the moment, how much do you want?"

"I want to see Bryson."

Schaefer shook his head. "You'll be dealing with me."

"Has to be Bryson."

"He's authorized me to handle this matter."

"Yeah, I know how authorized you are, Schaefer," Bistouri said. "You were the guy your boss took to Chicago. But I want Bryson."

The two men stared at each for a moment, unmoving. Then Schaefer said, "How can I reach you?"

Bistouri put a slip of paper bearing a telephone number on the desk and left without a word.

# 40

---

A S THEY APPROACHED DR. CHASE'S lab, a tall, heavy-set
man with a knapsack slung over one shoulder backed out
of the doorway, pulling the door closed behind him. Hearing
their footfalls, he turned. Renata had no difficulty recognizing
the man she had seen at Carmen's Cornucopia. His large glasses
were trifocals, and they seemed too heavy for his knobby nose.
The nose was about all she could see of his features; half his
face was covered, though not adorned, by his beard. It was the
patchy kind, sparse here, thick there, brown mixed with gray,
and badly in need of a trim. His blue jeans hung low under his
belly and his plaid sports shirt bared hairy, powerful forearms.

"Dr. Chase, may we have a word?" said Peter.

But Chase's gaze fastened on Renata. It was intent enough
to raise the butterflies in her stomach. Was this the man Reyes
had seen, the man who was not walking a dog? Was he the
murderer of Helen Stromberg-Brand?

"I've seen you on TV," he said. "You're the guy's girlfriend.
No, sister."

She nodded. She was too nervous to speak.

"Renata Radleigh, mezzo-soprano. Are you in this thing
tonight? How is it? My girlfriend is threatening to drag me."

Without waiting for a reply he shifted his gaze to Peter. "Who are you?"

"Peter Lombardo. We exchanged emails yesterday."

"Refresh me."

"About Dr. Stromberg-Brand's obit."

"Oh gawd. What did I say? No, never mind. What do you want today?"

"We'd like to talk to you for a few minutes."

"Haven't got 'em. I'm late for a meeting. You can ride down in the elevator with me if you want."

He set off down the corridor. They fell in on either side of him. It was like keeping pace with a bear. He had a hunched posture and a heavy, waddling gait. She wondered how much weight he had in his backpack.

"I'm sorry for your brother," he said to her.

She still could not find her voice, so Peter filled in for her. "Jail is tough on anybody."

"No, I mean having to sleep with Helen Stromberg-Brand. Gives me chills. He did it just for the money, I assume?"

"I don't know," Renata said. Such was the force of Chase's personality that he was towing them along, making them answer questions rather than allowing them to ask any.

Peter must have felt it too, because he decided to assert himself. "We've just been speaking to Dr. Patel."

"Oh gawd. Don't get me started." They had reached the bank of elevators. Chase pressed the call button, then looked from one of them to the other. "Say, what's going on here? You're trying to dig up dirt on Stromberg-Brand to drum up some sympathy for your brother. That's obvious."

He turned to Peter. "But why are you helping her? You're from PR. One of the dessert chefs. Forever circling the great big angel food cake that is Adams U Med, looking for another ass-kissing doc to squirt a little icing on."

He leaned confidentially toward Renata, "You must have

used your wiles to get this guy on your side. Doesn't he know he's toast?"

"I know," said Peter.

"Not that I'll rat you out. But they'll find out. They always do."

"In that case I might as well get some answers in exchange for my job. Was Patel's complaint justified?"

Chase gave a bark of laughter. "Let me make one thing clear. I never laid a finger on Patel."

"She didn't say you had."

Chase appeared not to hear. "It was strictly verbal harassment. That's the thing bothered me most about this whole mess. That some people got the idea I was hot for scrawny little Patel." The doors slid open. Two young Asians in lab coats were standing there, holding a caged white rabbit. There was a small bloodstain behind its ear. Chase took no notice of them as he got in. He pressed a button and leaned against the wall. "And what was the harassment? A few mild jokes about her Indian origins. Not that Patel even had much to do with India. You thought she clawed her way up from the slums of Bombay, or whatever they call it now? She was born in Houston. Her father's a cardiologist."

"Do you think Stromberg-Brand put her up to it?"

"Sure. But you'll never be able to prove that. The young girl network in this place is even tighter than the old boy network was. I know, 'cause I've had 'em both against me."

"Did it cost you the professorship?"

Chase put a thumb in a belt loop and hitched his jeans up the downslope of his belly. "Put it this way. There were a lot of people on my side. But they were just the rank and file. The people who think our job is to heal the sick. The big shots wanted Stromberg-Brand. Patel gave 'em the excuse they needed."

He raised his voice. "Want to know how you get to be a name professor in this place? It's simple enough. You kids listening?"

The two young scientists smiled nervously and looked at the floor.

"You bring in grant money. Lots of it. That's what keeps the wheels turning around here. So the committee weighed up my grant-earning potential against Helen's. They said, well now, Chase, if he finds the cure, it may save thousands of lives. Unfortunately, these are all brown or black people, in poor countries. The pharmas develop a drug for them, and what'll be their reward? These countries will start demanding they give it away for free. Now, Helen, if she finds her UTI vaccine, well, it won't prevent any deaths, but it will make millions of comfortable lives even more comfortable. The customers will be American and European and Oriental women. With health insurance. Helen was bound to bring in more grant money than me."

The elevator doors opened. They stepped out into a small, bare lobby. The young scientists were exchanging sidelong glances as the doors closed.

"So the committee made their decision," Chase went on. "I can live with it. A lot of people in Latin American couldn't."

"Aw, come on, Dr. Chase. You're saying you would have cured Chagas Disease?" Peter was taking obvious pleasure in waving the red flag at the bull.

"The stars were aligned. If I'd gotten the Blix chair, I could have afforded to hire a couple of particularly brilliant postdocs from Penn. One of them had studied under Lehrer at Ohio State, and he would have agreed to collaborate with me. Lehrer's in tight with the Brent Foundation and we'd have gotten a grant from them. Yes, by now we would have cured Chagas."

Chase crossed the lobby. He paused with his hand on the door. "But so what? I gotta admit, Stromberg-Brand delivered the goods."

"You're impressed with the vaccine she developed?" Peter asked.

"No, I'm impressed she snagged Keith Bryson as her venture capitalist. Running triathlons. Racing yachts. Screwing movie stars. The world thinks everything that guy does is cool. Now he's going to make investing in Adams U Med startups cool, too."

Chase had more to say on the topic, but he looked over Renata's shoulder and changed his mind. A shuttle bus was pulling up at the curb.

"Got to catch that." Before either of them could say anything, he was through the doors, pulling out his cellphone as he ran for the bus, his knapsack bouncing on his back.

They looked at each other in silence. It took a moment to calm down, after Ransome Chase left you. She felt short of breath, her heart was pounding, and her fists were clenched. The very air of the small lobby seemed to be sloshing around, like the water in a pool after someone has dived into it. Chase was one of those self-righteous people who had the ability to infect you with their indignation.

# 41

—

"WHAT NEXT?" RENATA ASKED.

They were sitting on a bench in the shade, on the edge of the Emerson Electric Picnic Lawn at SLO. It was only mid-afternoon, but already preparations were beginning for opening night: people were setting up tables and chairs on the lawn. Caterers' trucks were unloading next to the pavilion. Gardeners were kneeling and snipping in the flowerbeds.

Peter replied, "We go to the cops and tell 'em we think Ransome Chase killed Helen Stromberg-Brand. We give 'em what we have and tell 'em to take it from here. That detective you mentioned—"

"McCutcheon. A hard man to impress."

"He can laugh in our faces if he wants. But he has to file a report. And after that we keep the pressure on."

Renata smiled. "I love it when you say 'we,' Peter. But there's a problem."

"You don't believe Chase did it."

"The things he said to us today. Surely he wouldn't talk like that if he were guilty."

"Problem is, Chase has always talked like that. He's famous for it around the medical center. Maybe he figures, if he suddenly stopped slamming Helen Stromberg-Brand, it would be even more suspicious."

"You're convinced, aren't you?"

"I had my doubts, until I met him. Now I'm convinced. Where there's smoke there's fire."

"But … Peter, did you notice what Patel said about Chicago, right at the end of our talk?"

"You mean when she asked if Don slept with Helen that weekend?"

"She didn't ask that. She asked what happened in *Chicago*."

Peter's hazel eyes narrowed behind his gold-rimmed spectacles. "I'm confused."

"It keeps nagging at me, what happened here yesterday. Bert Stromberg-Brand was threatening the SLO bigwigs. He was going to tell the media what happened in Chicago. And right then Keith Bryson popped up, and they all went into a confab, and nobody mentioned Chicago again."

"Bryson didn't just happen to pop up," Peter said. "My boss Roger went over to his condo Sunday night and convinced him that as Helen's partner he should go to her defense. And he obviously convinced Bert to stop talking about your brother seducing Helen in Chicago."

"I'm not sure Don did that. Anyway I think something more important happened in Chicago." She thought for a moment. "So Bryson was in St. Louis on Sunday? I'd very much like to know if he was here on Saturday, too."

"Wait … you suspect *Bryson* killed Helen?"

She shook her head and winced. "I can't even get that far. I have no evidence. Not even a theory. I just can't help thinking, on one side of Helen Stromberg-Brand's life, you have an opera. An envious husband. A bit of money, a bit of sex. And that's the side everyone is paying attention to. But on the other side, you have her partner, a rich and powerful and famous man, and a vaccine that's going to change millions of people's lives and earn a vast fortune. I have this feeling everyone's barking up the wrong tree."

"Have you done anything about this feeling?"

She laughed. "Nothing effective."

"Except get yourself that shiner?"

"Aren't you the clever one? Yes, all right." She explained her misadventure of the night before. Peter listened gravely. He said, "Renata, please don't do anything like that again."

"Not to worry. I won't."

"This character, he may only have been spooked that you were following him. He probably had nothing to do with the vaccine or the murder."

"Yes, yes. Some crazed celebrity stalker or reckless paparazzo. Don explained it all to me. But I'm not convinced. I think this tattooed man is terribly important. Maybe it's just because I'm the one he hit. But I have the feeling something is going on. Something is in play. And if I could find out what, I could help Don."

Renata broke off, because she had suddenly remembered Archibald Henderson. He could have told her where he had found her purse. And if she hadn't been so busy being annoyed with him, she would have realized how important that could be.

"Peter, I've been thick as a plank."

"What?"

She had her cellphone out and was scrolling through stored numbers. "This man rang to say he'd found my purse. But he wanted too big a reward, and I told him to get stuffed. What time is it?"

"Almost three."

"He gave me till five to reconsider. Let's hope he's as good as his word." Archibald Henderson was presumably not behind the wheel of his truck, because he answered at once. "Well, hello, Ms Radleigh. You changed your mind?"

"Yes. Sorry I got shirty with you."

" 'Shirty?' That's what y'all call it, on your side of the pond?"

"In the mother country, yes. In fact, Mr. Henderson, I'm more interested in where you found the purse than in getting it back. You said it was quite a story."

"Yes, and I'll be happy to tell you, as soon as you pay me the hundred dollars."

"But I just want the story, not the purse."

"You just told me the story is worth more to you than the purse. In fact, it seems to me I've ... 'got you by the short and curlies.' " He chuckled happily.

"Oh ... all right. I'll send you a check. Now where did you find the purse?"

The syrupy drawl turned rueful. "Ma'am, I hope you won't put me to the embarrassment of explaining why that's an unsatisfactory arrangement."

"You sod!"

He chuckled. "I love it when Doc Martin says that."

Peter took the phone away from her. "Mr. Henderson, I'm a friend of Renata's, and I think we can work this out."

Renata rose and walked around the bench, trying to calm down. She did not attempt to follow the negotiations, which involved PayPal. On the fifth go-round, Peter handed her the phone with a nod. She sat down.

Henderson explained that his first delivery of the day had been in Ladue.

"A pair of fine wing-back chairs to a Mrs. Weiss on Picardy Lane. I've handed her the papers and I'm bringing in the chairs when her son, five or six, sharp as a tack, comes running downstairs. Says he looked out the window and saw a woman's purse on top of my truck."

Renata whispered to Peter. "It was on top of his truck."

Peter nodded.

"You mean that makes some sort of sense to you?" she said.

"Can I talk?"

"He's explaining how he retrieved the purse. At length."

"Okay," he said. "It's a way skells get rid of things. Like a gun that's been used in a crime, say. The hope is that it won't fall off until the truck is on an interstate hundreds of miles away."

"Oh. Well, my purse did get far enough, didn't it? This is no use to us."

"Ask him where he spent last night."

She did, and he gave her the name of a motel across from the airport. Then he said he would send her purse to SLO and waive the shipping and handling charge. She gave him a last thrill by saying "Ta."

Putting away the phone, she said, "You think that when the tattooed man finished with my purse, he just chucked it on top of the nearest truck. He was staying at the same motel. He could still be there. Peter, that's brilliant."

"It's a remote possibility at best."

Renata nodded. "I understand. I won't ask you to waste any more of your time on my desperate schemes. Thank you for helping me. Do you have a business card? I'll send you a check for a hundred dollars later today."

Peter locked eyes with her. "You're going to look for the man who almost bashed your head in last night. You are not going alone."

"You want to come? Fine. I hope you weren't expecting an argument."

# 42

———

ONCE THEY WERE ON THE highway to the airport, she swallowed hard and broke the silence. "Peter, I have something to say, sort of a confession to make. Please don't put me out by the side of the road."

"Okay."

"I've already been so difficult, I know. Out of sheer kindness you came to me with your idea, and I've dismissed it. Men don't like that sort of thing, I've noticed."

"I still say Chase is the guy. He did it. But you said you have to be back at the theater by six, so we're only going to waste a couple of hours. I figure what we'll do is drive around the motel's lot and see if we can spot the car. What's the year, make and model?"

"That's just it. I've no idea."

He glanced over at her. "But this was the car you were following last night. You must have gotten a good look at it."

"Yes. But I know nothing about cars. I've never owned one. When I rent one, I forget what it looks like. I have to walk up and down the street, pressing on the key fob till some car beeps and blinks its lights."

"Okay. Tell me everything you *do* remember."

"It was light gray or tan—I couldn't tell which at night.

Medium-sized, bigger than your car. Rather boxy silhouette." She struggled to improve on that. "Four doors. And it wasn't an estate, it had a boot."

"Translation?"

"You're taking the piss, aren't you?"

"I try not to in the car."

"I mean you're making fun of me. Archibald Henderson knew all these expressions. Don't you watch *Doc Martin*?"

"Okay, a boot is a trunk, right? But what's an estate?"

"A station wagon."

"We're narrowing it down. It was a sedan. What was the shape of the grille? How many headlights?"

"It was ahead of me. I didn't see the front."

"Okay. What was the closest look you got at it?"

"When I got hit, I was bending down to read the license plate."

"Did you get any numbers?"

"No. Oh, this is hopeless, isn't it?"

"Close your eyes. You're standing at the back of the car, looking at the trunk lid. Was there anything on it?"

"Like what?"

"Like the letters F-O-R-D, for instance."

"No letters." She squeezed her eyes tightly shut, which seemed to help her memory somehow. "There was a symbol. Emblem. Whatever you call them."

"A shield, maybe? Or a cross?"

"No. It didn't look like anything, really. Just a couple of lines."

With one hand on the wheel, he dug notebook and pen from his jacket pocket. She drew two curving, intersecting lines. Peter glanced at it and said, "Saturn."

"Oh. So this is supposed to be the planet Saturn?"

"Yes. They don't make them anymore."

"You mean they're rare?"

"Not as rare as we would like them to be."

The motel, across the highway from the airport, turned

out to be a sprawling four-story complex with a vast parking lot. They drove slowly up and down seemingly endless rows of cars, their chromework glinting under the afternoon sun. Jets thundered over from time to time, low enough to cast enormous shadows. The smell of aviation fuel was making Renata woozy. They found a tan Saturn sedan, but it had a bumper sticker that said, "I'm only speeding 'cause I have to pee!" and Renata said she would have remembered that.

They pursued their slow, zigzag course, drawing ever closer to the building. Renata kept glancing at the long rows of doors, expecting one of them to open and that tattooed man to step out. She was getting very nervous and had to keep reminding herself that she was in the car with Peter beside her.

Finally they reached the building. They had only to drive slowly around it, surveying the cars of the lucky guests who had been able to park in front of their rooms, and they would be done with this fool's errand. At least she would make it back to the theater on time. She was looking at her watch when Peter abruptly stopped the car.

"How about this one?"

She leaned forward for a better look at the car on their left. It was a dull, faded silver. It had the Saturn emblem. The license plate was from Illinois.

"Oh lord, Peter. This is it."

"You really think so?"

"The back of my head is throbbing. What are we going to do now? Knock on the door?"

"Hell no. Call the cops."

They found a space across the lot and while Renata watched the Saturn Peter called 911. Less than ten minutes later a patrol car pulled up beside them and a lean young black man got out, placing his uniform cap on his gleaming shaved head. His name plate said J. Thursby. With a face as impassive as Detective McCutcheon's had ever been, he listened to her story. She told him the truth, or part of it anyway, how she had been mugged, and her purse had been found, leading them to this motel, where she recognized the car.

She expected a lot of awkward questions about that last part, but Officer Thursby was a man of decision. He said, "Let's go see if you can ID the guy," and set off across the lot.

Renata decided to make the identification over Thursby's shoulder. She fell in behind him with Peter beside her. Her stomach seemed to bounce painfully around with each stride.

Thursby gave a resounding knock that would have done credit to the Commendatore's ghost in *Don Giovanni*. A voice inside said, "What?"

"Police."

The door was opened by a middle-aged man with a gray moustache. He was wearing a white undershirt, and his bare arms were well-furnished with hair but devoid of ink. A folded newspaper was in his hand. He took off his reading glasses and looked at them blankly.

Renata's heart sank. "It's not him. Sorry." She wasn't sure who she was apologizing to. All three of them, probably.

She was ready to turn away but Officer Thursby was maddeningly thorough. He verified that the man owned the Saturn and asked for identification. The man produced it: he was Louis J. Bistouri of Chicago, Illinois. He was traveling alone and had not lent his car to anyone.

At length they left the poor man in peace, but the diligent Thursby kept her and Peter for another ten minutes, verifying details for his report. Renata kept glancing at her watch. She was going to be late to sign in at the theater, for the first time in her career. And all for nothing.

# 43

—

Shane was lying in the bed in his room, watching television. It was a SpongeBob SquarePants rerun, and he was giggling feebly at it. He ignored the knock on his door, responding only when Bistouri shouted, "Open up."

Shane did and Bistouri strode past him, glowering at the messy room. He faced Shane, who could barely keep his eyes open. "So you're having a little party? Just you and your pharmaceutical pals?"

Shane sank down on the bed. "You got a better idea?"

"Yeah. Get dressed. I'm taking you to the airport and you're catching the first flight to Chicago."

"What are you talking about? We haven't seen Bryson yet."

"I am seeing Bryson tonight. It's all set. And I want you far away, where you can't fuck things up anymore."

Shane wiggled his head as if mosquitoes where whining around him. He shut his eyes. "I still don't know what you're talking about."

"You didn't do what I told you to do last night. With the purse."

Shane turned his attention to the television set. Bistouri picked up the remote from the bed and switched it off. "They were here ten minutes ago. The Radleigh woman, some guy, and a cop."

This brought Shane's head up. He squinted at Bistouri. "You got rid of 'em?"

Bistouri nodded. "Luckily for us, I know how to keep my head. What did you do with the purse, asshole?"

Shane got up and went into the bathroom. He plugged the basin and filled it with cold water. Then he plunged his head into it. When he returned to confront Bistouri, water was dripping from his brows and chin, but his eyes were wide and alert.

"Listen, Bistouri. I've had enough of your fucking Obi-Wan Kenobi routine."

"What?"

"Like you're the Jedi Master of the shakedown and I got to do everything you say or I'm out."

"They would be putting you in the backseat of a cop car right now if I hadn't—"

"I don't want to hear any more of that shit. I want to know what you're up to."

Bistouri's face went blank. He said nothing.

"You got something going on that you're not telling me about. That's why you don't want me there when you meet Bryson."

"I don't want you there 'cause we can't afford any more fuck-ups."

"No. What's the real reason? I brought you into this thing. And you took over. What's your game?"

"I'm seeing Bryson, and you're gonna be rich. Leave the details to me."

Shane shook his head. He went to the window and pushed aside the edge of the curtain. "I can see your car from here. You're not going anywhere without me."

Bistouri opened his mouth, then thought better of it. He turned and left the room.

# 44

—

A GLOOMY SILENCE REIGNED IN Peter's car on the way back to SLO. It was not until they left the highway that Renata said, "What a balls-up."

"Now there's a British expression I know." He shrugged. "It was a long shot. There are a lot of gray Saturns."

"Or possibly tan. We didn't even establish that for sure."

"I guess your brother's really counting on you? The pressure must be hard to take."

"Counting on me? No, I wouldn't say that. We've never been close, and this hasn't brought us together. We had a row this morning. I went to visit him in prison, comfort him, and we ended up fighting. People keep saying to me, 'Of course you think he's innocent, he's your brother and you love him,' and I want to say, 'You can't fob me off that easily, I *don't* love him. I don't even *like* him. If he was guilty, I'd be happy to see the back of him.' But that's it, you see, I can say quite objectively, he could never have killed Helen Stromberg-Brand. There, now you know what a horrid person I am."

She stopped because she was out of breath. Too much talking. Why was she telling Peter all this? She was appalled to realize that a sob was blocking her throat and tears were prickling her eyes.

Peter glanced over at her. "Hey, look. You couldn't be doing any more for the guy if you loved him to bits. So stop feeling guilty."

Renata swallowed hard. She straightened up and squared her shoulders. They were nearing the SLO complex. "Can you take me round to the rehearsal hall? I'm late."

"Just tell me where to turn." He hesitated a moment. "I'd like to stay."

"You mean you want to see the opera? Well ... I'm not important enough to merit house seats. I'll call the box office and see what's left."

"Thanks. Any seat will do."

"I'm afraid it's rather an odd production. Like no *Carmen* you've ever seen."

"I've never seen it. In fact I've never been to the opera."

"Oh ... you mean you want to see *me*?"

"Yes. I want to see you."

"But I'm only Mercédès. Blink and you'll miss me."

"I don't think I will."

HALF AN HOUR TO CURTAIN, and final preparations were proceeding smoothly. Renata was waiting in line for her turn at the makeup tables. She was wearing her costume and carrying a Styrofoam head with her wig on it. The costume was a red poodle skirt with violently clashing purple top, fishnet stockings, and high heels. The wig was blond, a stiff 1950s pageboy. Renata assumed that the director and designer must have explained to someone why this was an appropriate outfit for Mercédès, but she hadn't been included in the discussion.

Closing her ears to the excited chatter going on around her, she was concentrating on her role, summoning up every carefully prepared gesture. She had arrived at warm-ups ten minutes late, which was unheard of for her. Even worse, the stage manager had given her not a reproving glare but a melting, sympathetic look. Renata didn't think she was entitled to any special consideration. She was going to play Mercédès with full concentration tonight.

But it was hard to shut her mind to thoughts of the afternoon's events. Poor Peter Lombardo. She was certain Chase was going to grass on him. That would make for a difficult day at the office for Peter. She hoped he didn't lose his job on her account.

Only professionalism stood between her and an utterly degrading feminine flutter about Peter. He was dead dishy, for one, with his greenish-brown eyes and reddish-brown hair. He had all the qualities she liked in journalists: a well-stocked brain, keen ear for nonsense, unassuming, humorous manner.

It was a nice change, a real breath of fresh air, to meet someone who did *no*t think she was delusional. Pathetic. Irritating. In fact, she had given Peter good reason to lose his temper with her, and he hadn't. Aside from sympathizing with her predicament, he seemed to like her a bit.

Maybe more than a bit. There'd been that moment in the car on the way back. Ever since he'd instructed her to stop feeling guilty about Don, she had felt better. It was his stern tone that had made the difference. He talked to her the way she talked to herself. But he had kinder things to say.

A place opened up at one of the long tables and a makeup tech beckoned her. As she sat down, she noted that she was back to back with Amy Song. who was sitting at her own small table, attended by three technicians. Glancing in the mirror, Renata noticed that the Endeavor Rent-a-Car Endowed Artist was wearing breast makeup to create the impression of more ample swell and deeper cleft—an expedient Renata had never found it necessary to adopt.

The technician stood behind her, hands on hips, looking at her reflection in the facing mirror. "I'll have to get something special to cover that bruise," she said, and turned away.

Ray the irascible super was sitting beside her. He was wearing the khaki uniform of a security guard at a maquiladora, which had replaced a cigar factory as the setting for the first act. As a brutal hireling of American corporate imperialism, he was equipped with a large pistol, and a nightstick dangled from his belt. With his lined, ruddy face and short gray hair, he did look rather scary, and Renata complimented him on suiting the part. He offered a palm full of Hershey's kisses.

"No, thank you."

"A gift from the Commie, to all the supers."

"Oh, yes, directors do tend to realize on opening night that the show is in our hands now. They start to feel a bit guilty about being so beastly to us in rehearsals."

"I suppose he'll be taking a curtain call hand in hand with us, all smiles?"

"I don't know about the smiles," she said. "In Europe audiences have been known to boo von Schussnigg. Even throw things at him."

"Thanks, Renata. You've given me something to hope for."

Her technician wasn't back yet, and she had a question she'd been meaning to ask Ray. Since the fiasco at the motel, Peter's ideas about Chase were beginning to seem more plausible to her. "Do you remember at the party on Saturday night, when you were carrying the drinks tray, and I came up to you with Bert Stromberg-Brand—"

"I don't remember."

"Well, never mind about him. I wanted to ask about the man you were talking to."

"I said, I don't remember."

"A big man with a beard. His name is Doctor Ransome Chase. Do you know him?"

"No."

Ray's makeup was finished and he was eager to go. She reminded herself that he was easy to annoy and this was not the moment to do so, but she couldn't let it go. "Please try to remember. It seemed to me you and he were having a conversation when I came up."

"Maybe. Warmth of the evening. Cheapness of the white

wine. But I don't know the guy." She looked at his face in the mirror in front of them. What a short fuse the man had. He looked like he wanted to draw his prop nightstick and break it over her head. "This is about your brother again, isn't it? What does Dr. Chase have to do with that?"

"He's in the same department as Helen Stromberg-Brand, and it seems he bears a grudge—"

"So you're gonna try to make his life miserable. What right do you have to do that? *Christ*, Renata."

"Sorry I brought it up. Forget it. We've a show to do. Break a leg, as they say."

Ray stood and adjusted his gun belt. "Break a leg, Renata."

# 45

—

A QUARTER HOUR TO CURTAIN. Peter, who had paid for his ticket already and was in no hurry, stood watching the people at the tables packing up the remains of their picnics. New arrivals were coming up the path from the parking lot.

Being the approachable sort, Peter was always falling into conversation with strangers. In the line for the caterer's truck, he had starting talking to two elderly sisters from Bloomington, Indiana who seemed to know everything about opera. Sharing a table, they told him they were excited about seeing the rising star Amy Song. They'd seen *Carmen* countless times, but they knew Bernhard von Schussnigg would present a startling personal vision.

Now the sisters had gone to find their seats and Peter was leaning against a tree, thinking about Renata. Considering opera was her vocation, he probably shouldn't have told her that he'd never seen one. Especially since he had earlier scored some points with her by working that "britches, bitches and witches" line into the conversation. And maybe his advice to her in the car had been too personal. The British didn't like that. But it upset him when she started to cry over her brother. It was obvious to Peter, as to practically everybody in St. Louis County, that Don Radleigh was a jerk of the first water. Not that he deserved to go to prison for a crime he had not committed.

As much as Renata had tried to lower his expectations, he couldn't wait to see her on stage. He kept thinking about how different she was in real life than on screen. As Cherubino, she had a straight-ahead, heavy-footed male walk, but her real gait was light, swaying, feminine. Proclaiming her brother innocent on the TV news, she'd sounded like Queen Elizabeth II, but her informal voice was rather nasal. Neither speaking voice hinted at the beauty of her singing voice. He was also wondering when she played a guy, what did she do with her bosom? In propria persona, she had an awesome rack.

Peter straightened up, narrowing his eyes. Among the people filing down the path from the parking lot was Ransome Chase. He remembered that Chase had said this afternoon that he might be at *Carmen* tonight. If his girlfriend could drag him, was the way he'd put it. That must be the girlfriend beside him, a dandelion of a woman, tall and skinny with an aureole of frizzy gray hair. She looked about ten years younger than Chase. They were talking animatedly, but it didn't stop Chase from spotting him. The great hairy head turned his way, and the eyes behind the goggle-like glasses widened. Chase said something to the woman and headed his way. She captured his arm and spoke vehemently in his ear. But he shook her off and closed on Peter, arms swinging in arcs around his bulky torso, madras jacket flapping.

Back in Springfield, Peter had been confronted several times by people he had written unflattering articles about. That had been rather enjoyable. But he kept seeing Chase smashing a crystal bowl over Stromberg-Brand's head. While his mind stayed calm, his heart beat faster.

Chase started talking—shouting, really—from five paces away. "My girlfriend doesn't want me to talk to you. She says I was a fool to talk to you the first time. I should've done the cover-your-ass bureaucratic thing. Told you and the sister that I had no comment on my esteemed colleague Dr. Stromberg-Brand."

"I doubt you told us anything you haven't told a hundred other people, Dr. Chase."

By now Chase was looming over Peter. He smelled sweaty. "She also said I should've reported you to your boss. And that's an error I can still correct—if you don't give me some answers right now."

"Skip the threats. What do you want to know?"

"My girlfriend says I jumped to the wrong conclusion this afternoon. That you weren't just digging up dirt on Stromberg-Brand. Your plan is to distract the cops from her brother by giving them another suspect."

"No, it's simpler than that. I think you killed Helen Stromberg-Brand."

Chase fell back a step. He was breathing hard. As Peter himself was. They glared at each other in silence. Then Chase moved in again, raising his right fist, which made Peter flinch. But it was only to shake a stubby forefinger in his face.

"Who the *fuck* do you think you are? I have a complicated life. I have a lot of enemies. And I do not need somebody like you, with no standing whatever, trying to make trouble for me. Drop this now, or I will come back at you *hard.*"

He turned away.

Peter said, "You forgot something."

Chase turned back.

"The denial."

"You're not entitled to one, you little shit."

He stalked back to his girlfriend, who was clutching her purse before her with both hands and looking skyward. She was probably used to having her good advice ignored. Peter glanced around. Some people were studiously avoiding his eye; they must have overheard. He found that his fists were clenched and opened them.

# 46

—

THE ODDLY NAMED ST. CHARLES Rock Road, a broad but not busy street, passed through a run-down area in near-north St. Louis County. Bistouri's Saturn turned off it, onto a narrow track, and bounced over broken pavement into a stand of ailanthus trees and tall weeds. In just a few yards, the track came to an end next to a derelict shack with boarded-up windows and a collapsed roof.

"This is where we're gonna meet," Bistouri said to Shane. "But not yet. Don't get out."

He reversed back onto the road, then drove over a viaduct and turned into a large, empty parking lot. He crossed it and stopped next to the platform of a MetroLink station.

Without turning to Shane, he said, "Here's where you get off."

"What?"

"You're gonna wait here."

"No. That's not what we agreed."

"I said you could come along. This is as close as you get."

Shane made no move to get out of the car.

"This is a comfortable place to sit. And it won't be long. I'll pick you up as soon as the meeting's over. Now get out."

Shane did not take this turn of events well. He screamed

and cursed, spraying spittle in Bistouri's face. He pounded the window and kicked the dashboard until the car swayed on its springs. The tantrum went on for a good three and a half minutes, but Bistouri did not move or speak or show a flicker of reaction.

Finally Shane gave up and opened the door. He said, "Remember, I have the disk. You can't close the deal without me."

"I never forgot."

Shane got out and slammed the door.

# 47

—

THE CHARLES MACNAMARA III AUDITORIUM was full. The crowd was chatty and excited, but as the ushers stepped out and closed the doors behind them and the lights went down, an expectant hush fell. Peter, from his seat in the very back row, had not been able to spot Ransome Chase.

The house was in darkness for a moment, then a spotlight shone on the Ruth Baxter Irwin Mainstage and a man in a tuxedo stepped into it. The audience recognized him and applauded as he bowed and beamed. He had silver hair and a veritable cliff of forehead that would have made him handsome but for the dewlaps hanging over his black satin bow tie.

He welcomed the audience to the beginning of the Fidelity Investments Season of the Saint Louis Opera. Without saying anything specific about the murder and fundraising scandal, he thanked the audience for their loyalty, which brought more applause. Then he said that Endeavor Rent-a-Car Endowed Artist Amy Song was suffering from allergic inflammation (moans and grumbles) but had bravely decided to sing anyway (enthusiastic applause) and begged the audience's indulgence if her voice was not in tip-top shape (even louder applause). After plugging some more sponsors, he stepped down.

The Amy Song announcement struck Peter as distinctly bush

league. Maybe making pre-emptive excuses was acceptable in the opera world, but he was willing to bet that Renata had never done so.

He had already thought of warning her that Chase was in the audience, but he had no way of contacting her. Anyway, what would be the point? It would only distract her.

A recording asked everyone to silence their electronic devices. A scattering of tiny, bright screens appeared in the darkness as the audience obeyed. The conductor mounted the podium and was illuminated and applauded. He turned to the orchestra and raised his arms. The overture began and Peter recognized a few tunes. Maybe the performance wouldn't be too dull.

The Ruth Baxter Irwin Mainstage being a platform jutting out into the audience, there was no curtain. The lights just came on, very brightly, to show a grimy concrete factory wall with Hazmat decals and *peligroso* signs on it. The operatic sisters had told him that Carmen took place in Seville, but this didn't look much like it. Oversize video screens showed American tourists out of a '50s cartoon, fat people in shorts with straw hats on their heads and cameras around their necks, walking down a street kicking beggars out of the way. Other screens showed downtrodden women laboring on an assembly line. The sisters had said Carmen rolled cigars on her bare thighs. A bunch of guys in khaki uniforms with nightsticks swinging from their belts and "Ace Security" printed on their backs marched out. This was the Spanish army? They were singing in French. Then they stopped, and started talking in English. Peter was bemused.

A lot of light spilled into the auditorium from the thrust stage, and he saw a large man in the third row get to his feet and make his way down the row and over the feet of other spectators. When he reached the aisle and turned, Peter recognized Ransome Chase. Watching him go up the aisle and out the door, Peter wondered what to do. He hadn't a clue where Renata was, and he didn't like the idea of Chase prowling around the building. He rose and stumbled over knees and feet, muttering apologies.

The Emmanuel Gerwitz Lobby was quiet. The bartenders were checking their stock and the souvenir shop ladies were leaning on the counter and chatting. Chase was nowhere to be seen. Peter's heart was pounding, though he couldn't have said what he was afraid of. Pulling open a door at random, he found himself in a dim stairwell. He heard a voice and descended.

The familiar head of unruly hair came into view round an angle of the stairs. Ransome Chase was sitting on the steps, talking on his cellphone, giving orders to some intern or nurse in some hospital. Peter backed up the steps out of sight. He decided to keep an eye on Chase until he returned to his seat. He wasn't going to miss Renata. The operatic sisters had tipped him off that Mercédès did not appear in the first act.

# 48

—

Darkness had fallen on the St. Charles Rock Road. Traffic was sparse. Bistouri, slumped behind the wheel with his eyes on the rearview mirror, straightened up. A Porsche Cayenne turned off the road and drew to a stop behind him. The driver's door opened and Schaefer approached.

Seeing that he was alone, Bistouri shifted in his seat and muttered to himself. When Schaefer reached his open window he said, "Where the hell's Bryson?"

"Nearby. We have a couple preliminaries to take care of."

"Like what?"

"I'm going to search your car."

Bistouri laughed. "You think you're gonna find the disk? It's nowhere near here."

"That's not what I'm worried about."

"You're not searching my car."

"Mr. Bryson doesn't get in a car until it's searched. Ever."

"Okay. We'll talk standing next to the car. If that's the way you want it."

"Agreed. Now get out of the car."

"What for?"

"I'm searching you."

"I won't stand for a frisk. Forget it."

Schaefer stepped around so that he could look down through the windshield into Bistouri's face. "I want to make sure you understand. Mr. Bryson's safety is my top priority. Always. The way you keep insisting on meeting him personally has to make me wonder if you mean him harm. I'm going to get on the phone and advise him not to meet you."

"Good luck with that. He knows he's got to."

"If he decides to go through with the meeting," went on Schaefer as if Bistouri hadn't spoken, "I will observe, and I will be armed."

"Okay. But you stay twenty feet away."

Schaefer studied Bistouri through the glass for a moment. "It will be a lot simpler if you and I settle this. I have full authority to agree on the figure and deliver the cash."

"We've already been through all this."

"If you think you can scare Mr. Bryson and get more money out of him than you could get from me, you don't know who you're dealing with."

"I know what Bryson's capable of, Schaefer. That's why we're here. So let's get on with it."

Schaefer walked away, drawing his cellphone from its holster on his belt.

# 49

—

THE SUMMONS FROM THE STAGE manager crackled over the intercom, and Renata and the soprano playing Frasquita started to make their way through the dim, narrow, crowded passageways under the stage to where they would make their entrance. There were six or seven ways of getting onto the thrust stage, and von Schuschnigg had his cast using all of them. She was feeling the calm, deep joy that suffused her whenever she was about to sing to an audience. Real life was fading to a low hum at the back of her mind.

The assistant stage manager in her headset was dressing the ranks of the choristers. She placed Renata and Frasquita at the front. Then everyone went still as she listened for the cue. It came and she tapped Renata's shoulder.

Renata ran up the ramp, out onto the stage. As always she felt the warmth of the stage lights—purely imaginary, but she felt it all the same—and the presence of the audience out there in the dark. The choristers deployed, and she and Frasquita draped themselves artfully over the fenders of a mockup of an old Chevy. Von Schussnigg's version of Lillas Pastia's tavern was a roadside *taqueria*. Upstage Amy Song, clad in tight black jeans, was swinging her delectable hips and singing of a gypsy's life.

Renata kept her eyes locked on Carmen as she sashayed across the stage. On a stage like this one, where you performed in the audience's laps, there was always a risk of meeting an audience member's eyes and losing your concentration. She had resolved that there would be no nonsense about looking for Peter in the auditorium, about singing to him. Everything Renata did in her professional life, she did for an imaginary ideal audience, more demanding and more appreciative than any real audience could ever be.

In this scene, Frasquita and Mercédès were required only to look admiringly at Carmen and back her up with a tra-la-la now and then. But when tra-la-las were all you had, you needed to take each one seriously. Most of the characters Renata played spent longish periods onstage with nothing to do. Sometimes a director would give her a bit of business, but von Schussnigg hadn't, so she had worked up a little back story on her own.

Mercédès was thinking that she knew the smugglers were coming to meet them tonight with a new job, and Carmen didn't know that yet. Of course Carmen was more beautiful and had more lovers, but in this case Mercédès was one up on her and feeling smug. Renata liked to think she was adding a little daub of color to the stage picture. In any case, it helped her keep her concentration.

Carmen crossed the stage again, tracked by Mercédès, and Renata found herself looking into the eyes of Ransome Chase. He was sitting in the third row, only a dozen paces away. Renata jumped. She kept turning her head, watching Carmen, but she could feel Chase's gaze upon her. He wasn't watching the opera. He was glaring at her. He must have figured out that she and Peter suspected him of murder. It couldn't have been hard.

Renata's thoughts were in a whirl and she went deaf to the music. Not until Frasquita gave her a startled sideways glance and a nudge did she move to her next mark. All trappings of

Mercédès dropped from her and she was just Renata Radleigh again, who'd spent the last few days bungling attempts to help her brother. Under its coat of makeup, the bruise around her eye began to throb. She could feel Chase's gaze upon her, its weight and heat, and instinct told her that he intended to harm her and she must flee. Only sheer willpower kept her feet nailed to the stage. It was necessary to explain to herself, in detail, that there was no way Chase could get at her.

By the time she pulled herself together, Frasquita had guided her into the dimness at the very back of the stage. In the bright lights upstage, Carmen and Escamillo the bullfighter were flirting. So the opera had gone along smoothly without her. Here was a revelation, thought Renata. She could zone out completely for several minutes, in front of nine hundred people, and no one would notice. It made one wonder why one went to all that trouble.

As she watched Amy Song and Fred Kraus, the obnoxious baritone playing Escamillo, singing about how much everyone admired them and how much they loved themselves, she had a moment of resentment, pure as a child's, that the world was paying all this attention to someone else and none to her.

In her youth she had wanted to be a star, and now she was an aging journeyman mezzo-soprano, and in a few years she would probably be a piano teacher. Ordinarily Renata kept this thought padlocked in the cellar of her mind, but now it burst out into the living room and sprawled on the sofa. She gazed at Amy Song with sinful envy. Amy was singing beautifully but sloppily, as usual, contenting herself with an F when the score called for a G, drawling a half note when the score called for a crisp quarter note. Oh, Renata could kill her.

Well, could she?

Here was the relevant question. If she could answer it, she might learn how to deal with Ransome Chase, sitting out there in the darkness. After a moment's consideration, she decided that no, she could not kill Amy, who was not responsible for her fizzling-out career. It was the fault of many people over the years who had chosen to hire somebody else, of bad luck and bad decisions, some of them her own.

It was different for Ransome Chase. He blamed Helen Stromberg-Brand only. She had stolen the glory that should have been his. He had explained it all to them just a few hours ago. Renata wondered why she had failed to believe that Chase was guilty. Peter was right. Where there's smoke there's fire.

# 50

—

A MetroLink train was pulling out of Rock Road
Station. It was spanking new, white with bold red and blue
flashes, and was all of two cars long. It looked like something
that should be going around a Christmas tree, compared to the
El trains of Chicago, but if the comparison had ever amused
Shane, the novelty had worn off by now. The few disembarking
passengers went off to their cars in the lot or the bus stop,
and he had the platform to himself again. He slowly paced its
length. Twice he took his cellphone out of his pocket and put it
back. The third time, he made a call.

"I told you not to call," said Bistouri.

"Yeah, and you told me it would take fifteen, twenty minutes.
I been here for forty-nine minutes. Exactly. I know 'cause
there's a digital clock and I got nothing to do but watch it. Are
you just sitting there?"

"Schaefer's been and gone."

"Schaefer?"

"The right-hand man. He's taking a while to produce his
boss. Standard procedure. You make a guy wait. Let his nerves
work on him. Makes him easier to deal with. Well, it's not
gonna work this time."

"They got their recorded announcements on a loop. I know

'em all by heart. You want to hear what you're not supposed to do on a MetroLink train?"

"Just think about what you're gonna do with the money, Shane. And don't call me again."

# 51

—

RANSOME CHASE HAD RETURNED TO his seat and Peter had been able to see Renata. As she had warned him, she was one figure on a crowded stage, one voice among many. The scene played out and the stage darkened for a change of setting.

He had been able to tell, sort of, what locale the previous acts had been set in, but now he had no idea where they were supposed to be. As before there were banks of video screens, now showing news footage of Latin Americans trying to cross the desert or swim the Rio Grande. Stage left was a bulky object that in the dim light looked like nothing so much as an oversize slot machine.

Characters were drifting in from upstage, singing in French. The lights came up. It *was* a giant slot machine. The titles above the stage said they were singing that a smugglers' life is hard but fun. Oh. Now he got the border motif. The singers were carrying boxes and bundles, which they set down and sat on, except for Carmen and Don José, who were arguing. Then two women got up and ran over to the slot machine. They were Renata and her pal.

Peter straightened up in his seat. The operatic sisters had told him that this was Frasquita and Mercédès's best bit. It was very pleasant for him to hear her voice, less pleasant to look at her, for she was almost unrecognizable in another odd getup of blond wig, fluorescent orange tube top, short skirt, and fishnet stockings. The girls sang about telling their fortunes with cards, which made it a little strange that what they were actually doing was pulling the handle of the slot machine. Frasquita was going to marry a young handsome man. Mercédès was going to marry an old man—but very rich. Each thought hers was the more enviable future. Renata threw her head back and sang joyfully that her husband was going to die, leaving her a rich widow. Peter resisted the impulse to elbow the person next to him and say, isn't she great?

Then a spotlight picked up Carmen, who was slowly crossing the stage. She was wearing camouflage fatigue pants that fit her trim figure like designer jeans. The music and the lighting changed, becoming ominous. Carmen sang that she would try her fortune. She pulled the handle.

The video screens now showed hands flicking open glittering switchblades. An ace of diamonds the size of a highway billboard shot up from the floor. Another dropped from the ceiling. Peter got it: this was what Carmen was seeing on the slot machine. Up from the floor surged another giant card.

Halfway up, it froze. Then, with a metallic shrieking that drowned out the orchestra, it rose jerkily a few more feet and froze again. On the screens, the switchblades blinked out, to be replaced by the multicolored rectangles of the Microsoft Windows logo.

The metallic racket ceased. There was complete silence. The orchestra had stopped playing. Only now was Peter sure that this wasn't all part of the show. The performers who were sitting on bags and boxes stood up. Carmen, Frasquita, and Mercédès stared helplessly at each other. It was the moment to drop the curtain, but this theater didn't have one. The lights went out. In the darkness the jabber of the audience seemed very loud. A couple of people took it upon themselves to boo, but this was St. Louis, and it didn't catch on.

The house lights went up. Under cover of darkness the performers had fled the stage. A man in a tuxedo was running down the aisle. Peter recognized the SLO bigwig as he clambered onto the stage and disappeared into the wings. Most of the audience members were on their feet, some in the aisles already. The conversation was loud and animated, and there was even laughter. Everybody seemed to be having a good time.

By the time Peter reached the lobby, it was packed. Some people were heading out the doors toward the parking lot, but most seemed to be in no hurry to leave. There was a long line at the bar. The smokers were stepping out and lighting up. Little knots of people were forming to laugh and compare speculations. Many others were on their cellphones, reporting the disaster to the folks at home.

He spotted Renata at the same moment she saw him. She was still in her fluorescent tube top and short skirt, and people turned to look at her as she made her way over to him.

"I'm not supposed to be out here in costume, but—"

"I don't think it matters now."

"No, I suppose not. Listen, Chase is here."

"I know."

"The way he's been looking at me .... Peter, I don't know why I didn't believe you straightaway."

"He did it," Peter said.

"He did it."

"All right. Let's go to Clayton PD."

"I have Detective McCutcheon's home number."

"Even better."

As Peter handed her his phone, he looked over her shoulder and said, "Uh-oh. Brace yourself."

She turned. Ransome Chase was just emerging from the auditorium. His girlfriend was not with him, but another man was, one of the cast, a red-faced, gray-haired man wearing a T-shirt with an American flag on it. His arm came up and he pointed at them. Chase's eyes bored into Peter's. He started toward them.

Peter said, "Who is that guy?"

"His name is Ray. He's a supernumerary. We'd got to be quite matey, but he's very annoyed by what I'm doing, trying to help Don. Um … hang on a minute."

"What?"

"An hour ago he told me didn't know Chase."

Chase was upon them. Glaring from one to the other he said, "Planning your next stupid move?"

"Back off," Peter said. "I mean it. Stand somewhere else until the cops get here."

Chase looked at the phone in Renata's hand. "You've called the police?"

"I'm about to," said Renata. "Detective McCutcheon of Clayton PD, on the Stromberg-Brand investigation. It time he knew about you."

Chase raised his eyes to ceiling. They were left to look at his hairy throat while he struggled with his temper. After a minute he was ready to talk to them. "I really don't need any more trouble at the med school. So I'm going to offer you one last chance to avoid the consequences of your stupidity. Come with me."

"Come with you where?"

"My home. It's not far."

"We'll wait here for the police," said Peter.

"I don't want the police and neither do you. If you'll give me fifteen minutes, I can prove that I had nothing to do with Helen Stromberg-Brand's death."

Peter glanced at Renata. He could tell that her doubts about Chase's guilt were stirring again. She said, "All right. We'll follow you in our car."

# 52

—

Bistouri was slumped at the wheel of his car, head against the headrest, perfectly still. He would have looked to be asleep except that his eyes were open. Over the noise of insects and tree frogs came the sound of an approaching car. Bistouri raised his eyes to the rearview mirror but made no other movement until the car turned onto the dead-end pavement, its headlights sweeping the trees before they were switched off. Bistouri opened the door and got out.

Both front doors of the Porsche Cayenne opened. Schaefer got down from the driver's seat and stood next to the car. His hand slipped into his jacket. Bryson got out. He hesitated a moment, then approached Bistouri.

"Mr. Bryson—" Bistouri began.

"Schaefer said to remind you of the warning he gave you before."

"Right. He's armed and dangerous. Mr. Bryson, your guy has the wrong idea completely. I don't mean you any harm. In fact—"

"Let's not waste time. How much are you asking?"

Bryson stopped an arm's length from Bistouri. He took a step to his left, so that he was not blocking Schaefer's sight line. Bistouri said, "I'm sorry about what your guy has been saying to you, Mr. Bryson. Obviously he's got you kind of keyed up."

"Come on, what's your price?"

"Everything I've done so far was so I could get a minute alone with you. Let's calm down. Start over."

"What the fuck are you talking about?"

"Your man thinks this is a shakedown. The dumbshit kid I have to work with thinks so too. But it's not. I have something to say to you we don't want anyone else to hear. Something important. That's what this is about, and that's all."

"How much for the disk?"

"You can forget about the disk. It's not a problem."

Bryson stared at him and repeated, "How much?"

"Mr. Bryson, I don't want any money from you."

*"What?"* Bryson stepped toward him.

"Sir, please back away."

It was Schaefer's taut voice from beside the car. Bryson glanced at him and stepped back. Bistouri had not moved at all. His arms hung at this sides. In the same soft, mild voice, he said, "Some people sent me to see you. They're paying me very well. I'm not looking for any money from you. They'll pay off the dumbshit, too, so he won't trouble you again. Money is not the issue."

"Who are you working for?"

"Some people who have some good advice for you."

"Good ad*vice?*"

"Yes. You're right at the beginning of this. It hasn't cost you much yet. Now's the time to back out."

"What are you talking about?"

"The vaccine."

"The vaccine?"

"Here's where you stand. You have a vaccine that works great … in mice. You have to get through human trials. And everything else the FDA can throw at you. You don't know about side effects. This drug could cause women's hair to fall out. Have psychotic episodes. You're years away from putting it on the market. From seeing a profit. Assuming there ever is one."

"You're not telling me anything I haven't heard before. Who are you working for?"

"Just back out of the deal, Mr. Bryson, and it's all over. You don't even have to see me again. I'll be watching the news. When I see the announcement you're shutting down Ezylon, I call your guy Schaefer and return the disk."

"Who are you working for?"

"It'll be so easy. Dr. Stromberg-Brand's death gives you the perfect out. You just say you don't want to continue without her."

"How can I say that, when I've already said I have the obligation to bring her work to fruition?"

"Aw, your guys can write you out of that one."

"But that's what I believe. That I have the obligation. That Helen developed a wonderful drug that's going to do a great deal of good in the world."

"Mr. Bryson, remember. You're a rich man, enjoying a great life. You don't have to take chances."

"Who are you working for? You might as well tell me. There were several people who were very interested in backing Helen. I beat them out. All I have to do is make a few phone calls and I'll know the names of the fuckers who sent you."

"You can't make those calls." Bistouri's soft voice had a pleading note now. "You can't start people wondering and asking questions. You can't … can't operate in the way you're used to. Because you're not the man you were. And you won't be till you get that disk."

"So you're back to threats already."

"I regret that, sir. But you know what's on that video. You don't have a lot of options. There's really only one."

"Who sent you? A piece of shit like you, to dictate terms to me. Tell me!" Bryson lunged, grabbing Bistouri's collar. Bistouri stepped back, throwing up his own hands, trying to break Bryson's grip.

A small bright green spot appeared on Bistouri's left temple, followed an instant later by a light, dry crack. His head jerked as the bullet ploughed through and blew out several square inches of the right side of his skull, spewing blood and brains and bone fragments over Bryson and the hood of the car. He dropped in a heap at Bryson's feet.

# 53

—

PETER AND RENATA FOLLOWED CHASE up Big Bend Boulevard. He turned into the lot of a small brown-brick apartment building. They parked next to him. He waved at the building. "An imposing residence for an eminent physician," he said, with his usual lively sense of grievance. "Alimony. Child support. Her lawyer picked me clean."

He led them into the lobby and up the stairs to his apartment. It was both cluttered and bare; it had the same unlived-in look as her flat in London W. 11. That was one thing she and Chase had in common: they had a career instead of a home.

Going around his mare's nest of a desk, Chase switched on his computer. While it booted up, Renata wandered over to inspect what was on his wall. It was hung with his degrees and licenses and pictures of him shaking hands with hot-country presidents and ministers in ornate uniforms or tribal dress and with suit-clad CEO donors. On the desk itself, where one might expect to find pictures of children and grandchildren, there were snapshots of patients: people in hospital beds, grasping Chase's hand and smiling at the camera. Shots of children were pasted to letters laboriously printed in Spanish, or to crayon drawings.

"I snuck out of that party at the opera on Saturday night

before the speeches even began. I was back here about quarter after nine. He pointed to his computer screen. "There we are. My first email is timed at nine oh seven."

"Was anyone else here?" asked Peter.

"You're not listening. This is my alibi witness." Chase patted the top of the monitor. "I was sitting right here, receiving and answering emails and texts, until well after one in the morning. I was not at Helen Stromberg-Brand's house in Clayton. Just check the times of the messages in my in- and out-boxes."

Renata sat down before the screen.

"All this tells us is that someone was here, clicking and sending," said Peter. "We don't know if it was you."

"Let me open some of the messages," Renata said.

"You're asking me to violate patient confidentiality. But why would I expect any decency from you people? Go ahead."

Renata grasped the mouse. For the next few minutes, she clicked through messages. The contents were arresting.

So this was what had happened to the ancient custom known as "talking to your doctor"—it hadn't disappeared, just gone into cyberspace. She could never get more than a few minutes face to face with her gatekeeper and other care providers, and never wasted any of it on personal chat. Her doctors were strangers to her. But anyone who suffered from Chagas Disease or had a relative who did, and had access to a computer, seemed to be able to find a friend in Ransome Chase. In English, or in good Spanish, he answered questions and advised, offered hope, told hard truths. Often it went beyond expertise. There were people here he must have been corresponding with for months or years. He condoled with them on their sufferings or the deaths of loved ones. He enlisted them in his feuds; he wanted them to hate his enemies as much as he did—especially Helen Stromberg-Brand.

Abruptly Chase leaned over her and grabbed the mouse. The screen went blank. "You've seen enough. It's obviously me writing these messages."

She stood. "Yes. I'm convinced. You're not much on collegiality with fellow doctors, are you?"

"Don't you condescend to me. My life isn't singing pretty songs. It's saving lives. The people who blocked me have deaths on their consciences. Or would if they had consciences."

Renata sighed. "All right, Dr. Chase. You were here on Saturday night. That's all that matters. I don't suppose you want my apology, but you have it."

She turned and walked out, followed by Peter. If he said anything to Chase, she didn't hear it.

# 54

—

A TRAIN PULLED INTO ROCK Road Station. Its doors opened, but no one got on or off. The only person on the platform was Shane. He held his phone to one ear, while his finger blocked the other. He was shifting from foot to foot. He shouted, "Goddamn you, Bistouri, pick up!" but there was no response, and he shoved the phone in his pocket. He started walking up the platform. Soon he was running. He crossed the parking lot and scrambled up the slope to the viaduct.

At the turn-off into the woods he stopped, breathing hard. There was nothing to see. He advanced. The overhanging trees blocked the streetlamp and he was in the dark. He bumped into something and grunted: Bistouri's car. He felt his way along the fender to the door and opened it. The interior light came on.

The car's hood was dotted with blood spots. Bistouri's body lay on the ground a few feet away. His face was turned away. Shane reached down. His fingers touched brains in the gaping hole in the side of Bistouri's skull. He gasped and backed away.

He slammed the door and the darkness returned. Propping his elbows on the car, he buried his face in his arms and muttered incoherently. Then he ran back the way he had come. Tripping over a crack in the pavement, he fell full-length. He scrambled to his feet and ran out to the edge of the road. He looked both ways. There wasn't a car in sight. Shane just stood there for a while, breathing deep and swallowing, pulling himself together. Then he went back into the darkness.

Opening the car door again, he leaned in. The key wasn't in the ignition. He didn't hesitate. Leaving the door open for the light, he went down on his knees next to the corpse and began to search the pockets. He found the keys in the left pants pocket. His hands had gotten bloody and he wiped them on Bistouri's coattail.

Then he got in the car, switched on the lights and engine, and reversed out onto the Rock Road.

THE PORSCHE CAYENNE WAS PARKED on a side street, just far enough down to be out of the streetlight and invisible. Schaefer started the engine and made a U-turn to follow Bistouri's car. Only then did he turn on the headlights. Bistouri's taillights were tiny red flecks far down the dark road.

"Get closer," said Bryson.

"Can't do that. Not till there's more traffic."

Bryson was slumping into the seat and against the door. In the dim light from the dashboard his face looked wan, the features drawn. There were still blood spots on his shirt. He said, "How sure are we this is the accomplice?"

"One hundred percent. He knew the rendezvous point."

"Yes, of course." Bryson shut his eyes and said nothing more. He was swaying with the motion of the car. He did not open them until several minutes later, when Schaefer made a sharp turn and accelerated up an on-ramp.

"What's going on?"

"He's heading north on I-170."

Bryson made a sound between a sigh and a moan. "You said, there's two of them. One sits on the disk while the other goes to the meet."

"That made sense to me."

"Well, what if you're wrong? What if they left the disk in Chicago and that's where he's headed?"

"Too early to say where he's headed. Excuse me, sir, I need to concentrate."

The interstate had more streetlights and traffic was thicker. Schaefer closed the distance with the gray Saturn, but not too much. He kept two or three cars between them. The driver gave no signs of wariness. He was driving in the right-hand lane, a few miles under the speed limit. His turn signal began to flash, and a moment later the car went under the green sign that said, I-270 NORTH—CHICAGO.

"Looks like he's going home," said Schaefer.

"He's what? That's not what you said he'd do."

"No. I couldn't figure out what this kid had to do with it. I mean, why Bistouri brought him along, if it wasn't to sit on the disk while Bistouri came to see us. I was wrong. Sorry."

"What do we do now?"

"Follow him."

"To Chicago? But that's ... how many hours?"

"Five or six."

"But I can't drop out of sight for that long. Too many people will miss me. Start asking questions."

"I'm very sorry about that, sir. But here's the situation." Schaefer lifted his forefinger from the wheel and pointed. "This guy up ahead, I thought the first thing he'd do—after he got over the initial panic, I mean—was go back to the hotel or wherever and re-establish contact with us. There'd be some threats and curses but I could get him through that and then he'd deal. His heading home suggests one probability. The disk is in Chicago. And he's decided he's not going to deal with us anymore. He's spooked. I don't know what he's going to do next. Maybe try to sell the disk to CNN. But if we lose him, there goes our only chance to get it back."

The workings of Bryson's normally quick wits were slowed by shock. It was not until they were on the bridge crossing the Mississippi River into Illinois that he feebly echoed, "We can't lose him."

# 55

—

PETER AND RENATA WERE SILENT in the car, contemplating their failure. It was getting to be a habit with them.

"Look," Peter said. "Chase was my idea, and—"

"Peter, shut up. It isn't *your* fault."

They continued to drive aimlessly up Big Bend Boulevard for a while. He glanced over at her: she was still in costume. "You want to go back to the theatre and change?"

"No. I can't bear to look another human being in the face today."

She directed him to Don's house. As they drove through the dark, empty residential streets, she wondered if she would be able to sleep. She had never felt so exhausted in her life. It was possible that she would fall into a crevasse of unconsciousness so deep that her anxious thoughts would not be able to drag her out of it for several hours.

"Turn here. The house will be on the right."

Peter's headlights swung round and settled on a white car parked in front of the house. In glistening green reflective letters, its door said, WEBSTER GROVES POLICE.

"Oh my God," Renata murmured. "What now?"

Peter stopped behind the car. As they got out, the

policewoman came to meet them. She looked at Renata. "Are you Renata Radleigh?"

Never had she felt so much like denying it. "Yes."

The officer glanced at Peter. "Your name, sir?"

He gave it.

She nodded, satisfied. "You need to come with me. Or you can follow in your own car."

"We'll follow," Peter said. "What's this about?"

"A call you made to Bridgeton PD this afternoon. About an individual named Louis Bistouri."

POLICE VEHICLES WERE LINED UP along the side of the wide, dark, empty road—patrol cars, unmarked cars, technicians' vans. Peter followed the Webster Groves car to the head of the line and turned in. Renata opened the door and stood up, dizzy with fatigue. She had a fleeting impression of a narrow track running into the woods and halogen lamps on stands, casting a brilliant light on a group of standing or kneeling men. Then the scene was blocked out by Detective McCutcheon striding up to her. His face, normally so expressionless, was livid with anger.

"Need you to make an ID, Ms Radleigh," he said in a low, strident voice.

"I can do it," Peter said, but McCutcheon had already seized her arm and was dragging her into the pool of bright light. She nearly fell over a man who was down on one knee, examining a tire track. When she got her feet under her, she was standing over the corpse.

The man she had seen at the motel lay on his back, limbs outstretched. His head lolled, revealing a gory crater where his temple and the top half of his ear had been. Brain matter like gray scrambled eggs trailed across the blood-soaked shoulder of his jacket.

"Is this the man you saw this afternoon?" McCutcheon asked.

She could not answer. She was going to be sick and there was nothing she could do about it but turn away. One of the other men who were standing around the body heard the sounds coming from her throat. As she was bending down he took her arm less roughly than McCutcheon had and pulled her away. *Mustn't contaminate the crime scene*, she thought. She was dimly conscious of him putting something in her hand before he left her to her convulsions. When they were over, she found that it was a Handi Wipe. She supposed the police were prepared for such reactions from people they called to identify bodies.

She staggered back into the glare, wiping her chin. Peter was talking to McCutcheon. Seeing her, the detective turned to address her. "What can you tell us about this guy? What's he doing in St. Louis? Who shot him? Why?"

Renata shook her head.

"That's what I figured. We have a thorough report from Officer Thursby, Bridgeton PD. Based on that, I would say the only thing you know about the victim is, he has no connection to your brother or Helen Stromberg-Brand. He just drives a car similar to someone who might have some connection. That right?"

She nodded.

"You know *nothing*. You blew off my warning not to interfere. You lied to a police officer. And you found out *nothing*."

"We didn't lie," Peter said.

"Shut up," McCutcheon barked, and turned back to Renata. "I should have arrested you long ago. But I kept trying to talk sense into you, which was a *fucking* waste of time."

"That's enough," Peter said. Raising his voice he went on, "Who's in charge of the scene? This man is way out of line."

McCutcheon paid no attention. "Are you convinced now, Ms Radleigh? That this is serious business? That you ought to leave it to people who do it for a living?"

A gray-haired, uniformed man stepped forward. "Detective McCutcheon—"

McCutcheon swung around. "You woke me out of the first sound sleep I've had this week to drag me up here, to a crime scene that turns out to have nothing to do with my case. Not that I'm blaming you. I'm blaming her."

"Detective, you want to stop talking and cool off."

"You have no idea what I've put up with from this woman. Demanding reports from me, like she's the fucking prosecutor. Telling me what I *would* be investigating if I wasn't such a stupid asshole. Accusing me of railroading her brother. Calling me at home in the middle of a fucking ballgame to accuse me of stealing her panties—"

"That's enough. Come with me." The uniformed man put a hand on McCutcheon's shoulder.

But McCutcheon shrugged off the restraining hand and thrust his face in hers. "We're not stupid assholes. We don't need your help. There's nothing weird going on in this case that we don't know about. We put your brother in jail because he killed Helen Stromberg-Brand, and he's gonna stay there. Get used to the idea."

Finally McCutcheon was through. He allowed the uniformed cop to lead him away, restoring Renata's view of the bloody corpse. She turned around and leaned her forehead against a tree trunk. Peter was talking to the other policemen but she didn't try to follow what they were saying. Eventually he came up beside her, took her elbow, and steered her toward his car.

# PART V

—

## WEDNESDAY, MAY 26

# 56

ORNING LIGHT AWAKENED PETER. HE could hear Renata
in the kitchen: the clink of plates and cups, the running
of water. He'd been living alone for so long that it was odd to
hear someone else in his kitchen. Not unpleasant, though.

Last night, in the car, they had both been silent for a long
time. When he glanced over at her, she was scowling so fiercely
that he didn't dare speak to her. He wanted to, though. It had
not escaped his notice that Renata had a tendency to beat up
on herself. It was she who broke the silence. "Where are we
going? Your flat?"

"Yes."

He braced for an argument, but she said only, "What a jolly
evening you're going to have."

In his living room she sank down on the sofa. He asked if she
wanted anything, and she said a cup of tea. When he returned
with it, he found her slumped with her head back, asleep. He
didn't think that either the tea or anything he could say would
do her as much good as sleep, so he turned off the light and
went into the bedroom. Pausing only to take off his coat, tie,
and shoes, he flopped on the bed.

He woke in the darkness to find her lying beside him, fully
clothed, on her back. He raised himself on an elbow. Her eyes

were closed but her brow was furrowed. Could she be frowning that hard in her sleep? No, her breathing told him she was awake. Nothing good to say had yet come to him. He reached out tentatively and stroked her forearm. She tolerated it well.

Now, hours later, he rose and went to the kitchen. Renata was pouring water into the coffee maker and did not notice him. So he just looked at her: this statuesque woman in fluorescent tube-top and miniskirt, barefoot and mostly bare-legged. Her makeup had worn off to reveal her empurpled eye, the bruise now yellowing around the edges, and her hair was tousled. He thought she was beautiful.

"You're feeling better," he said.

"Oh, hello, yes. I've thought it over. Of all the things that could have resulted from my amateur investigating, what happened last night is only the third worst."

He nodded. "You're still alive, and you still believe your brother's innocent."

She gave him a look. "You know how I think. I've noticed it before. Yes, well, I spent most of the night going over Detective McCutcheon's little lecture. Trying to think up answers to his accusations and failing. I mean … we find this man Bistouri at the motel, and a few hours later he's dead. It's not a coincidence. It's something to do with Bryson. But of course McCutcheon would have said such vague musings were no use to him. He was so angry. I wish I'd never accused him of stealing my knickers."

"You'll have to tell me about that sometime."

"When this is all over." She sighed. "That's the point I reached about dawn. It *is* all over. Don is going to spend the next twenty to thirty years in prison. Unless I do something."

"What?"

"I'm going to the jail, where I will ask my brother what really happened in Chicago, the weekend he took Helen to see *Carmen*."

"You've asked before."

"This time he's going to tell me."

"What are you expecting to hear?"

"Haven't a clue. Nor a theory. Nor a plan. But he's kept it back for too long. Now he will tell me."

"I'll drive you to Clayton."

"Thank you. It'll be SLO, actually. They'll be wanting my costume. I've got the sack."

This confused him. He had an image of Renata taking off her costume and pulling a gunnysack over her head. "Which sack is that?"

'I've lost my job. The radio said that the show did go on, after a long delay. Which means I'm out."

"Are you sure? Just like that?"

"Of course. One can't leave the theater in mid-performance. Of all the people who've been sacked by our general director, I'm one of the few who actually deserved it. Anyway, thanks for putting me up. It was lovely sleeping with you. Or beside you, rather." She paused, and continued in a voice different from her usual firm tone. "I'd like to see you later on. Assuming you'd like to. I realize my behavior last night was absolutely hopeless, from your point of view."

"As a man?"

"Well, and an American. I should have cried on your shoulder and blathered on endlessly about Don's and my childhood and begged you to tell me what to do. Then after you'd got it sorted for me, we could have spent the rest of the night having athletic sex."

"I'm afraid I have no ideas about what you should do. As for the athletic sex, however, my mind is a good deal more fertile."

Renata smiled. She stepped up to him, put her arms around him, and brought her lips to his. The next moments passed agreeably.

As they broke from the embrace, Peter said, "I'd like to stick with you today."

"Don't you have to go to work?"

"I haven't bothered to listen to my messages. I'm sure I got the same sack you did."

# 57

—

IT WAS QUIETER IN THE visiting room today. The chairs on either side of them were empty. Don looked glum. It was sad to see him so. What an overpowering presence he had been in his glory days, with his bright avid eyes and voracious smile, the sheen on his blond hair, the aroma of expensive soaps and lotions that wafted from his well-tailored suits and crisply pressed shirts. Now he smelled like old sweat and disinfectant. He was a jailbird already.

He was eager to talk, though. "Have you done anything about the guest list? The possibility the killer was there on Saturday night?"

"That turned out to be rather a dry hole."

He did not pursue it; he had something else on his mind. "I heard about what happened at SLO last night. Naturally I rang a few people, wanting to get the inside story. No one would take my call."

"I'm sorry."

"I know there's that awful recording, telling people they have a call from a prisoner, but I thought surely one of my friends would pick up. No one did."

"Don, you're no longer part of the happy SLO family."

"Yes, you've been telling me so all along. You have no idea

how hard it is for me to accept. You're just sitting there, waiting for me to get down to business. You don't understand me. You and I are just too different."

True. She was impatient to ask her question, but she let him talk.

"The last few years, you've been more baffling to me than ever. How could you keep doing it, flying off to the Timbuctoo Opera to sing Kate Pinkerton. Carrying on even though everyone says you're well past your sell-by date. I thought you didn't know what they were saying, but you do, don't you? You simply don't care. You have such a hard time winning your own approval, you can't pay attention to what anyone else thinks of you."

"I guess that's true."

"Too bad you're not the one in here. You'd do well. But I … I'm driving myself mad, thinking what people must be saying about me. You have no idea what it's like. No use expecting sympathy from you."

Right. She had let him talk long enough.

"Listen, Don. I know you'd prefer to have a sister who's as silly as you are, who thought that your biggest problem was that you are no longer in with the in-crowd. But at least you have a sister who is trying to clear you of murder. So make the best of it."

"What do you want from me?"

"I want to know what happened in Chicago."

"We've been over this before. I'm not keeping back anything that will help my case. So why go into it?"

"Because I'm asking. I've been knocked on the head and humiliated and have lost my job, and now you will tell me the truth."

Don sighed and shrugged, and listlessly began the tale. "I didn't think the trip was going to come off, even the day before—"

"This was Friday, May fourteenth?"

"Yes. Bert wasn't even talking to me by this point. Helen was willing to see *Carmen*, but she kept asking, does it have to be Chicago? Why not somewhere else?" He smiled sourly. "She seemed to think operas were like movies, that they were playing everywhere."

"Why was she reluctant to go to Chicago?"

"I don't know. I sang the praises of the hotel and the restaurant where we'd have dinner, and she came round. And there I was, eleven a.m. Saturday morning, pacing the concourse at Lambert airport, and she walked in alone.

"She was in a filthy mood. She'd had a flaming row with Bert, saying they were not going to give to an opera company, and apparently throwing in a lot of abuse aimed at me personally. It was a bad moment. But then I thought, *Hang on a moment, she is here. The husband's against SLO and she's mad at the husband. I can work with this.*

"So I was jollying her along, saying, well, sucks to Bert, we'll have a lovely time in Chicago. And it seemed to be working. It got her through security and onto the plane. But then I put a foot wrong. I said, 'We're of age. We don't need a chaperon.' And her face turned to stone. She looked out the window and didn't say a word to me all the way to Chicago. When Helen ignored you, were you ever ignored."

"Did you ever find out what offended her?"

"I think I made a mistake mentioning age. Reminded her she was a good deal older than me. Women worry about that sort of thing."

"I doubt Helen Stromberg-Brand did."

"I'd laid on a limo, and kept it a surprise, and that turned out to be a mood-changer. She livened up a good bit on the drive into town. The hotel was a hit—she'd never been to the Palmer House, and she liked the painted ceiling in the lobby. The restaurant too. I suggested New York strip steak with a side of frisée salad sprinkled with shaved beef tongue, which was risky, but she adored it. And she laughed at the Bizet anecdotes I'd swotted up."

Renata was finding her brother's conversation as jejune as ever. She reminded herself to bear down and pay close attention.

"We get to the gorgeous Civic Opera House, are shown to seats down front, and the overture begins. By the time the curtain rose, she had zoned out."

"Zoned out of *Carmen*? You're joking."

"You remember, one of Bert's nasty lines was that she never listened to a piece of music lasting more than five minutes. Well, I'm afraid he was right."

"She fell asleep?"

"No. But she wasn't applauding when everyone else did, and she was looking everywhere but at the stage. Her thoughts were elsewhere. I was wondering what I could say at the interval. Turned out I didn't get the chance. She said she was going to see somebody."

"What did you do?"

Don shrugged. "Saw her to the limo. Once Helen made up her mind, you could not get in her way and live to tell the tale. She didn't say when she'd be back, and I thought she would not be returning to the theatre in any case. So I walked back to the hotel. I thought I could at least save the cab fare. This weekend was looking like a complete waste of a lot of money. Those were two-hundred-fifty-dollar seats we'd abandoned.

"SLO simply had to have a large gift soon. The alternatives wouldn't bear thinking on. So I sat in the lobby, with a view of the entrance, and made calls, trying to set up meetings with other possible donors, while I waited for her to come back."

"And did she?"

"Yes. Two hours later." He smiled unpleasantly at the memory. "I almost didn't recognize her at first. It was the same red silk opera frock, but the face was different. She looked ... deflated."

"I don't understand."

"Like she'd been taken down a peg or two since I'd last seen her. She was actually looking to me for a kind word, and I thought, *Right, I'm back in business. I've been given one more crack at her.*"

His expression was grim. Even vindictive. Not kind at all.

"She tried to dismiss me at the door of her room, but feebly. She didn't really want to be alone. The minibar had Bailey's Irish Cream, her favorite late-night drink, and I gave her that and ordered a big bottle from room service. Then I helped her out of her pantyhose—"

"Don, tell me now. Does this end with you being Don Giovanni?"

"You've known that all along. Haven't you?"

"No. I wasn't sure."

"She was feeling low. I was trying to make her feel better. I knew her favorite movie was *Dirty Dancing* and when the hotel couldn't provide it, we watched it on my laptop in bed. And she kept getting cuddlier." He shrugged.

"And afterward?"

"Once she fell asleep I went back to my own room. I called her at nine a.m. and it was obvious she'd woken up feeling like Scrooge on Christmas morning. Happy as could be. She wrote out the check on the airplane. Didn't even make me go through the paperwork with her."

"That's it?"

"I told you there was no point going into it."

"You never asked where she went? Who she talked to?"

"I've already told you, I was trying to make her feel better. Answering those questions wouldn't have done."

"She didn't want to talk the thing through? Americans love to talk things through."

"Couldn't take that chance. Might have got quite messy, and I'd have been out of my depth. I'm not a psychotherapist."

"But later … I mean, you had a love affair, didn't you?"

"I wouldn't say it amounted to that. We met a couple of

times. But once she got back home ... well, she had a lot on her plate."

"And you'd cashed her check."

Don sat up straight and folded his arms. "This is what you really came for, isn't it? Another chance to feel superior to me. People like you have plenty of time to cultivate their finer feelings. You think singing about love is a *living*."

# 58

—

IT WAS ONLY MID-MORNING BUT already the sun was baking
the plaza of St. Louis County Government Center, across
the street from the jail. The benches between planters full of
marigolds were unoccupied, except by Peter. Seeing her, he
smiled and rose.

Renata had a flashback: one day last winter she had been
walking by a bench in Hyde Park, and a young man had stood
up, smiling past her at his approaching girlfriend, and she'd
been transfixed by a cold shaft of loneliness. Now she took
a moment off from thinking that her last chance to help her
brother was gone and she had failed completely, losing her job
in the process. Instead she thought: *This handsome young man
is waiting for me.*

"Let's sit," she said, taking his hand.

"Oh. I was hoping we might be going someplace."

"No. He told me about Chicago, but it was nothing
useful." She shook her head. "He knows *nothing* about Helen
Stromberg-Brand. Aside from her taste in liqueur and films. I
don't think he knows anything about anybody, really. He isn't
even curious."

"Easy, Renata. We don't want him to go to prison just for
being shallow. Tell me what he said."

"Well, something did happen. She walked out of *Carmen*, got in the limo SLO was paying for, and went to see someone. Two hours later she was back, looking glum. Apparently she'd got some bad news. But that's all we have."

"If we could track down the limo driver, maybe—"

"Grasping at straws."

"Start from the beginning. Tell me everything he said."

"Oh, all right. I warn you, it's not an edifying story." She started, and soon her gloom and irritation faded as she concentrated on reproducing the conversation as near verbatim as she could. Peter was one of those good listeners who made a talker of you. He sat very still, looking at the ground, and said nothing apart from an occasional "uh-huh." The sun was hot upon her head, and she was sweating freely by the time she got to the end. "There you have it," she said. "And sordid enough."

"Not especially. I kind of figured it went something like that. Though *Dirty Dancing* was a surprise. Tell me again what he said to her on the plane. His 'faux pas,' he called it."

"He said they were of age. He thought he shouldn't have mentioned age. She went silent for the rest of the flight."

"He said something else."

"That they didn't need a chaperon."

"That was the word that got to her. Age had nothing to do with it."

"Chaperon?"

"It's a term they use in the lab. It's something in a cell, a protein that guides pilus subunits to their assembly point and makes sure they fit together."

"Pilus subunits. You've lost me."

"In Helen's research, it's the pilus that bacteria use to cling to the bladder lining and inflict a UTI."

"Oh, what Bryson compared to a grappling hook."

"Right."

"So Don's chance use of that word … I'm still not with you."

"Earlier, Don said she was willing to go see *Carmen*, but she preferred not to see it in Chicago."

"Yes."

"Let's say there was someone in Chicago, a colleague, someone connected to her research. And she figured she ought to see him but she didn't want to."

"What? Sorry to be so thick."

"These big shot research docs, they have more to do than people like us can imagine. People they ought to talk to but don't want to talk to naturally fall to the bottom of the list and don't get called for months. I know, I've been that person a few times. But if she was actually in Chicago—"

"Yes. It can be harder not to go see someone when you're there than to avoid calling them long-distance. You're thinking that this person and Helen talked about the research, and he told her there was some problem with the vaccine."

"It's a guess." He stood up. "Let's go."

"Where?"

"To see Dr. Patel. She's the only person we know who worked on Helen's project."

As they walked to the car, Peter took his iPhone out of his pocket and tapped keys. He handed it to her. The little screen was dense with print. It was Helen's article in *Nature*, he explained, the big one announcing her discovery.

"Oh, I see. You want me to read it and figure out what problems there could be with these pilus whatsits. By the time we get to the medical center."

"No. I want you to see if any of the co-authors live in Chicago."

All through the drive to the medical center, Renata picked at tiny keys and squinted at the screen. There were eight co-authors listed, all researchers at great universities, none of which were located anywhere near Chicago.

# 59

—

Aɴɪꜱʜᴀ Pᴀᴛᴇʟ ᴡᴀꜱ ꜱɪᴛᴛɪɴɢ ᴏɴ a stool with her back to them when they entered her lab. It was busier today, full of students and technicians who stopped what they were doing and stared at Renata and Peter. Patel noticed and swiveled round. Stuffing her hands in the pockets of her lab coat, she came toward them frowning.

"We agreed yesterday that I would not speak to you again."

"Things have changed," said Peter.

"They certainly have. We've all received an email from your boss Roger, saying that we are not supposed to talk to you. Except to tell you that Roger is waiting for you to go to him and explain your recent conduct."

"That's decent of him. In his position I would just fire me."

"The email also said that if you refuse to leave, we should call security."

"You weren't entirely honest with us yesterday, Dr. Patel," said Renata.

The narrow dark face turned to her and the large eyes fastened on hers. "I told you all I know about Ransome Chase."

"No, I mean that bit at the end. You asked us what happened in Chicago. But you knew more about that than we did. Didn't you?"

Patel dropped her head. She was silent for a moment, thinking. Then she turned and led them into her office. She shut the door behind them but did not sit down. "What have you found out?"

"Helen went to see somebody in Chicago the night of May fifteenth," Peter said. "It seems the meeting did not go well. Do you know who that person was?"

"It did not go well?"

"Don said that Helen looked dejected when she got back," said Renata. "That's all we know. She went to see someone connected with her research, didn't she?"

Patel took a deep breath and made up her mind. "I think so."

"Is there some problem with the vaccine?" Peter asked.

She looked at him blankly. "What? Oh … no, it was nothing like that. The vaccine's fine. It was … I guess you'd call it personal. I'm sorry to hear it didn't go well."

"Is this a friend of yours?"

Patel dropped her eyes. "I would say yes. He would say I wasn't much of a friend to him."

"Dr. Patel," Renata said, "how much longer are we going to dance around this?"

She flinched. "His name is Jeff Csendes. He was a postdoc in Helen's lab, like me. I don't know for sure that it was him Helen went to see. But I think it was. Since you came to see me yesterday, I've been trying to reach him, by phone and email. He hasn't responded."

"Only one thing to do, then," Peter said. "Knock on his door."

Patel blinked at him. "You mean go to Chicago? Now?"

"Dr. Patel, you have nothing else this important to do today."

Patel shrugged out of her lab coat and hung it on a hook, then took her purse out of a desk drawer. She said, "Let's go."

# 60

—

THE RAILSPLITTER REST STOP ON Interstate 55, midway between St. Louis and Chicago, was busy. The lot was three-fourths full and people were streaming into the building to check the map and visit the bathrooms or vending machines. Some were even reading the plaques about the area's connections with Lincoln. Schaefer was on the far side of the building, pacing in a small circle as he talked on his phone. He put it away and walked quickly back to the Porsche Cayenne. He was wearing a baseball cap and he kept his head down.

Schaefer got in the driver's seat. Bryson, who was also wearing a baseball cap, was slumped against the other door. The line of demarcation of his beard was blurred; he had not shaved, and his eyes were bleary. He had on a fresh T-shirt, without bloodstains. At another rest stop, one hundred miles to the south, Schaefer had gone shopping while Bryson kept an eye on Shane as he napped behind the wheel. Now Schaefer looked through the windscreen at the gray Saturn parked a dozen spaces away. It was empty. "He still in the men's room?"

"Yeah. No, here he comes."

The kid was walking down the path, rubbing his eyes. He got back into the Saturn and started the engine. Schaefer fastened the seatbelt and twisted the key.

Bryson raised his iPhone and looked at the screen. "Twelve p.m. precisely. I'm supposed to be Skyping Angelina Jolie. She's been after me for days for advice on her UN ambassadorial duties."

Schaefer hesitated. Bryson had been looking at his phone regularly and reciting what his schedule called for him to be doing. Schaefer had explained several times that he had called a staffer, not Jayson but someone competent and tactful, and this person was covering for him. That didn't seem to help Bryson, so this time Schaefer said, "You'll Skype her tomorrow."

This didn't seem to help either. Bryson put away his phone. The Saturn was backing out of its space. Schaefer waited until it was halfway down the ramp to the highway, then followed.

"You find out anything?" Bryson asked.

"Yes. My friend ran the plate. The car belongs to Louis J. Bistouri, D/B/A Bistouri Surveillance and Security, with an office address in the South Loop."

Bryson straightened up. "Then that's where the disk is."

"Could be. I'm not sure enough of it to let this guy go."

"Do we have anything on him yet? Does Bistouri Surveillance and Security have employees?"

"No information yet." Schaefer gazed thoughtfully through the windshield. "If there weren't so many people around back there, I maybe would've grabbed him. If he stops again—"

Bryson looked over in alarm. "No. Forget it."

"The thing is, sir, once we get to Chicago, it's going to be a lot harder to follow him. And if we lose him, and if the disk's not at Bistouri's office, we got nothing."

"My God, Schaefer, do you realize what you're saying? Are we going to beat him till he tells us where the disk is? Waterboard him in some motel bathroom?"

"You wouldn't be directly involved."

"Involved enough. No, Schaefer. There are things I am not prepared to do."

"Sir, I have no right to give a person like you advice. But

I have been in situations like this before, and you probably haven't."

"I don't think anyone has been in a situation like this before," said Bryson bitterly.

"I just mean a situation where, uh, an objective has to be attained."

"All right. Give me your advice."

"Just this. These things you're not prepared to do? Better start preparing."

# 61
—

IT WAS A SHORT FLIGHT to Chicago, and the airlines assigned mini-jets to the route. The plane was cramped and noisy. Patel told her tale across the aisle to Renata, and in the far seat Peter. She spoke softly, seeming to find this a difficult story to bring out, and Peter had to lean uncomfortably forward and sideways to hear. There were frequent annoying breaks as flight attendants or passengers walked down the aisle between them. Unregarded out the windows, the flat green landscape of Illinois spread out 30,000 feet below.

"I feel so disloyal, telling you about this," Patel began. "Helen was a wonderful person. She did nothing that men in her position haven't been doing for years."

"Feminist point taken, Doctor," said Renata. "A woman has just as much right to be a ruthless bastard as a man. Now let's proceed."

"We were freshly minted PhDs, postdocs working in Helen's lab. Jeff was a nice enough guy, but difficult. Brilliant and driven. Wound really tight. I guess we all were. It's an amazing feeling, being in a lab that's close to a great discovery. You know you may never have such an opportunity again. Helen was a wonderful mentor to me. She was the opposite to Jeff."

"What did he have to do with the chaperon?"

"A lot." Patel's brow was cleft as she mentally translated the scientific terminology. "He headed the team that isolated the chaperon that escorts the pilus subunits to assembly. He set it up as the target for our vaccine."

"But that was the whole ball game, wasn't it?"

Patel gave him a tolerant smile. "Your department specializes in simplifying scientific research, Peter from PR. There were many, many other problems to be solved to create the vaccine. And that was the difficulty. Jeff wanted to publish his part right away. Helen told him to hold back until she was ready. If he gave away that key part to the entire world, one of her competitors might beat her to the vaccine."

"How long did she tell him to wait?"

"It was always a few months more. A science project goes slowly, but the lives of individuals move quickly. His stint as a postdoc with her was drawing to a close. He was applying for faculty positions. That publication would have done him a lot of good. He felt he deserved the credit, and he did. But Helen was the boss. I could see both their points of view. I was trying to keep the peace, which wasn't easy. Jeff turned very bitter toward Helen."

"He let her know it?"

Patel nodded "Threats were exchanged. He was going to wreck her project. She was going to wreck his career. He really did believe that she was sabotaging him when he went on interviews. I don't believe that. I just think everybody could see the chip on his shoulder and didn't want to hire him.

"He ended up in a diagnostic lab in Chicago. Dealing with blood tests and urine samples. He was off the map as far as Helen and everyone who mattered was concerned. But I tried to keep in touch by email.

"When our paper was in final preparation for publication in *Nature*, I found out Helen had left him off the list of authors. I told her that was unjust. She *had* to include him ... it was really the biggest fight we ever had. But she said there were always too few people who could be authors, of the many who'd worked on a project. The distinction had to be kept for those who had promising academic careers, and Jeff didn't."

"Pretty cold."

"Yes. It was. I don't know how he took it. He stopped responding to my emails and calls. Finally I made inquiries at his lab, and they told me they'd had to let him go because he'd become unreliable. They thought he was using drugs."

"And Helen?"

"I thought she'd forgotten him. Then, just a few months ago, we were passing in a corridor and out of the blue she asked if I'd heard from him. I told her he was working for the lab in Chicago. Not that he'd been fired or why. I don't know who I was trying to protect—her or him. She asked me to email his contact information. And that was the last I heard."

"She felt guilty?" asked Peter.

"Yes. I think she did."

"But not terribly guilty," said Renata. "She didn't actually contact him."

"Until she happened to find herself in Chicago. True."

"So she said to herself, as long as I'm here for an evening, I'll go see Jeff and make it up to him. Put his life back on track," said Peter.

"She'd have been perfectly confident that she could do it. You have no idea how much power somebody like Helen had in academic medicine. She could make a call and get a job."

"Not for an unemployed drug addict."

"No. But I hadn't told her that Jeff had gone off the deep end. She didn't know what she was walking into, and it was my fault."

The intercom came to life, and the pilot announced that they were beginning their descent into Chicago.

# 62

—

THE SUN WAS IN THE west and the overcast was thickening as Schaefer and Bryson drove through Joliet. Countless lights shone through the drifting clouds of white smoke around a sprawling oil refinery of spindly towers and labyrinthine pipes, a foretaste of the great city's skyline half an hour to the north. Crossing a bridge over a canal, Schaefer accelerated, moving closer through heavier traffic to the gray Saturn.

Lanes multiplied, "exit only" signs flew past overhead, and the lanes disappeared toward other destinations. The Saturn bore on toward downtown Chicago. Bryson was becoming more agitated. He gripped the belt across his chest with both hands and twisted it. Schaefer took off his sunglasses and narrowed his eyes, watching the Saturn.

Traffic slowed as they passed vast warehouses. Their lane turned into an exit, forcing them to shift behind a truck that blocked their view of the Saturn entirely. Bryson leaned forward, as if a few inches would make a difference in his view of tires, mud flaps, and glowing brake lights. Schaefer sat back comfortably, holding the wheel at quarter to three.

Spotting a half-car-length gap opening to his left, he spun the wheel and stamped on the gas. The Porsche Cayenne swung neatly into the lane as the car behind bleated in protest.

They crawled, a little more quickly than the lane beside them, moving up alongside the truck until they inched ahead and the Saturn was in view once more. Traffic loosened up and began to move faster, and they slid in behind the Saturn again. Schaeffer allowed a car in between them.

"Sir?" said Schaefer, breaking a silence that had gone on for forty minutes, "Can you keep your head down, please? I'm worried about him seeing your face."

"Aren't you giving him too much credit? It hasn't entered his mind he's being followed."

"I don't know what's entered his mind. But his driving's been kinda squirrelly."

Bryson obeyed, ducking his head. The highway was urban now, running between sloping concrete walls. Big, bright signs advertised radio stations and restaurants. Far off to the left they had occasional glimpses of the Loop, its more famous skyscrapers becoming recognizable.

"Not much longer now," murmured Bryson.

As if, even in his reduced circumstances, Bryson could still order events, the Saturn's right taillight began to blink. It shifted from lane to lane. Schaefer matched the movements. By now Bryson was chewing his bearded lower lip.

The exit lane, curving up to an overpass, was solid with cars. Still on the highway, the Saturn reached the end of the line and stopped dead. Two other cars had fallen in behind him by the time Schaefer steered over and braked.

"This'll take a while," said Schaefer. He set the handbrake and took his feet off the pedals, his hands off the wheel. He shifted in the seat, rolling his head, flexing his fingers, efficiently wringing the tension from his body. He had been trained for long periods of immobile waiting followed by sudden action.

Even so, he was taken by surprise. The Saturn pulled onto the shoulder and accelerated past the motionless cars in the traffic lane.

"Shit!" Bryson yelled. Schaefer grabbed the controls and

rotated the wheel and with a squeak of tires went after the Saturn. By luck or by design it reached the top of the ramp just as the light changed. The intersection was fleetingly clear and the Saturn veered left across it, cutting off the first cars in the line and earning furious horn blasts as it accelerated down the street.

Seconds later, when Schaefer reached the intersection, there was no room to get through. He could only turn right and go in the opposite direction. He punched the accelerator so the Porsche shot ahead of the car to the left, swept the mirrors with a glance, and wrenched the wheel. Tires squealing, the Porsche swerved across the road in a U-turn and returned to the highway overpass. The traffic signal was against Schaefer but he went through it anyway, earning more honks.

"Shut up," muttered Bryson at the indignant drivers.

Lurching and swerving, the Porsche picked its way through traffic. The Saturn came into view, half a block ahead.

"There he is!" said Bryson. "Good work!"

"No. He's made us for sure." Schaefer kept closing, cutting off one last honking truck to get in the lane directly behind the Saturn, feet from its bumper. They could see the driver's eyes in the rearview mirror.

Bryson braced himself against the dashboard. He was expecting the driver to pull into the left lane and accelerate. But he didn't do that.

The Saturn drove along with the heavy traffic for a couple of blocks, until it came to a small shopping center. It pulled into the parking lot and stopped. The kid got out.

Schaefer pulled in behind and jumped out of the Porsche, which was blocking a truck that was trying to back out of the space. A man leaned out and shouted in Spanish. Ignoring him, Schaefer watched the kid. He was approaching a crowd of boys lounging in front of the 7-Eleven. Homebound from school, with heavy backpacks and pants drooping below their underwear, they were guzzling Slurpees and chewing Slim

Jims. The kid picked his way unhurriedly through them and entered the store. Schaefer bent down to speak to Bryson.

"Sir, I need you."

But Bryson, chin sunk to collar, was trying to hide under the visor of his ball cap. "No. Somebody'll recognize me."

"I'm going in. You gotta go around, see if there's a back door."

Bryson looked furtively at the lolling teenagers. "I can't."

Schaefer ran across the lot. The truck driver was out of his vehicle, calling after him. Schaefer moved overhand like a swimmer through the teenagers and flung the door open.

Inside an alarm was shrilling. A line of customers stood at an unmanned cash register, craning their necks and looking toward the back of the store. Schaefer ran that way.

At the end of the aisle a stack of soda cans was half-knocked over and cans were rolling in every direction. Behind a counter, a door stood open on an alley. A store clerk and a security guard were looking out the door. Schaefer was just in time to glimpse the kid, running flat-out down the alley, turning a distant corner. Schaefer leapt the counter. The guard swung around, blocked his way, and gave Schaefer a warning look. The clerk was pulling the door closed. It latched and the alarm ceased, giving way to a hubbub of talk and laughter. Schaefer turned around, vaulted the counter, and ran out of the store.

Outside the truck driver was leaning in the window of the Porsche Cayenne. In a mix of Spanish and English he was imploring Bryson to move. Bryson was slumping and hunching, raising his arms to cover his head. He looked like a man who had stumbled onto a hornet's nest. Seeing Schaefer approach he said, "Get me out of here!"

Schaefer swallowed an exasperated reply with a visible tremor of cheek and throat. "Sure, no problem. Except we lost him. We got to hope the disk's at Bistouri's office."

# 63

—

THEY TOOK A CAB IN from O'Hare, Peter up front with the driver, Renata and Patel in back. The driver was telling Peter about the Chicago Cubs' latest loss to the St. Louis Cardinals. Peter was one of those approachable people, Renata thought. Not like her at all. His face radiated affability and competence. In Lambert and O'Hare, hurrying as they were, they'd been stopped by people asking Peter questions, which he paused to answer.

How many trains of thought, how many contradictory emotions, the mind was able to process at the same time. Even as she was wondering what they would find at their destination, turning over all Patel had told them on the plane, there was still one track in her mind for Peter. Her feeling for him was growing steadily, and she was avid to know everything about him.

Patel was silent through the drive. She had a slip of paper with Jeff Csendes's address pinched between index finger and thumb. Renata, being given to compunction herself, knew what Patel was feeling. Having dismissed worries about Jeff she should have acted on long before this, she was now over-eager, and afraid that it was too late.

Renata looked around. She didn't know Chicago at all.

From the wide, busy expressway, the flatness of the land and the soaring height of the center-city skyscrapers distorted her sense of distance. It was like approaching a mountain across a plain: they seemed to be driving quickly toward downtown without getting any closer. The driver flicked his signal and eased onto an exit ramp.

They descended to a street lined with parking lots behind chain-link fences and old, blank-walled factories and warehouses. On a steel bridge they crossed a river, its rocky banks and black waters choked with rubbish, jolted over railway tracks and passed more warehouses. Then the street narrowed and they were passing between terraces—row houses, she mentally corrected herself—old, worn buildings, some with little barbed-wire barriers between upper windows, others scrawled with graffiti. It was late afternoon, and the sidewalks were busy. It was always startling, when she left St. Louis with its empty sidewalks, to see pedestrians again. Here was the usual big-city mix of races and ages and sizes: an old lady in bulging stretch pants rolling a trolley full of grocery bags, lovers entwined against a street lamp, each talking on a cellphone, two cops standing together, laughing, with a morose black man sitting on the curb at their feet.

The cab pulled into a space between parked cars at the curb and stopped. Swaying forward, Renata felt her heartbeat pick up and stomach tighten. They were here. She glanced at Patel's dark, craggy face. Her eyes looked enormous, her lips compressed. The women got out as Peter paid the driver. They were in front of a brick apartment building. It wasn't tall, five stories, but looking to right and left, they saw that it took up the entire block. Even on a warm May afternoon, it made you think of winter. The color of the bricks suggested they were made of ashes and mud.

They went under a low, broad entrance archway into a courtyard where children were playing around parked cars. There were double doors with wired-glass windows, covered with warnings and notices. Next to them was a panel of doorbells. Patel bent over to read them and pressed Jeff's. They waited. A young Latina holding a little girl by the hand used her key to open the door and went through, pulling it shut quickly behind her to prevent them from following.

Patel tried again. After a minute, she shook her head. Peter said, "I'll get the super" and walked across the courtyard. Another thing Renata had noticed about him was that he knew how to do all sorts of practical things, like where to find the super of a strange building. In a moment he was back, leading a short, pear-shaped man in bib overalls.

"You been calling B-two eighteen and he don't answer?" he said to Patel. "For how long?"

"It's a day and a half now."

"You tried his cellphone?"

"I don't know it."

"Maybe he's just out. Keep trying." He turned away.

Peter said, "I'd hate to think Jeff skipped out on the rent."

The super looked at him, then turned to open the door. The tile floor was worn down to cement in many places. They climbed a narrow stairway filled with smells of cooking and sounds of television. A short way down the corridor was the door marked B-218. The super knocked loudly, and without waiting for an answer pulled a big key ring off his belt and opened the door.

The apartment was dark, warm, and musty. Patel walked in a few steps, calling Jeff's name. The super switched the ceiling light on. The apartment was only one room, plus a bathroom Patel looked into and shook her head. Jeff wasn't here. The few sticks of furniture and appliances looked undisturbed, except that a small rug lay rumpled on the linoleum floor. Peter walked over and pulled it flat with his foot. Patel gasped at the wide, red-brown stain.

Peter took out his phone and touched in 911.

# 64

---

THE SIREN FLUTED, SHRILL AND thin, through the rush-
hour clamor of traffic. Cars and trucks didn't pull over
and stop, but gave way grudgingly as the white police car,
lights flashing, horn braying, passed them. It bounced on its
springs as it landed on the steel plate of the bridge over the
river and raced away. A pedestrian who had been standing
with his back to the roadway turned. It was Shane. He walked
on, in the direction the police car had gone.

People were giving him second glances as he passed. His
eyes were unnaturally wide and he was muttering to himself.
He was wearing jeans and a T-shirt that revealed the tattoo
that swirled up his left arm. As soon as he was off the bridge,
he stepped into an alley and dug a container from his jeans
pocket. He shook pills out and popped them in his mouth, his
Adam's apple bobbing in his scrawny neck as he swallowed.

He continued on his way. Either the more crowded sidewalk
made him feel less conspicuous or the drug worked very
fast, because in a few minutes his pace slowed and he ceased
muttering. Another police car went by. Its lights were flashing
but the siren wasn't on. It passed and Shane watched it cross
the intersection and turn a corner. His eyes narrowed. At the
curb he stopped, though he had the walk sign. He stood still

for a minute, thinking hard. Then he followed the police car.

A hundred feet from the entrance to Jeff Csendes's building, he stopped.

There were three police cars double-parked in front of it with lights flashing. One patrolman stood near the door, talking on his radio. As Shane watched, a large white van with CRIME SCENE UNIT lettered on its door pulled up, blocking the street entirely. Traffic piled up and horns began to honk. A patrolman moved unhurriedly into the street to deal with the mess.

Shane backed up a few steps and ducked into an alley. He leaned his back against the wall and stuck his hands in his pockets. He waited.

# 65

—

SCHAEFER HAD NO DIFFICULTY PICKING the lock on the door of Bistouri Surveillance & Security. Once in the small office, they set to work immediately searching the filing cabinets and desk drawers. After a while Bryson went to the window, gazing out at the black tubes and wires of a neon sign and the brown brick wall opposite. He dropped his gaze to the outer window ledge covered with pigeon droppings. The expression on his face was baffled, as if he could not believe he was in a place like this.

Schaefer was squatting, riffling through a bottom file drawer. He glanced up. "Sir? You okay?

"I don't think the disk is here. Only that fucking kid knows where it is."

"We gotta keep looking."

Bryson didn't move.

"Sir, uh, the position is clear to you, right? If the cops get hold of that disk, we're going to prison. For a long time."

"I'll provide you with the best legal representation."

"Mr. Bryson, nobody can talk a way out of this for us. We got to get the disk." He went back to work.

Bryson returned from the window and sank into the chair behind Bistouri's desk. Cards and scraps of paper were stuffed into the edges of the desk blotter. Bryson leaned forward, examining them.

"Shane Komarovsky."

"Sir?"

"That's the kid's name."

"How do you know?"

"This is his business card. He's a rep for Pryor Lab, a diagnostic medical lab over on the West Side."

"So?"

"Pryor Lab is where Jeff Csendes worked, too."

Schaefer straightened up and came over to look at the card. "So the kid didn't work for Bistouri. He was friends with Csendes."

"Yeah. Or he was supplying pills to Jeff. I guess it comes to the same thing. When you're a drug addict, your dealer is your best friend." Bryson turned the card over. "It doesn't have his home address. Too bad. I doubt he hid the disk at the lab."

As he talked Schaefer had been tapping keys on his smartphone. He looked at the screen and grinned. "No prob. He's listed. His home address is also on the West Side."

# 66

—

THE CHICAGO POLICE PROCEEDED IN the same manner as the Clayton police: they asked questions, they did not answer them. After interrogation, uniforms had herded Peter, Renata, and Patel to the end of the hall as the Csendes apartment filled with cops. They sat on a cold radiator beneath a dirty window and waited. A uniform standing at the apartment door with a clipboard, writing down the names and badge numbers of all who entered, kept a watchful eye on them. The wait was hardest on Patel. She kept her eyes on the floor and did not respond when Peter spoke to her.

A short, broad-shouldered woman with brown hair pulled back tight and turquoise eye shadow came out of the apartment and approached them. She had a detective's shield clipped to her shirt pocket and carried a folder under one arm. "I'm Detective Gutierrez," she said. "You're Doctor Patel?"

Patel nodded.

Gutierrez held up a photo. "Is this Jeff Csendes?"

Renata could see the photo too, and the first thing she realized about the man was that he was dead. His eyelids hung slack over glassy eyes. His face was battered. His mouth was half-open and two of his teeth had been knocked out. Bloodless cuts with pallid wrinkled edges marked his forehead and cheeks. It was hard to believe that he had been a young man when he died.

"Yes, it's him," said Patel hollowly. "He must have suffered terribly."

"Most of the damage was postmortem," said Gutierrez, not unkindly. "He was in the river for between six and nine hours before we found him. He got entangled in a shopping cart. The current drove things into him."

"How did he die?" asked Patel.

"He was in a fight. It wasn't one-sided. He had broken knuckles, cuts, and bruises on his hands. We're finding blood in the apartment. The fight was here. He died by strangulation."

"When did this happen?"

"He was found Friday morning. It happened late the previous night."

"Thursday the twentieth?"

Peter glanced at Renata: Csendes had died five days after Helen had left Don at the opera and come to see him.

"Do you have any idea—" Peter began, but Gutierrez interrupted.

"I can't tell you much at this stage. Frankly, the investigation was stalled because we couldn't identify the victim. Now that we have the ID and the crime scene, I expect we'll know a lot more soon. Especially because of one strange thing. It was wired for sound and image."

"Jeff's apartment?"

"Yeah. Hidden cameras and mics were set up to cover the whole room. It was done by a professional. You know anything about that?"

Renata and Patel shook their heads. Peter said, "Did you find a recorder?"

"No. Wireless remote. Whatever was recorded, there's no telling where it was sent." She waited a moment, and when they said nothing more, she addressed Patel. "Doctor, I'd like you to come with me. To the medical examiner's office. Make the official identification."

"What about us?" asked Renata.

She handed each of them her card. "Why not get something to eat? Then come over to the station and we'll take your statements."

"Ma'am?" a uniform called from the door, and Gutierrez left them. Gripping the arm of the taller, more slender Patel, she took her along.

Renata and Peter headed for the stairs. She said, "She doesn't seem terribly interested in us."

"She wants to call the Clayton police before she talks to us."

She frowned. "They can tell her how annoying I've been. But we're getting somewhere at last. Aren't we?"

They began to descend the stairs. Peter said, "Here's what we know. Eleven days ago, Helen Stromberg-Brand left your brother at the Civic Opera house and came down here to talk to Jeff Csendes. We think it was to make peace after she screwed him out of his share of credit for the vaccine. We think she wasn't successful. Six days ago, somebody came to see Jeff, who was expecting him and had the room wired for sound and video. They ended up fighting and Jeff lost. I have a guess or two about what happened—"

"So do I."

"Let's get something to eat and talk it over. We're probably in for a long night of waiting around at the cop shop."

"Yes, I'm starving." She had been running on coffee all day. "You know, it'll be our first meal together."

"I don't guarantee this neighborhood will have a restaurant worthy of the occasion."

They passed under the archway to the street. The sun had dropped below the cloud layer and slanting evening light graced Jeff Csendes's bleak neighborhood. They walked by the parked police vehicles. She had her head down and was lost in her thoughts. It took a moment to realize she had come to a stop. Someone was blocking her path.

As her head came up she saw the bare left arm covered

with swirling multi-colored ink, recognized the girl with the rosary in her mouth. This was the man she had passed in the revolving door of Bryson's building Monday night. The man who had knocked her out. She fell back against Peter. His solid form was reassuring. At least she didn't take to her heels.

"Hey," he said. The hollow-cheeked face was smiling. "You're the guy's sister, right? We got to talk."

"You hit me," Renata said.

Peter stepped between them. "Who are you?"

The man was looking over Peter's shoulder at her. His eyes were wide open, unnaturally so. Excitement or amphetamines or both. "Yeah, well, I'm sorry about that. I didn't know who you were and wanted to find out. Anyway, plenty has happened since then. I can do you a lot of good. And your brother."

"He's the guy from Monday night," she told Peter.

"Let's have it," Peter said. "Start with your name."

"Shane. You don't need to know the rest of it. But I got something for you. Come with me."

"Where?"

"Just around the corner. Please. These cops are making me nervous."

He turned and shuffled away. Peter glanced over his shoulder at Renata and she nodded. They followed the man around the corner of the nearest building. Peter was scanning the street. The man noticed.

"Don't worry. I'm alone." He gave a nervous bark of laughter. "I'm as alone as a guy can be."

"Where do you come into this?"

"Me and Jeff, we worked at a diagnostic lab. We got off at the same L stop. So we became friends." He hesitated. "See, I live near here. Just ten minutes' walk. Go with me there and I'll give you what you need to clear your brother. Just ten minutes' walk."

"What is it?" asked Renata.

"A disk." The man raised his hand and spread his fingers, as if holding a disk by its edges. "I'm giving it to you free. I just want you to take it away."

"Is it a video recording?" Peter asked. "Made in Jeff's apartment?"

"I'm not gonna stand here explaining the whole fucking thing. I want to get off the street." His gaze shifted to Renata. "And I don't want to be outnumbered, so the guy stays here. Understand?"

"Renata, don't go with him."

She did not need to think about it. "I have to."

Peter looked into her eyes and gave it up. He stepped back and bowed his head.

Shane set off at a rapid clip. She could keep up because her stride was longer. She was several inches taller than he and probably outweighed him. He was wearing a T-shirt and tight jeans: nowhere to carry a weapon. She told herself these things because she was scared. She was keenly conscious of that group of police cars and men with guns, sworn to protect the law-abiding citizen, whom she was leaving behind. She had the feeling, now that she had committed herself and it was too late, that she was taking a stupid risk and it was going to turn out badly. She'd had that feeling several times in the last few days, and she'd been right every time.

"Keep talking, Shane," she said. "Tell me about Jeff Csendes."

"When we get to my place."

"No. I'm not going into your place until you convince me it's safe."

"Lady, I am not gonna hurt you. This fucking thing has been a nightmare and you're my way out."

"You say you were Jeff's friend. He told you Helen Stromberg-Band came to see him?"

"She just turned up at his door. He couldn't believe it. He never expected to see her again. She says she's sorry she fucked him over. She wants to make it up to him. He says, 'You mean give me the credit I deserve for *our* discovery?' That *our* pissed her off. She says, 'I was gonna get you a job. But you can't expect me to recommend a guy who's living in a shithole like this, who's high on something right now.' "

"Jeff must have been hurt."

"Nah, he was happy. He'd been planning what he'd say to her for years. Never thought he'd get a chance. But here she was and he let her have it. He told me the last thing he said as she was trying to get out the door was, 'There are a hundred people who hate your fucking guts as much as I do, but I'm the only one who has nothing to lose and can tell you so.' "

No wonder Helen had been grateful for Don, Renata thought, with his soothing compliments and bottle of Bailey's Irish Cream.

Shane had been glancing nervously around as they walked. Now he looked over his shoulder, cursed and stopped. Renata turned to see Peter, standing on the curb of the street they had just crossed. Shane took a step toward him and waved his arms, as if trying to make a vicious dog retreat. The people on either side of Peter began to cross the street, but he stayed where he was.

"What's with this guy? He your boyfriend?"

"Yes," said Renata. It was the first time she had said so. Might have been a bit nicer to make the announcement to her best friend rather than a scuzzy small-time criminal, but there it was. Peter would keep trying to follow them, of course. She mustn't look back.

Shane was unpleasant to be around. He stank. Worse than his sweat was a nasty chemical smell, as if he had so many drugs in his system that they were oozing out of his pores. Or maybe this was the smell of fear that they talked about in bad movies. Shane kept glancing around, and his Adam's apple was bobbing in his throat. He was more frightened than she was. She had to find out of whom.

"Why were you trying to get in to see Keith Bryson on Monday night?"

Shane shut his eyes and wagged his head, as if in physical pain. "I can't believe how this thing with Bryson turned out. It would've been so simple, if Jeff had just taken my advice."

"Jeff contacted Bryson?"

"No. Bryson called him. Not some secretary or assistant. Keith fucking Bryson himself. Jeff told me he sounded just like he does on TV. He said Helen had called him the morning after she saw Jeff. "

"She knew she hadn't handled it well, and she wanted her partner to try again?"

"Yeah. Jeff told me Bryson's exact words: 'Helen wants you to feel better about the contribution you made to this wonderful discovery.' Well, I told Jeff, you got a billionaire who wants to make you feel better. How much you gonna ask for?"

"Sounds like you were expecting Jeff to give you some of it."

"Hey, look. By that time Jeff was into me for three thousand two hundred fifty bucks."

"Yet you continued to supply him with drugs."

"Right. Like I said, I was his friend."

"Uh-huh. But he wouldn't take your advice?"

"He wasn't interested in meeting Bryson. He said if it was just a pay-off, he didn't care. So I talked and I talked, and finally I found a way to get him to meet Bryson."

"You suggested bugging the meeting."

"Yeah. I told Jeff, we'll get him on tape, admitting that your idea was the key one that made the vaccine possible. Now he and Stromberg-Brand are gonna make a fortune and you get nothing. You make him hand over plenty of cash if he wants you to keep quiet. Then you double-cross the son of a bitch. You go public with the tape. Nobody would be interested if it was just some professor who fucked you over. But when it's Keith Bryson who did it, that's news."

"Jeff agreed to your plan?"

"That wasn't my *plan*. I was hoping once he had the money, Jeff would forget about exposing Bryson and the lady doc. He was kind of weak on follow-through in most things. I should've known this time was going to be different, because he didn't want to talk about the money, only the video. I said we could do it ourselves, go to some spyware store. I'd advance him the money for camera and mic. But he says no. We don't want any mistakes with this tape. We want a professional. So that's how Bistouri came into it. Guy called Lou Bistouri—"

"We've met."

"Oh yeah. You came to the motel yesterday. He told me. Man, that was close. I was in the room upstairs. Anyway, Bistouri knew his business, I'll give him that. The video is top quality. You can see and hear everything that happened."

"Which was that Bryson killed Jeff."

Shane nodded. "Never should've happened. Bryson started out by telling him the money was in the car. He's begging Jeff to name his price. But Jeff's only thinking about the video. Trying to get Bryson to admit Helen couldn't have done it without him. That she fucked him over. And Bryson ... my God, he starts defending her. Jeff lost it. Lost it completely. Bryson was trying to get out of there and Jeff wouldn't let him leave. They're throwing punches. Rolling around on the floor. Bryson gets on top, gets his hands around Jeff's throat—"

Renata didn't want to hear anymore. "So that's why you came to St. Louis. To sell Bryson the disk."

"That was Bistouri's idea. Or part of his idea, anyway. I had a feeling he wasn't telling me everything. But he wasn't as smart as he thought, 'cause he got himself killed."

"By Bryson?"

"Or somebody working for Bryson. I don't know. I wasn't at the meet. When I got there, I found only Bistouri, with his head half blown off. That was it for me. I knew from the start, you don't want to fuck with a billionaire. I headed for home. Only Bryson and his guy were following me. The guy is very good, because I didn't know it till I got to Chicago. I lost him, though."

"You're sure?"

"Yeah. But I know they'll track me down. A guy like Bryson can do just about anything. There's only one way to take the heat off me. I'm giving you the disk. Free. No strings. 'Cause it clears your brother. It was Bryson that killed the lady doc."

"What?"

" 'Course it was. He went to tell her what happened with Jeff. Had to. She sent him to Jeff in the first place."

"Okay," said Renata slowly. "But why—"

"Obviously, he said she had to keep quiet about the murder. And obviously, she refused. That's the only way it could've gone. You mean I have to talk you into this?"

"No. I'll take the disk." Now she understood. Clearing Don, she would incriminate Bryson. And he would have too many other worries to continue a pointless hunt for Shane. "You've worked it all out, haven't you?"

"You see you got no reason to be scared of me, right? The faster you hand that disk over to the cops, the better."

They had covered some distance since she had last looked around. The old brick houses on this block were better maintained and graffiti-free. Some had small gardens in front. Shane stopped in front of one of these, opened a low iron gate, and motioned her through. As he shut it she risked a glance down the street but did not see Peter. She followed Shane down a short flight of steps under the stoop. Evidently he lived in the basement. He unlocked the door and opened it.

There was a flurry of motion. It happened so fast that she did not even have time to feel alarm, let alone think of turning and running. She was pulled into the room and shoved against a wall. Shane was sitting on the floor. She did not know how he had gotten there. His hand covered his nose. Blood was pouring between his fingers. A man was standing over him, a man she had never seen before.

She understood that he had been waiting behind the door

to pull Shane in and hit him hard enough to break his nose and send him sprawling, then pulled her inside and slammed the door behind her, but it did not seem possible for anyone to move so fast. Shane was groaning and whimpering. The man standing over him said, "Shut up"—not loudly, but it terrified Shane into silence.

Another man was sitting slumped in an armchair. He had matted gray hair and bloodshot eyes. Not until he spoke did she recognize Keith Bryson.

"Who is she?"

"Radleigh's sister," said the other man. His gaze returned to Shane. He reached down, grabbed handfuls of his shirt, and pulled him to his feet without visible effort. "Where's the disk, asshole?"

Renata realized that the apartment—one long, low-ceilinged room—was a mess. The contents of closets, cabinets and the refrigerator were spread all over the floor. Framed posters had been pulled from the walls, furniture upended. Dripping blood, Shane bent to flip over the welcome mat. The silver computer disk was lying on the floor. He picked it up, and carrying it at arm's length, brought it back to the man.

"Why didn't you think of that, Schaefer?" said Bryson hollowly.

"It's too goddamn stupid a hiding place is why. Anybody stepping in the wrong place would've snapped the disk. You are such a fuck-up." He glared at Shane with disgust. "Now the copies. Where are they?"

"Didn't make any copies," muttered Shane. He picked up a T-shirt that was lying on the floor and held it to his face. His eyes fixed on the man who'd hit him. "There's only one and you got it. I swear. Just take it and go, okay? I wasn't gonna do anything with it. That was all Bistouri. All I want to do is disappear. You'll never hear of me again."

Bryson and Schaefer were paying no attention to him. Bryson took the disk and started to put it in his pocket. Schaefer shook his head and held out a hand. "I'm gonna have to look at it, sir. Verify it's the one."

Bryson reluctantly handed over the disk. He said, "Turn off the sound. I don't want to hear any of it."

"Yes, sir." Schaefer glanced at the far end of the room, where a computer with a large flatscreen was sitting on a table. He turned to Shane. "We're going over there. I'll turn on the computer and you type in your password. Then you sit on the floor and keep quiet." He shifted his eyes to Renata. "Can you handle her, sir?"

"Yes," said Bryson, gazing at her also.

The man strode over to Renata, righted an upside down chair, and shoved her into it. Then he turned and walked to the end of the room with Shane following him. The shirt was already soaked with blood. He was badly hurt but no one was doing anything about it. Renata thought that once Schaefer verified the disk, he was going to kill Shane and herself. He had made up his mind. Another flurry of motion, a moment's pain, and she would know nothing more. But still she felt numb, disbelieving. She told herself that Bryson was her only hope of getting out of this room alive.

She said to him, "You've seen me before. But you don't remember. I was standing next to Bert Stromberg-Brand while you were talking to him. I wasn't important enough to introduce to you, and you never noticed me. My full name is Renata Radleigh. You are going to remember it for the rest of your life."

Bryson watched her steadily with his red-rimmed eyes. He seemed to be fumbling to grasp what was about to happen, too. They gazed at each other in silence. There were clicks and whirs from the computer. Cars passed in the streets. Horns sounded. Then footsteps passed over the ceiling, six feet above their heads. Both Renata and Bryson looked up.

Schaefer returned and handed the disk to Bryson. "This is it. You can go. Wait for me in the car."

Bryson shook his head. "There are people upstairs."

"Sir, this asshole's a drug dealer. They're used to being deaf to what goes on down here. Just go, please."

Bryson was staring at the disk in his hand. "What can the asshole do without this? Make a nuisance, no more."

"I don't believe him about there being no copies. Leave him alive and he could start the shakedown all over again."

Bryson sighed and looked at Renata. "What about her?"

"She's here, so she's a problem."

Bryson continued to look at her. Something was changing in his face but she could not guess what he was thinking.

"Sir, if we walk out and leave them, you won't know a moment's peace."

"I won't know a moment's peace either way."

"Sir, you have to go now."

Bryson smiled bleakly. "No. I don't. Keep an eye on the asshole. I want to talk to her."

Schaefer's face was flushed, his mouth set. But he said nothing. He pivoted on his heel and walked back to sit in front of the computer and gaze at the hunched figure of Shane.

Bryson said, "I'm willing to accept your word that you'll keep quiet and let you go."

"Why?"

"Because I can convince you that it's the right thing to do. That you should not try to destroy me."

She gazed at him and waited.

"This thing with Jeff Csendes was not my problem. I took it on as a favor to Helen. She was upset about the bitter things he'd said to her. She was shocked by the way he was living, how low he'd fallen, and I couldn't convince her it wasn't her fault."

"Probably because it was."

He went on as if he hadn't heard. "She said, you go to him, don't send some underling. If it's you, he'll know we're sincere. That we want to make him whole. And I walked right into a trap. I suppose this little pill-pusher told you about the conspiracy they'd hatched against me."

"Yes."

"I'm willing to let you look at the video. You'll see. It wasn't my fault. How could I possibly cope—"

"With the sort of person who is usually kept away from you."

He narrowed his eyes, appraising her. "Can I get you to see that there is more at stake here than one self-pitying drug addict?"

"The one who made the key discovery, and whose reward was to have his career destroyed?"

Bryson slowly shook his head. "This involves millions of people. You know nothing. Let me tell you what this whole thing is really about. Did the pill-pusher tell you about Bistouri?"

"I already knew about Bistouri. I saw his body. Did you kill him?"

"Not me. Schaefer made a mistake. Not that I blame him. It was Bistouri's own fault. You know who he was?"

"Some kind of private investigator, Shane said. Bugging expert."

"Yes. He was smart. He had an idea too good to tell the asshole about. He went to Newton-Drax. You know who they are?"

"Of course. The big pharmaceutical company. I don't understand."

"They sell Sūthyne. The most prescribed drug for UTIs."

"Oh."

"It kills enough of the bacteria to relieve the symptoms. The itching and burning stop. But then the surviving bacteria multiply, the itching comes back, and the patient has to take more Sūthyne. Very crude compared to Helen's elegant solution, which arms the immune system. You take it once and never have to worry about UTIs again. Not good for Newton-Drax. They make forty-seven point five million dollars a year from Sūthyne. Every year. That will drop to zero if Helen's drug reaches the market."

"Bistouri was trying to blackmail you into pulling your money out of Helen's company? He told you that?"

"He didn't tell me who he was working for. But I've thought about practically nothing else since. I'm sure it was Newton-Drax."

"I don't believe you. How could they be so sure getting rid of you would stop Helen's vaccine from being developed?"

"At this point, it's a long way from the market. And when I drop a project, other people are reluctant to pick it up." He smiled bitterly. "It was my enviable reputation that got me into this mess. So what do you think, Renata Radleigh? Two people are dead, but it was more their own fault than mine. If I am destroyed, the vaccine development will stop, and Newton-Drax will be rewarded for what they have done. Is that what you want to see happen?"

"You mean I owe it to medical science and millions of women with itchy bladders to keep your secret. Keep talking, Bryson. Explain to me how it's somebody else's fault that you killed Helen Stromberg-Brand."

Bryson's face went as blank as a concrete wall. She had to hand it to him, he acted surprise and bafflement very convincingly. "Where on earth could you get the idea that I killed Helen?"

"You went straight from Chicago to St. Louis. She was eager to hear how it went with Jeff Csendes. You told her, but she wouldn't promise to keep your secret. So you killed her. You've had only one idea from the start: you'd do anything to save your precious arse."

"Helen was my partner and friend. I would never harm her. Not even burden her with the knowledge of what I'd been forced to do."

"You lied to her?"

"I told her what she wanted to hear. My turning up mollified Csendes. He accepted the money. She could forget about him."

Renata shook her head.

"You stupid bitch!" It was Shane, wailing from across the room. "Why couldn't you promise him *any*thing and save our fucking skins?"

Bryson looked at him, then back at Renata. He said, "He brought you here to give you the disk. Didn't he? You'd make it public to clear your brother." He pointed at Shane. "And he'd be safe from me."

Schaefer rose from his chair. "She's not going to leave here without the disk."

"It's futile, Renata Radleigh," Bryson said. "Such a waste. You will destroy me, and Helen's discovery, and you won't save your brother. I did not kill Helen Stromberg-Brand."

Shane moaned again. "No, don't say it, you dumb fucking bitch."

"I won't leave without the disk," said Renata, and turned to Schaefer. "Stay right there, Schaefer. One more step and I'll scream. I have quite good lungs. I can scream the bloody house down."

"Nobody'll pay any attention," said Schaefer. "And you won't scream long." But he was holding still, his eyes on Bryson.

Renata turned to Bryson too. "It's simply not on. Two more murders. And you won't get away. A friend was following us. When he lost us, he'll have called the police. They're out there looking already." At least she hoped they were.

"It's true," said Shane, grasping at any straw. "A guy followed us."

Bryson looked at him, then bowed his head. He gave an exhalation of breath that might have been a sigh, or a laugh. "Schaefer?"

"Sir?"

"I owe you a head start. More than that, but it's all I can give you. Go."

For a moment Schaefer stood paralyzed, but only for a moment. Then, in a split second, he was across the room and out the door, which he left swinging slowly in his wake. From outside came the sound of sirens.

"So the friend was real," said Bryson. Noticing that he was still holding the disk, he grimaced and dropped it. Renata snatched it up. He looked at her with bleak amusement. "You know, Renata Radleigh? You and I are going to be talking about each other for years. But this is probably the last time we'll talk to each other. I'll tell you one last time. I did not kill Helen."

# PART VI

—

## THURSDAY, MAY 27

# 67

THE GENERAL DIRECTOR WAS WAITING for her at the door of the Peter J. Calvocoressi Administration Building. She was not surprised. It was the sort of treatment she had gotten used to in the twenty-four hours since she had handed the disk, and Keith Bryson, over to the Chicago police.

Congreve opened the door with his left hand and held out his right to her, a cordial but wary smile on his jowly face. "Well, the heroine of the hour!"

He had obviously given his opening a lot of thought, and that was the best he could do? But she took his hand and said, "It's been hectic, yes."

"Come on up."

It took rather a long time to ascend the stairs and go along the corridor, because people kept appearing to shake her hand and ask how she was. They sent their best to her brother, too; Don was mentionable again. Finally the door was closed and she was seated upon the plush sofa, facing him in his armchair and saying no thanks to a coffee as well as to "something stronger."

"I hope you'll forgive me for getting right to it, but of course I'm anxious to know. What is Don's status at the moment?"

As soon as her plane had landed at Lambert Airport an hour

before, she had called Detective McCutcheon of the Clayton police. To her surprise, he had taken the call. He had been civil and informative, which she supposed was his way of making up for his rant of Tuesday night.

To Congreve, she said, "The Clayton police have sent detectives to Chicago and they've tried to interrogate Bryson, but so far his lawyers are doing more talking than he is."

"But there's no doubt," Congreve said, "that he killed Dr. Stromberg-Brand?"

"No doubt at all. But the St. Louis County Prosecutor is being bloody-minded about dropping the charges against Don until she can charge Bryson. There's good news, though. Don goes before the judge tomorrow, and the lawyer I've hired for him is confident he'll make bail."

"That's great. I'm very glad he'll be out of jail." Congreve sat up straight, laid his hands flat on his pinstriped thighs, and looked at her in silence.

This was such a novel experience, Renata thought. Having important people wait with bated breath for her next word. She rather liked it. She went on, "Rachel—that's Don's new lawyer—is quite keen to meet with Dick Samuelson. She wants to discuss his representing Don while working for SLO. It was all too technical for me, but she used terms like 'conflict of interest' and 'disbarment.' "

"Renata, I'm as baffled as you are by this legal stuff. More so, because Dick kept me completely in the dark about his dealings with Don. I'm suspending him without pay, as of today."

So this was how it was done, she thought. You threatened Congreve, and he served some underling's head up on a plate. She had expected a bit more finesse. "We can avoid unpleasantness, and Samuelson can keep his job, if you will accept a suggestion from me."

Again the general director waited meekly for her to go on.

"When the media call you for comments about Don, I would like you to say helpful things. We were in a cash-flow crisis. We made mistakes. Basically, I'd like to hear a lot of 'we.' "

Congreve smiled with relief. "Of course. Have Rachel call me directly. We'll work out a statement."

They shook hands and Renata went out. In the corridor, she paused before a window looking down on the Emerson Electric Picnic Lawn. Night had fallen, and the tables were empty: the evening's performance of *Carmen* was well under way in the theater. She gazed down on the white-and-green-striped pavilion in which, five days before, it had all begun. The corridor was reflected in the dark glass, and she saw her friend Mike Joyce, the head of production, come out of his office. She turned and they hugged.

"I saw you on the news this morning. What is it like, being you now?"

"Oh, my celebrity is bound to be fleeting. I'm just flickering in the light as Keith Bryson crashes and burns. How are things going round here?"

"*Catch-22* has its world premiere tomorrow night. I will personally shake the hand of every audience member who manages to sit through it. *Carmen's* fine. Iris Kortella is doing a creditable job as Mercédès."

"Glad to hear it." Renata wasn't, actually. She was tempted to ask for her part back. SLO would deny her nothing. Worse luck for poor little Iris. She smiled: amazing how quickly power corrupted. She hugged Mike again and went down the stairs and out the door.

The parking lot was full. She picked her way among the cars of opera-goers in the darkness. Peter was leaning against the fender of his car, talking on the phone. She had watched him on the phone a lot in the last twenty-four hours. He was very Italian about it, nodding his head and gesturing with his free hand. Seeing her, he ended the call.

"That was a Hollywood agent," he said as they got in the car. "He says he can get me a six-figure sum for the rights to my life, just the last few days of it."

"You'd think some newspaper would offer you a job."

"Doesn't seem to be happening. I think I'll take an hour off from phone calls." He switched off his phone and put it away. "Where to?"

"Don's. I have to pick up the deed to his house for bail and his courtroom suit. Turn left here. Then there are phone calls to return. Then I have to pack."

"You don't want to be there to welcome him home?"

"No. I've done enough for Don. Can I stay at your place? It will facilitate the untrammeled debauchery I have planned for the next few days."

Peter grinned and nodded. They hadn't made love yet. They'd had countless questions from reporters to answer last night and this morning, and they had not wanted to be asked why they were sharing a hotel room, so they hadn't. Fame had its drawbacks.

As they pulled up in front of Don's house, Peter said, "Shall I come in with you?"

"No, thanks. It'll take a while. You must be dying to get home. Have a drink and a shower and something to eat. I'll drive over in Don's car, soon as I can. You ought to be ashamed of yourself, Peter Lombardo."

"Why?"

"You're not thinking about sex. I can tell. What's the problem?"

"Uh … can we talk about Bryson?"

"Oh lord. Do we have to? I've done nothing else for the last night and day."

"Well, I wasn't about to say this to the media, but I believe him. About the pharmaceutical company being behind the attempt to blackmail him. Newton-Drax did make forty-seven point five million off Sūthyne last year. I checked."

"Of course you did. You're a journalist. You love a conspiracy. Go ahead and believe him. Fine with me. It doesn't alter the fact that he killed Helen Stromberg-Brand."

"I wonder why he denied it to you, when he admitted everything else."

"It's bleeding obvious why he denied it. Because there's no video of him doing it."

"Yes, of course. Sorry. What I meant to say is, what Bryson told you—about how he told Helen what she wanted to hear, that Jeff Csendes accepted the hush money and she could forget about him—that sounds plausible to me. So there was no reason for Bryson to kill her."

"It sounds plausible because he's a good liar. But now that the Clayton police know what to look for, they will find evidence. He killed Helen."

"Okay. I expect they will."

He was looking through the windshield. He knew he'd annoyed her and wasn't expecting a kiss. Compunction poked Renata: she was going to have to do something about her filthy temper. She said, "Sorry. There'll be plenty of time to talk about this tomorrow morning." They kissed and she got out of the car.

In the Charles MacNamara III Auditorium of the Jane B. Pritchard Theatre, intermission was just ending. The "turn off your cellphones" announcement was repeated for the benefit of the hard cases. The house lights went down. Maestro stepped into the spotlight, bowed to the applause, and swept his arms to share it with his musicians. Then they began to play. Images of the U.S. Border Patrol rounding up illegal immigrants popped up on the big screens. The smuggling party entered, led by Iris Kortella in the orange tube-top and miniskirt and Ray the super in American flag T-shirt. Act III of *Carmen* was under way.

# 68

—

PETER WAS DRIVING NORTH TOWARD home on Big Bend Boulevard. A traffic signal ahead turned red and he brought the car to a stop. A hundred yards down the street, he could see Ransome Chase's apartment building. The light was on in Chase's second floor window.

There was no reason why Peter could not pay Chase a visit, as he'd planned.

Peter had a moment of weakness. He took off his glasses and rubbed his eyes.

He had wanted to talk to Renata about Chase before confronting him; unfortunately, she had not been in the mood. Nor was he, really. He was so tired. Home beckoned to him. Renata's list—a drink, a shower, and something to eat—sounded wonderful.

The light turned green. Peter drove through the intersection, and found out that it was impossible to continue on by. He swung the car into the parking lot of Chase's building. This being Webster Groves, the street door was unlocked. He climbed the stairs.

Chase didn't respond to his knocks. He shouted "Doctor Chase!" until the door opened.

"Look, I'm Skyping a colleague in Peru. Come back later."

"No. You need to talk to me now."

Chase frowned. Only now did he seem to recognize Peter. "Lombardo. That business is all over with, I heard. What can you possibly want to talk to me about?"

"What's the word for an operatic extra?"

Chase froze. Peter waited.

"Supernumerary," Chase said at last.

"Right. I want to talk about a supernumerary who seems to be a friend of yours."

On stage, Mercédès and Frasquita were taking turns pulling the lever of the giant slot machine and singing about their fortunes. Iris Kortella ably handled Mercédès's little number on becoming a rich widow. Amy Song sashayed over, swinging her slender hips in her tight camo fatigues, to pull the lever and receive a prediction of imminent death.

The first ace of diamonds descended swiftly and smoothly, in perfect unison with the second ace of diamonds, arising through the trap. "*Carreau!*" Amy sang. As it locked in place the first ace of spades dropped. It landed with a thud, catching the edge of the slot into which it was supposed to fit. The hooks holding its top edge disengaged. The twelve-foot high, eighty-pound structure of canvas and wood tottered and fell forward. Amy Song, trying to get out of the way, was a step slow. The card caught her on the shoulder and knocked her flat on the stage. The giant card lay lopsidedly, half on top of her.

The orchestra stopped playing. Gasps and cries arose from the audience and here and there people stood. The house lights came up and stage hands rushed out to help Mercédès, Frasquita, and Ray, who were lifting the card off Amy Song.

# 69

PETER SAT AND WAITED PATIENTLY while Chase, leaning over his computer with headphones on, ended his Skype session, which took rather a long time. Finally he pulled off the headphones and crossed the room to loom over Peter. "I don't know what supernumerary you're talking about."

"Going back to Tuesday night—"

"You mean, when you were falsely accusing me of murdering Stromberg-Brand? I wouldn't think you'd want to go back there. If you insist, perhaps a lawsuit for slander can be arranged."

"Remember, they stopped the opera, the lights came on, and everybody headed for the lobby. Renata and I were talking to the cop, and you came to the door of the auditorium with a super in an American flag T-shirt. And he pointed us out to you."

"He told me he knew Renata Radleigh, and she'd told him she was trying to make trouble for me. He came to warn me."

"Right. Renata explained that much. She also said Ray told her that you didn't know each other."

"We didn't."

"You don't know his name?"

"No."

"It's Ray Costello. Does that help?"

Chase advanced on Peter, bumping into his coffee table and sending a stack of medical journals slithering to the floor. "I don't have to answer your questions, Lombardo. This is my home and I don't want you in it. Get out."

"Ray Costello had a daughter named Michelle who died two years ago at the age of twenty-six. She died of Chagas Disease. You are one of the leading authorities on Chagas Disease. It wasn't hard for me to find these facts on the internet. It won't be hard for the police, either. And they're bound to look, once they figure out that Keith Bryson didn't kill Helen Stromberg-Brand. Sooner or later you'll have to talk to them about you and Ray Costello. So you might as well talk to me now."

Chase backed away from Peter. He sank down heavily on the sofa.

# 70

---

IN THE CROWDED WINGS OF the Ruth Baxter Irwin Mainstage, Congreve was pacing, his face locked in a rictus of anguish. Amy Song was seated on the crate to which she had been helped five minutes before. Two EMTs were attending her. Mike was standing nearby with his hands in his pockets. Even now, he radiated calm competence. One of the EMTs turned to speak to him. He nodded and walked over to Congreve

"Well?"

"The EMTs say no broken bones, just bruises. But Amy says she's in considerable pain. She wants to go to the hospital for X-rays."

"Can't it wait? What about the rest of the show?"

"We really, really don't want to aggravate her anymore."

"But where's her professionalism? Her sense of responsibility? I'm going to talk to her."

Mike stepped in front of Congreve and placed his hands flat on his chest. He said, quietly but emphatically, "No."

"Well, shit, Mike. What are we gonna do?"

"We call in Amy's understudy, of course."

Congreve's eyes opened wide. He was speechless.

THREE-QUARTERS OF A MILE AWAY, in Don's kitchen, Renata

was making a glass of iced tea. The phone on the wall beside
her was ringing, but she ignored it. Word had spread quickly
among reporters that she was reachable at this number. But
when her cellphone emitted its tune, she thought it might be
Peter and took it out of her pocket. The little screen told her
that it was Mike. Puzzled, she pressed talk.

"Hello?"

"Renata, can you come to the theater?" said Mike, in the
please-pass-the-potatoes tone he used in a crisis.

"What for?"

"To sing Carmen."

Renata did not ask if he was joking. Nor did she take the
Lord's name in vain.

She was neither incredulous nor dismayed. Not even
flustered. She had been waiting for this moment for years—all
her life, really. She said, "I'll drive right over."

"We've sent a car. It should be pulling up outside now."

"On my way."

She pocketed the phone. Was there anything she needed to
bring with her? No. It was all at the theater. She walked to the
front door and out. The car was parked in front, lights on and
engine thrumming. The driver was rounding its front end at a
trot, headed for the house. Seeing her, he grinned and waved,
and went to open the car's back door.

As the car accelerated away she leaned back in the seat and
closed her eyes. These were the last calm minutes she would
have. She used them to breathe deeply, feeling her throat open
and relax in several yawns. She made a few experimental noises
to confirm her cords were healthy and began to hum softly. In
a little while she would sing to nine hundred people, and they
would all hear every note and syllable.

Abruptly she remembered that there was now somebody
else in her life, to whom this moment would be almost as
important as it was to her. She called Peter. His phone was
off. She waited through the recording and said, "Come to the

theater as soon as you get this, my love. I'm singing Carmen.
They won't make you pay for your seat this time."

Already the bright lights of the SLO complex were filling the
windshield. The car pulled up at the stage door. As she got out
there was a rattle of applause and shouts of "*Brava!*" A few of
the more savvy audience members had come round from the
lobby to await developments. She waved to them and went up
the steps. Mike was waiting in the doorway. A repetiteur was
standing by with the heavy folders of the score, in case she
needed to refresh her memory. She didn't, but she did think to
ask, "Where are we taking it from?"

Mike put his arm round her shoulders and they started
down the hall. "*Voyons, que j'essaie à mon tour.*"

"Oh. Those bloody cards again?"

"One of them fell on Amy."

"Is she all right?"

"I think so. But she's too pissed off to continue."

Renata noticed a dresser walking beside them. "You'll never
get Amy's camo fatigues to fit me."

"We're going with a basic black dress from another
production."

"Bernhard von Schussnigg won't like that."

"Bernhard von Schussnigg will never work in this town
again," said Mike. He pushed through a door.

The supers and choristers lining the corridor burst into
applause and cheers. Renata smiled and nodded as Mike
rushed her past them, trying to meet every pair of eyes for at
least a split second. One face was not smiling.

It would have brought her up short, but Mike and the others
bore her along. Ten feet down the corridor she realized that it
had been Ray. She had not given him a thought for the last two
days. Now she recalled that their early friendship had rather
cooled and thinned lately. He'd thought Don was guilty and
disapproved of her attempts to clear him. Well, if he apologized,
she'd forgive him. She was in a magnanimous mood tonight.

And that was all the time she had for Ray. He vanished from her thoughts as the door of the wardrobe department slammed shut behind her and four dressers closed in and began to tear off her clothes.

# 71

—

"MICHELLE COSTELLO WAS NEVER MY patient," Chase said. "And the first time I met Ray Costello was last night."

"Okay. That might delay the cops for a while. Did you delete his emails?"

Chase said nothing.

"If you did, it probably won't help you. The cops can work miracles when it comes to recovering deleted emails. Not to mention that Ray probably didn't delete your replies. They must have meant a lot to him."

Chase gave a heavy shrug.

"All right. Ray emailed me, out of the blue. Like hundreds of people do. He was an engineer at the Boeing plant. He was used to knowing how things worked. With what was happening to his daughter, he felt helpless."

"How did she contract Chagas? We don't even have it in this country."

"On a spring break trip to Cancun. It was her first trip out of the country. He said he could never forgive himself for letting her go. On the brochures it looked just like Myrtle Beach and all her friends were going, so he said okay."

"It's not exactly Myrtle Beach."

"No. An insect they have down there—Reuviidae, commonly called the assassin bug—bit her and passed on a protozoa called Trypanosoma. At the time it was only a little soreness and redness. She didn't even mention it when she got home. Years went by. Michelle felt fine. She graduated and went to work and got engaged. And all that time the parasite was multiplying inside her, spreading through her blood, invading her organs. Including her heart.

"When she started feeling sick, it took a long time to find out what was wrong. Chagas isn't a possibility that occurs to American doctors. I would have asked about the trip to Mexico; they didn't. She was put through lots of useless tests as she got sicker and sicker. By the time they tested for the parasites, they found too many. Her heart was about worn out."

"Ray Costello couldn't accept the diagnosis, I suppose. He contacted you."

"All I could do was confirm that it was hopeless."

"But you kept in touch."

"Michelle's doctor was hiding behind his secretary. Afraid of being sued for malpractice. Or just plain squeamish about death. Somebody had to answer Ray's questions. Comfort him. His beautiful daughter. Twenty-six years old. To die like that. No parent ever gets over it. We exchanged a lot of messages."

Peter said, "When you were comforting him, what did you say about Helen Stromberg-Brand?"

# 72

―

THE CAST WAS WAITING IN the wings when Renata came up the steps. Dressers flanked her, titivating her costume and hair. She could not see the stage over heads and shoulders, but she could hear the sonorous voice of Congreve, who was saluting the spirit of his company. The audience was cheering and applauding whenever he paused. Many had been at the bar during the unscheduled interval, obviously. *Oh, shut up and let us get on with it*, Renata pleaded. This wasn't one of the big crowd-pleasing numbers from earlier in the show. This was a quiet moment, with Carmen calmly and courageously resigning herself to death. Anyway, that had always been Renata's interpretation of the character, and in tonight's performance, that was how it would be.

Dismissing the dressers, she moved through the crowd. People made way with encouraging smiles. As she got closer to the stage, she saw with pleasure that the giant aces were gone and the video screens were off. They'd even got rid of that wretched slot machine. She and Georges Bizet's music would be on their own.

She realized that she was standing next to Ray. She glanced at his doleful profile. He wasn't acknowledging her; they stood like rush-hour passengers on the Underground.

"Hello, Ray. We're on speaking terms, aren't we?"

He actually jumped, then turned to her with his old sardonic smile, though it seemed a little forced. "Didn't know if you were still talking to us peons."

"Oh, after tonight I'll be back to peonage again."

He looked at her for a moment longer, with an expression she couldn't make out, then faced front. *Go ahead, be that way*, Renata thought. This might have been a good moment to apologize for all those snarky things he'd said about her brother being guilty.

She had no time for petty annoyances. Congreve was leaving the stage. Over the applause the stage manager called out, "Places, everyone!" The cast went out and deployed to their marks. Renata stepped into the center-stage spotlight reserved for her. The silly people applauded again. She wished they would let her sing first. She did not look out in the audience to see if Peter had arrived yet. Peter was not her boyfriend, Don José was. She had just told him she no longer loved him. Now she would face the consequences.

Maestro's head floated above the edge of the stage, lit from below like a horror-movie villain. He lifted his hands and the music began. Filling her lungs with the breath that would leave them as song, Renata set off across the stage toward Mercédès and Frasquita, who were sitting at a table on which playing cards were laid out. She gathered them up, listening for the eighth G-note that was her cue. And here it was.

> *Voyons, que j'essaie à mon tour*
> *Carreau, pique—la mort! J'ai bien lu.*

> Let's see, it's my turn
> diamond, spade—death! That's what it says.

She turned and walked slowly away from Mercédès and Frasquita, folding her arms and hunching her shoulders against the cold mountain air and the premonition of death.

> *Mais si tu dois mourir, si le mot redoutable*
> *est écrit par le sort …*

> But if you must die, if the fearful word
> is written by fate …

She was approaching the group of smugglers squatting by the campfire. One of them was looking at her. That was wrong. Nobody should be looking at Carmen now; she should be utterly alone. Her concentration faltered. The smuggler turned back into Ray, and Carmen into Renata. What was his problem tonight? But the number was reaching its climax. She put her back to Ray and face to the audience, and gave herself to the music as Carmen gave herself to death.

> *la carte impitoyable répétera la mort.*
> *Encore! Encore! Toujours la mort!*

> the pitiless card will repeat death.
> Again! Again! Always death!

# 73

—

"L OMBARDO, I HAVE NO IDEA what you're accusing me of."
"I believe that, Doc. At least I believe you've been trying really hard not to think through the consequences of your behavior."

"I don't recall what I said about Stromberg-Brand in my messages to Ray. Probably nothing."

"That I don't believe. This was two years ago. Only four years after you lost the Blix chair to Stromberg-Brand. I mean, after she and Patel stole it from you."

Chase shifted uncomfortably. He had stopped looking at Peter. "I certainly wouldn't have gone into any of that."

"We've read some of your emails to patients." Peter gestured at the computer across the room. "Remember, we were here Tuesday night. We know how they go. You care for them. You're fighting for them. But you have enemies."

"This is pointless. I can't remember what I wrote to Ray."

" 'The stars were aligned.' Does that ring a bell?"

"What?"

"You explained it all to us down at the med center, the first time we met. If you'd gotten the chair, you would have gotten the postdocs, the collaborators, the grants. You would have cured Chagas Disease, if not for Helen Stromberg-Brand."

Peter leaned forward. "And what Ray thought was, my daughter would be alive today, if not for Helen Stromberg-Brand."

"Get out of here, Lombardo," said Chase, but there was no force behind the words. "It's no use tormenting me. I have no idea what you're accusing me of."

"Of being self-indulgent, Doc. Of rubbing salt in the wounds of a man whose wounds were too deep." Peter stood up. "I don't know what section of the penal code covers that. I'll let the police figure it out. Better lawyer up."

Chase said nothing. Peter left the apartment.

CARMEN WAS FEELING BETTER. HER superb vitality had banished the premonition. Now she and Frasquita and Mercédès were singing of how they would fool the customs men, who were just men after all and would fall victim to their charms. Some smugglers joined in. It was a fast, intricate ensemble, requiring her to nail her cues, but Renata knew the score so well that she could do it automatically. The trick was to take the lower line intended for Carmen rather than joining Mercédès in hers. Once again she was being distracted by Ray.

He ought to be upstage with them. She was supposed to pick up a backpack of contraband and hand it to him at the end of the number. Otherwise she'd have to carry the bloody thing off-stage or it would be in the way in the next scene, when Micaëla was singing her big number.

She turned and looked downstage. Ray was still squatting by the campfire. He had forgotten his blocking, which he'd never done before. Was it stage fright? At that moment he raised his head and their eyes met. It wasn't the audience he was afraid of. It was *she*. But why—

Oh God. Why hadn't she listened to Peter? Bryson wasn't the killer.

In a split-second it all came together in Renata's head, the key memories falling into place more neatly than Bernhard von Schussnigg's giant cards had ever done. Tuesday morning in the costume department, she had told Ray about the man Luis Reyes had seen walking down Helen's street the night of the murder. Ray had told her Don was the killer, that it was too much of a coincidence that this man should happen to come along in the brief period that Helen was alone in her house.

But it wasn't a coincidence at all. On Saturday night in the pavilion she had seen Ray, clinking a glass for silence before Congreve's speech. He had been standing six feet away when Helen had stood and said, *I want my house to myself.* He had recognized his opportunity. The man Luis Reyes had seen had been Ray, walking away from the house after killing Helen Stromberg-Brand.

She broke Ray's gaze and turned toward the audience to sing her next phrase, wondering if her face had given her away. If he knew that she knew.

PETER CAME OUT THE DOOR of Chase's apartment building. He took the phone out of his pocket to call Detective McCutcheon. Switching it on, he saw that there was a message from Renata: "Come to the theater as soon as you get this, my love." The beautiful voice brimmed over with excitement. "I'm singing Carmen. They won't make you pay for your seat this time."

He stood frozen as his thoughts raced. She was in the theater with Ray Costello. Call 911? But he was five minutes from the theater. He could get there more quickly than he could explain.

He ran to his car and jumped in. Reversed out onto Big Bend Boulevard. Brakes squealed and horns honked behind him as he swung the wheel, shifted gears, and stamped on the accelerator.

RENATA WAS STANDING IN A spotlight. Nine hundred people were staring at her. Ray couldn't harm her now even if he wanted to. She thought ahead to her exit, only a minute or so away. They were all clearing the stage for Micaëla. Ray was a good ten paces downstage at the fire. He would join the smugglers and exit downstage left. She, Frasquita, and Mercédès would run down the ramp upstage right. It turned into a passageway underneath the stage. She just had to make it to her dressing room. Lock the door and call the police.

She and her friends finished their song. They hugged and walked upstage. The smugglers left them, moving downstage. The music grew softer. The lights dimmed.

She'd forgotten that lighting cue, forgotten the stage went almost dark before Micaëla entered. She looked over her shoulder. Ray wasn't following the other smugglers. He was coming toward her. She turned away from him. Mercédès and Frasquita were already running down the ramp. Renata went after them, running flat-out.

The applause began as she left the stage, descending the ramp. Even in the darkness under the stage she could see Mercédès's back, clad in the orange tube-top, only a couple of paces ahead. She was thinking that this was going to be all right when Ray's hand clamped down over her mouth and his other arm wrapped round her waist. Her feet left the floor as he swung her off the ramp, then half-dragged, half-carried her down a dim, narrow side corridor. She wriggled and kicked and tried to bite. He slammed her head into the concrete wall. Lightning flashed behind her closed eyelids. She was dazed for a moment, incapable of resistance.

PETER SKIDDED TO A HALT at the main doors of the theater, startling the two parking attendants, who arose from their chairs but did not approach. Flinging the door open, he ran into the lobby. It was empty. The performance was still going on. He ran toward the nearest auditorium door. Pulling it open, he heard applause, an ovation just dying down. He could hear music but there was no one on stage.

An usher was approaching.

"Has anything happened?"

The usher just looked at him, wide-eyed. He wondered fleetingly what his expression must be like. He ran down the dark aisle, tripping and nearly falling full-length over unexpected steps. A woman walked on stage. A spotlight illuminated her: she was not Renata. She began to sing.

*Je dis que rien ne m'epouvante—*

I say that nothing will terrify me—

She broke off as Peter ran up the steps and onto the stage. The conductor froze and the orchestra collapsed into silence. There were murmurs and exclamations from the audience. The singer stared at him as he ran past her into the wings.

"Where's Renata?"

Everyone just looked at him, except for a tall black man who approached him with arms outspread, saying in a calm tone, "Renata's fine. Everything's fine."

"No, it's not. I'm—"

"You're Peter Lombardo. I saw you on the news. I'm Mike Joyce. You think Renata's in danger?"

"Yes. Where is she?"

"She just exited down the ramp a moment ago. She's probably in her dressing room."

"Help me find her."

Mike looked confused but did not hesitate. Gesturing to Peter to follow, he ran down the steps.

RAY HAD HIS HANDS UNDER her arms and was dragging her backward down a corridor of sleeves. They were in the costume storeroom, a dark musty room filled with racks of garments in plastic bags. There was no reason why anyone would come in here during a performance. Her head struck concrete again, not so hard this time. She found that she was sitting, leaning against the wall, her legs stretched out in front of her.

Ray crouched beside her and his hands began to close around her neck.

"No, Ray. You can't get away."

"I have a better chance with you dead."

She could feel his fingertips probing through her hair, locking and tightening against the nape of her neck, his thumbs pressing into her windpipe. But he was hesitating. She could still talk. "You don't want to do this to me."

"I have to. I'm not going to jail for killing Stromberg-Brand. I'm not sorry."

His eyes were locked on hers. Even in the dim light she could see them harden as he talked himself into it. His thumbs dug in.

DESCENDING THE STAIRS WAS LIKE going down into a rush-hour subway station. They shouldered their way through a pack of costumed performers who had just left the stage. In the corridor, a woman was standing in a doorway, a dress over her arm, looking the other way.

"Kim, have you seen Renata?"

She turned to them and shook her head. "She's supposed to be here for—"

Mike continued down the corridor. There was room to run now and he and Peter did, shouting "Renata!"

The corridor narrowed and dimmed. Up ahead, two young women in bright mini-dresses were standing in uncertain postures.

"Iris, where's—"

"She just disappeared."

"She was right behind us coming down the ramp," said the other woman.

Mike plunged down a corridor turning to the left and Peter followed. The first door they came to was ajar. Still calling Renata's name, Mike pushed it open and flipped on the ceiling lights. Racks of clothing in plastic bags, neatly arranged in rows, filled the room. Peter dropped prone so that he could see under the hanging garments. Movement caught his eye. Several rows down, at the back wall, he saw struggling limbs.

He jumped to his feet. Sweeping garments aside, he plunged through to the next aisle, and the next. At the third he knocked the whole rack over and had to clamber over a mound of plastic-wrapped clothing, barely keeping his feet. Against the wall he could see Renata's legs, kicking at the back of a man kneeling over her.

"Mike!" Peter roared as he ran down the aisle. Now he could see that the man's hands were around Renata's throat. He threw his arms around the man's torso under his arms, pulling him back with all his strength. Mike's hands came into view, grabbing the man's wrists, breaking his grip. Peter fell backward, taking the man with him. Panting, they scrambled to their feet. The man tried to get by him and Peter hit him in the face. Hard. A shockwave of pain ran up Peter's arm. The man dropped to his knees.

Blood was running from Ray Costello's mouth to his chin, dripping onto his American flag T-shirt. He looked past Peter, who turned and saw that people were pouring into the room.

"Call the police!" Peter shouted, louder than he needed to.

"They're on the way," someone in the crowd answered. Most of them were moving to surround Renata and Mike, who was kneeling beside her. She was coughing and massaging her throat. She caught his eye and nodded reassuringly before people got between them.

Ray Costello sank down on his haunches. He looked at Peter with narrowed eyes, recognizing him. "I almost killed Renata for nothing, didn't I? You knew."

"I found out about Michelle."

Ray nodded. "I was afraid somebody would."

"It wasn't true, what Chase told you."

"Sure it's true. Medicine's a racket like everything else. Only Dr. Chase was different. That party Saturday night, that was the first time I met him face to face. He remembered me. He remembered Michelle."

"That meant a lot to you."

"Everybody else forgot her. Expected me to get over it. Dr. Chase is a fine man. But nobody at the party noticed him. They were all too busy kissing Stromberg-Brand's ass. And she loved it. I kept thinking, she doesn't even know who I am. Or what she did to my daughter."

"Then you heard her say she was going home alone. It was your chance to kill her."

"I wasn't planning to kill her. I just thought she ought to know who I was. But she wouldn't listen, wouldn't let me in the door. She thought I was just some crazy old man who wasn't worth her time. She wasn't afraid of me, not even when I pushed my way into the house. She just ordered me out. I wasn't taking orders from her. That big bowl was sitting right there on the table."

Ray hung his head. He was through talking.

Mike was kneeling beside Renata, brushing the hair from her face. She was taking in great whooping breaths, her hand at her neck. He said, "Are you all right?"

"No," she croaked. "Can't do the last act. Sorry."

# 74

—

PETER WAS STANDING AT THE door of Clayton Police Headquarters. There was no light in the sky yet, and downtown Clayton was so quiet that he could hear a mockingbird singing, probably from the park three blocks away. The bird sounded ebullient and carefree—the way he had been feeling ever since Renata called from the hospital to let him know that the doctors said she was fine, and she was on her way.

A police car approached down the empty street and pulled over to the curb. Renata, in the front passenger seat, smiled up at him. He stepped forward to open the door. She had barely got to her feet before a uniformed officer came out of the door behind Peter. "Ms Radleigh, Mr. Lombardo, please come with me. Detective McCutcheon is waiting for you. And Lieutenant O'Brien and Chief Schmidt."

"Ms Radleigh just needs to change clothes," said Peter, lifting his arm, which had slacks and a jersey draped over it.

Renata was still wearing her black silk dress from the performance. She pointed to the bruises on her neck. "I'd like to cover these, if you don't mind."

Peter held the building door for her. "There's a room over here you can use."

They went in and crossed the lobby. An open door led into a little office with a bare desk and empty shelves. Taking her clothes from Peter, Renata noticed that the young cop had followed them. He looked very alert and determined for this ungodly hour.

"Uh … you're not supposed to be alone together before questioning."

"Don't worry, we won't talk about the case."

The policemen hesitated.

"I'm about to take off my dress," Renata said. "You'd best wait outside."

The cop pressed his lips together in annoyance, but went out and pulled the door closed. Peter dropped his eyes to the floor as she unzipped.

"How charmingly Midwestern of you, Peter," she said with a laugh. "You know I'm going to be naked in your arms as soon as we can get well shot of the police."

"Until then, I'm trying to concentrate. In fact let's do what we just promised we wouldn't."

"Coordinate our stories? Good idea. One contradiction and they get excited and the questioning goes on and on."

"Okay. It began as it ended, with *Carmen*."

"The Lyric Opera, Chicago, May fifteenth. Helen Stromberg-Brand, bored with *Carmen*, ditches my brother and goes to see her former research associate, Jeff Csendes. Her conscience has been troubling her about him and she wants to make peace."

"Instead she finds an embittered drug addict who tells her how much he hated her. She returns to your brother in need of soothing."

"He soothes her. They begin a love affair that lasts long enough for her to sign a check to SLO."

"Renata, that's awfully harsh."

"Right. It lasts a couple of days longer. And unfortunately her husband Bert finds out." She was dressed now, adjusting the turtleneck of the jersey. "Does this hide the bruises?"

"You look fine. Meanwhile, Helen's conscience is still bothering her about Csendes."

"Or she is afraid he's going to go public with his accusations."

"Well, that too. She hopes that her friend and partner Keith Bryson will be able to succeed where she has failed and mollify him."

"Pay him hush money."

"Well, that too. Bryson calls and asks for a meeting. Csendes isn't interested in money. But his friend Shane Komarovsky, who supplied him with uppers and downers, is. He persuades him to meet with Bryson."

"Bryson walks into a setup. Csendes has hired a sleazy bugging expert named Lou Bistouri to wire his place for audio and video. Bryson offers money. Csendes doesn't want it. He wants Bryson to admit that he's made the key contribution to the vaccine and that Helen has screwed him. Bryson won't. They get into a fight. Bryson kills Csendes."

"Bryson's bodyguard Schaefer is waiting in the car. He dumps the body in the river." Peter paused. "The cops tell me, by the way, that they have identified him as Duane R. Schaefer, former sergeant in Special Forces. But they haven't caught up with him yet."

"I doubt they will. He's a man of impressive skills." Renata shivered. "Let's move on. The Chicago police find the body. But they can't identify it and their investigation stalls."

"Shane was holding the tape, probably because he didn't trust Bistouri. According to the Chicago cops, Bistouri had a history of petty extortion, which kind of goes along with being a sleazy bugging expert. This was going to be his big score. He and Shane headed for St. Louis to sell the video to Bryson. But somewhere along the line, Bistouri has a more lucrative idea he doesn't let Shane in on. He makes a deal with somebody at the pharmaceutical giant Newton-Drax. They pay him to blackmail Bryson into stopping development of Helen's vaccine, which threatens their own highly profitable drug."

"They must have paid him a lot."

"Yep. They were protecting a drug that brought in fifty million a year, every year."

"The splendid thing about it was that it wasn't all that effective, so people had to keep buying more of it."

"Right, where Helen's vaccine actually prevented UTIs, killing the goose that was laying the golden eggs for Newton-Drax. So. Act Two. The scene shifts to St. Louis. Bryson lies to Helen, telling her Csendes accepted the money and she doesn't have to worry about him anymore. Relieved, Helen goes off to what she expects to be a delightful evening of champagne and accolades at SLO. But Bert is planning to humiliate her and Don."

"Carmen's Cornucopia. A night I'll never forget. Peter, straighten me out on something. When Bert and I went looking for a drink and found Ray Costello talking to Ransome Chase, that was the first time they'd met?"

"Yes. But they'd been exchanging emails for a couple of years. And we know that Chase has intense email relationships."

"He ranted and raved. He wrote that Helen had prevented him from curing Chagas Disease. Which killed Ray Costello's daughter."

"Horribly. Poor Ray."

Peter raised his eyebrows. "Considering those bruises on your throat, you're very magnanimous."

"I can't help feeling sorry for him. He was a lonely old man. All that anger and nothing to do with it."

"Until Carmen's Cornucopia, when he overhears Helen getting up, saying she's going home and wants to be alone."

"He waits for Don to leave and goes in and confronts her." Renata sighed. "You'll answer their questions about the next part. Please?"

"Of course. I'll tell them what Ray told me. And that brings us to Bert, being driven home by his gardener and finding the body. The police arrive, and he tells them about Helen's affair with Don. They go to arrest Don."

"Enter his sister—barefoot, sleepy, utterly clueless."

"You got the important thing right away—that he was innocent. So you fought the cops over him." Peter flashed her a grin. "In the end, you won."

# PART VII

—

## TUESDAY, JUNE 18

# EPILOGUE

EVERY DAWN, AND NOT A few noons, of the lovely month of June had found Renata and Peter in bed—naked, sated, and asleep. But today she was going to have to leave, and the dread of it awakened her early. Pulling on a robe, she left him sleeping and went into his book-lined living room.

St. Louisans took for granted apartments that Londoners would unhesitatingly kill for. Peter's was in a beautiful old building north of Forest Park, and not only was it quiet and spacious, but it had a broad balcony. She opened the French windows and stepped out into the slanting sunlight. It wasn't hot yet, so she sat on a bench. After a few minutes, Peter came out in T-shirt and shorts. He'd been awakened by her absence from his side. They kissed and he sat beside her. She was thinking how desolate she was going to feel tonight, going to bed alone. He was thinking the same—funny about that, she just knew he was, so there was no need for either of them to say anything. She would have liked to sit with him like this for, oh, the rest of her life, but it was necessary to make an announcement.

"I have to leave in an hour."

"No way. Your plane isn't until three thirty."

"I'm meeting Don for breakfast."

"Oh. I'm not coming?"

"No. He'll be pumping me for the names of people I know who might give him a job. I'll be trying to convince him opera is a small world and he should try some other line of work. It'll be grisly."

"He'd show more gratitude, Renata, if you'd let him."

"So you keep telling me. But as far as I can see, Don is still Don. Impressive, in a way, after all he's been through. Have you got your tickets yet?"

"Plane ticket to Santa Fe, and ticket to the July tenth performance of *Faust*. Finally, my first opera."

"You'll see that ordinarily they go right through to the final curtain without the scenery falling down or any cast member trying to kill another."

"Just so I get to see you play a guy."

"You'll see me for about ten minutes. Siebel isn't much of a part. And you've already heard my only number. About a thousand times. Sorry."

"I like listening to you practice. You know, you have a pretty nice voice."

"Nice it's not. It's driven me all my life. Now it's making me leave you. Can't you demand that I quit the stage? Say I've got to choose between opera and you? Please?"

"Don't forget, you're the one of us who has a job."

She reached over to caress his face. "I can't believe the *Times* wouldn't hire you for that special task force to investigate Newton-Drax and whether they were behind the plot against Bryson. If anyone was qualified—"

"It's just as well. I've heard that the special task force is funded under the table by Bryson."

"What?"

"It's also being rumored that they're making progress. Newton-Drax is offering them a scapegoat. Some hapless vice president who negotiated with Bistouri without telling his superiors."

She shook her head. "Newton-Drax thinks like Phil Congreve."

"In fact there's quite a lot of Bryson money and influence being applied to the media. The counter-offensive is about to begin. He's the real victim of this whole affair, and so forth. His lawyers are even helping Shane out with his legal problems, in exchange for his testimony that Jeff Csendes was crazy."

She blew out an exasperated puff of air. "It'll end up being all his fault that Bryson killed him."

"Probably. Meantime Ezylon is humming along. Bryson hasn't pulled his investment and Bert Stromberg-Brand is turning out to be an able bioscience tycoon."

She raised her hands to the heavens and shook them, as if to praise the Lord, Baptist style. "Good news for the UTI sufferers. I wouldn't bet against Bryson. But I still think Ray Costello is the real victim."

"It sounds like his lawyer is doing a good job of putting the blame on Chase. With Chase's help. The guy still hasn't learned how to keep his mouth shut."

Renata stood. It was time to start packing. But her eye was caught by the rows of small basil and tomato plants along the front of the balcony. She had bought them last week and they were making a good start.

"Peter, don't forget to water these."

"I won't."

"When I get back from Santa Fe they'll be three feet tall. I'll use them when I cook for you."

"You mean my days of eating microwaved tater tots are numbered?"

"We're going to reintroduce you to your Italian heritage, Peter Lombardo. First, pesto and marinara."

"Second, Verdi and Puccini."

"Oh. I was planning to break that to you later."

"I'm on to your tricks," Peter said. "Hurry back."

**D**AVID LINZEE WAS BORN IN St. Louis, where he and his wife currently reside. Earlier in life he lived near New York, where he sold several stories and published mystery novels from the '70s through the '90s: *Final Seconds* (as David August), *Housebreaker, Belgravia, Discretion,* and *Death in Connecticut.*

Moving back to St. Louis, Linzee turned to other forms of writing, selling articles to the St. Louis *Post-Dispatch* and other publications and teaching composition at the University of Missouri-St. Louis.

Retired from teaching, Linzee has continued to write more than ever. He also serves on the boards of various community organizations and has been a supernumerary at the Opera Theatre of Saint Louis.

Linzee is a former marathon runner (two in New York, one in St. Louis). He prefers to cycle rather than drive, and also enjoys scuba diving. Eager travelers, he and his wife have been to Ecuador, India, and Israel, but his favorite destination is London, explaining why English characters keep popping up in his novels.

For more information, go to www.davidlinzee.com.